Wind Whisperer

Book 1
Spellbound in Sedona

Anna Lowe

Contents

Free Books

Get your free e-books now!

Sign up for my newsletter at *annalowebooks.com* to get three free books!

- *Desert Wolf*: Friend or Foe (Book 1.1 in the Twin Moon Ranch series)

- *Off the Charts* (the prequel to the Serendipity Adventure series)

- *Perfection* (the prequel to the Blue Moon Saloon series)

Chapter One

ERIN

"Hurry up, Erin!" Pippa hollered.

My sister was all the way over on the porch of the main house, but she had the lungs of an opera singer, as her father liked to say. That, and we three sisters — Pippa, Abby, and I — had always been tuned in to one another in a way the laws of physics couldn't explain.

"Coming," I murmured, though I didn't budge. The sunset was too spectacular to miss.

Well, every sunset in Sedona was a miracle of color and light, but this one was especially bold. Streaks of orange, pink, and yellow split the sky and made the rocky red landscape glow.

I closed my eyes and took deep, deliberate breaths, soaking in the peace. A trick my dad had taught me at a young age when it was abundantly clear I hadn't inherited his easygoing nature.

Mind over matter, he liked to say. That and, *It's the journey, not the destination.*

Easy to say for a guy who roamed the West with a motorcycle gang — er, club.

The first stars winked just like my dad's eyes, telling me, *One thing at a time. You'll reach your dreams... eventually.*

My stomach rumbled, hinting that dinner should be first on my list. Still, I stood there, hugging myself against the cold. The stars were so bright and clear on our ranch, miles away from the nearest paved road.

Roscoe, our speckled Australian shepherd, leaned against my legs, scanning the desert for a jackrabbit to chase. Nothing so far, though, just the dry winter breeze that made the scrub whisper and sway. A lone wren trilled a cheery tune, while a chorus of crickets hummed in the background.

As serene as it all was, a sense of unease prickled my soul. As if trouble was creeping up from around the corner, and chaos was about to erupt.

Roscoe didn't seem concerned, though. Should I be?

I sniffed the air again, then turned to the base of the cliff, my favorite sunset lookout point. The rocky red surface glowed back at the sun in a beauty contest that could only end in a tie. One patch of the cliff — aligned with the summer and winter solstices, or so legend claimed — was full of petroglyphs etched by ancient artists.

Some of the rock carvings were enigmatic squiggles. Others were deer. A few resembled turtles, and another was a centipede, crawling across the same inch of rock for all eternity. Pippa always claimed to see a penis, but I didn't. Just squares, stick figures, and lighting bolts. It was all a jumble, but one symbol stood out to me — the one in the middle, exactly at the height of my heart.

It was a spiral, or rather, a spinning galaxy, with two loose ends that spun around in a tight design.

The one you weren't supposed to touch.

Actually, you weren't supposed to touch *any* of the petroglyphs, but especially not that one.

So, of course, as a kid, I had.

One touch. Once. Never again.

I shivered as electricity tingled through my arms. Or was that just in my memory?

Roscoe laid his ears back as I inched my hand between the sun's last rays and the spiral. I felt nothing...nothing...

Then, *wham!* My hand jerked back, blasted by an invisible force. I snatched it away, staring at the cliff.

Roscoe whimpered and backed away.

I wiggled my fingers, then tried again.

Whoosh! The invisible jet slammed my hand back.

Roscoe growled and paced nervously.

"Come on, Erin!" Pippa called in the distance. "Time to go!"

A car door slammed, and an engine revved in a not-so-subtle hint.

"Roscoe! Time to come in." Pippa whistled.

He whimpered once more, then shot off.

"Erin! Come on, already!" my sister yelled.

I stared at the spiral a minute longer, then stepped away.

"Coming," I murmured, crunching over frosty ground on the way back home.

∞∞∞∞

"One Bitterroot IPA, one Mile High Lite, and an iced tea." The waiter winked, delivering drinks and nachos. "Let me know if you need anything else, ladies."

Pippa held her glass up to him, flirting back. "We will." Then she looked around the bar and muttered, "Well, that's not encouraging."

Her sigh of disappointment hinted at bad news. I looked around then and shut my eyes, reminding myself to keep things in perspective. As long as *bad* didn't involve vampires, demons, or my mother popping in for a surprise visit, I could cope.

"What?" Abby asked.

"Not one halfway attractive guy here to dance with tonight," Pippa lamented.

I snorted. Not a priority. And anyway, we were treating ourselves to a night out for a totally different reason.

I raised my glass. "All right, already. Time to toast. Happy birthday, Mom."

"Wherever you are." Abby, my younger sister, sighed.

Pippa chuckled as we all touched glasses. "What do you think she's up to right now?"

I preferred not to speculate, but Pippa loved letting her imagination rip.

"I bet she's celebrating in a fancy condo in Tahoe."

"With a view of the slopes," I added.

"And a glass of wine that cost more than our three drinks combined," Abby chimed in.

"In a hot tub," Pippa added with a laugh.

"With a man," I sighed.

Pippa clinked heartily. Abby and I, less so.

"Go, Mom," Pippa cheered, gulped her drink, and scooped a huge portion of guacamole with a chip.

I took a smaller helping with a lot less gusto, then sighed.

"What's wrong with her?" Pippa asked Abby as if I wasn't right there.

Abby shrugged then looked at me. "Let me guess. You still didn't get that hour you need."

I jutted my jaw, silently shaking my head.

"One lousy flight," Abby commiserated. "One little hour. That's all she needs."

Pippa halted her next chip halfway to her mouth. "You still don't have that last hour?"

"Don't rub it in," Abby hissed.

I stared silently into my drink.

"I'm not rubbing it in," Pippa insisted. "I just don't get it. You earned your pilot's license ages ago, and you've been up in balloons loads of times since."

"It's not the license," Abby explained. "It's the insurance company. They only cover commercial pilots with 250 hours flying time."

I looked at her, surprised. Whenever I talked to Abby, I had a feeling she wasn't paying attention. . . much like our mom. But, wow. She'd actually been listening.

"Well, that sucks," Pippa declared. "I mean, seriously. One hour. Couldn't your boss just round up and sign off on your logbook?"

I gave her a firm look, but Pippa wasn't swayed. "Seriously. Let's hunt him down right now and talk some sense into him." She started to stand.

"We ordered burgers, remember?" Abby pointed out.

Pippa plopped back down. "Right. After the burgers, then."

Good old Pippa, always getting riled up by a good cause — then getting sidetracked by something else.

"And if that doesn't work, we could get your dad to convince him." She punched one hand into the other, hinting at how that *convincing* might go.

I shook my head. "Uh, no. My boss is right to do things by the books. Thanks for the sentiment, though." I took a sip of beer, then added lamely, "Besides, my dad is four states away."

My sisters cracked up, and Pippa tapped Abby's arm. "We could call *your* dad. He's as badass as Erin's."

Abby scowled. "We don't need him."

Her tone slammed a nail through that coffin and locked it away forever.

I winced at the word choice. Locked away... Her dad wasn't back in jail, was he?

With Abby, it was better not to ask.

"Could you just go up as a paying guest?" Pippa tried. "Would that count?"

"Are you kidding?" Abby hooted. "Do you know how much those flights cost?"

I munched another chip, resigned to my fate. "I'll get that hour, sooner or later."

I managed a casual note, but in truth, I was getting more and more desperate. I needed a flight, and not just for insurance. What the ocean did to sailors, what mountains did to climbers, the sky did to me. I needed to feel the wind in my hair, on my skin, in my soul. All around me, in a way only possible from aloft.

"I know you will." Pippa patted my arm the way she petted Roscoe. "Oh! Our burgers!"

Ah, to be Pippa, always ready to sweep the bad under a carpet of good cheer.

"Here you go, ladies." The waiter was all smiles, especially for Pippa. "Three burgers."

She was the youngest, cutest, and bubbliest of us three, and as such, a man-magnet. Abby, on the other hand, could chase a man away with a single, piercing scowl — except the roughest, toughest types drawn like moths to the flames tattooed on her arms.

I was the eldest sister. The most disciplined. The most practical — on the relative scale of a balloon pilot, a glass artist, and a blacksmith/part-time welder.

Sometimes, I felt we had nothing in common except our mother's half of our genes. Other times, I felt my sisters knew me better than I knew myself.

Pippa mushed down her double cheeseburger and ate, smearing her face with ketchup. Abby snipped at hers in quick, decisive bites. She used to eat as if every meal might be her last — yes, parts of her childhood had been that tough — but her dining style had mellowed slightly since we'd all moved to the ranch permanently. As for me, I turned my plate this way and that, considering the best angle of attack. Then I spread my napkin in my lap and took my first bite.

We ate in silence, staring into the open fireplace in our corner of the bar rather than the football game on the big-screen TV.

The candle on our table danced and swayed. Behind me, I sensed the bar door open with a new customer. Pippa's bright-blue eyes lit up, and she squeaked.

"Whoa. Stand aside, boys. I think we have a ten."

A ten was the veggie burger I was currently savoring, which was where my focus remained. Pippa was always vigilant for a possible hookup. Abby and I were a little more reserved.

But the candle flickered, as did the fire in the hearth. And, huh. Something inside me quivered in the same way.

"Ooh, la la. Where did this guy come from?" Pippa gushed.

Abby scowled, then did a double take. "Not bad — if you like hair cut like that."

"I like, I like!" Pippa chuckled.

I could already picture him. A tall, built, cowboy type. Maybe a tall, built, lumberjack type. Or a tall, built, athlete type...

Yes, there was a clear pattern when it came to Pippa's man hunts.

I wasn't convinced, but I did turn for a peek. And, oh.

Oh.

Wow.

I meant, er... not bad.

Mystery Man stood at the door. Strong jaw, I noticed. Strong shoulders. Heck, strong everything, all looming a couple of inches over the man closest to him. Brown hair curled to just under his ears, a shade darker than mine. His comfy, fleece-lined denim jacket sported a tear on one sleeve. The guy would have fit in perfectly with a construction crew — the kind that inspired Diet Coke ads.

Hollow, brownish-green eyes swept the scene before he stepped to the bar. Whoever he was, the guy moved like a cat. Or better yet, an assassin.

Pippa wiped her mouth, threw down her napkin, and stood. "I'll be back, girls. I'll be back."

"You'd better," Abby warned. "It's all fun and games until the morning after."

"Having a drink with a guy doesn't mean I'm spending the night with him," Pippa protested, sashaying away.

I believed her. Pippa liked to flirt, but I wasn't aware of her really fooling around with anyone since breaking up with the love of her life. She claimed to be over him, but I doubted it.

Abby watched her go, frowning. "Ever worry she's too much like Mom?"

I worried constantly — and not just about that. Ranch finances were just as high on my list. Our great-aunt had sold us the ranch for a song before moving to Palm Springs, but we struggled to keep the place up, what with taxes, maintenance, and routine operating costs. Developers kept knocking on our door, but we refused to sell.

Abby and I were hashing out ideas when Pippa returned and plopped into her chair. "Huh."

"No luck?" I asked.

She shook her head, dumb struck.

Now, that was a first.

As was my strange sense of relief. Apparently, Pippa wasn't Mystery Man's type. So, who was?

As I peeked over at him, the candle flickered, just like that undefinable *something* inside me.

Chapter Two

NASH

The waiter thumped a glass on the bar. "One water. You sure you don't want a whiskey with that?"

I shook my head. Water was fine. Unlike other drinks, it was easy to know when to stop.

Still, he stood there, grinning at me. "You're either crazy, stupid, or gay."

I cocked my head, waiting for the punch line.

"A man's gotta be one of those three things to turn down a woman as fine as Pippa." He chuckled.

I shrugged. *Burned out* — by work, by women, by life — was more like it, but let the guy think what he wanted.

"Oh, I get it," he went on. "Bad breakup and you're not ready."

Close, but no cigar. Still, I kept my mouth shut.

"Or maybe her sister is more your type." He motioned to one of the two women Pippa had joined. "Erin."

I barely glanced over, then jutted my jaw. "I just came for a drink."

My eyes must have flared, because he stuck up his hands and hurried away.

I turned my glass, adding wet circles to the bar. Heading to an out-of-the-way bar on my first night in town had not been my plan. But something had kept my blood stirring, and I'd had the same itchy feeling I'd been getting lately — the one that insisted I had to be someplace in particular at a certain time, even if I didn't know why.

And, hell. That feeling had brought me to Sedona. It had made me pull over to a strip mall and wander toward a supermarket exactly as an older guy was posting a *Help Needed* sign. Five minutes later, he took the sign back down, and I had a job — starting tomorrow — and a place to stay.

So I'd figured I ought to go with that feeling one more time, and here I was.

Old habits died hard, so I studied the place, counting entrances and exits and sweeping my eyes over the crowd. All were human, from what I could tell — except three grizzled old shifters engrossed in a hand of poker across the room. Two wolves and a cougar, if my nose was right. It took a while for them to spot me, and when they did, their nostrils twitched. One huffed and the scruff on his chin thickened, but the others elbowed him.

I raised my glass in a subtle motion that said, *Live and let live, right?* After all, I was no longer in my previous job.

They held up their beers in a silent toast and went back to their cards.

I sipped my drink, relieved to have encountered shifters old enough not to give a damn about a dragon minding his own business.

I checked the rest of the crowd, finding nothing else of note — except the three women by the fireplace.

Just relax and watch the game, I ordered myself.

I tried to, but my eyes kept dropping to the mirror under the screen — a long one that ran the length of the bar, reflecting all the bottles on display — and among them, glimpses of the tables behind me. Lots and lots of tables, though my eyes landed on Pippa's every time. Not for Pippa, but the woman next to her.

Erin, my dragon whispered, if what the bartender said was right.

One of those tough, brunette cowgirl types with intriguing, kaleidoscope eyes and something on her mind. Something I doubted she would find a solution to in the fire, but she kept staring there.

I towed my focus to the TV, but it wandered back to her again and again and noticing tiny, unimportant details. How she munched her burger, deep in thought. The way she dabbed her lips before reaching for her drink. Her eyes swept through the place, then over to the—

I jerked my gaze down to my drink a split second before her eyes met mine in the mirror.

Minutes later, I peeked again. She was in animated conversation with the third woman — the one with the tattoos.

Which made me think. Did Erin have a tattoo? She didn't seem like the type, unless it was one she hid.

And, zoom — my imagination took off on that thought. A four-leaf clover on her ankle. A dolphin in the small of her back. A yin-yang symbol around her belly button...

I gulped and stared back at the game. Who was playing? Miami and...some other team.

Then I cussed, catching myself spying on that woman again. What was it about her?

She stood, heading to the restroom. As she did, my eye caught on a detail, and I froze.

The flame of the candle on her table tilted as she moved, following her. It tilted...tilted...went sideways, then gave up and snapped upright.

Which could have been anything, but the candlelight on the next table also bent when she passed. And the next one, and the next, like so many wobbly toys tipping, tipping, tipping. When Erin disappeared down the hallway, the candles went back to flickering normally.

I squinted into the mirror. Just an optical effect?

When she returned, I swiveled to watch. And, *bing! Bing! Bing!* Like a row of lights in Las Vegas, each candle flared as she passed. The fire in the stone fireplace sparked too.

And it wasn't just her. When Pippa wandered over to chat to someone else, every flame in the place wandered with her.

All barely noticeable, except for someone trained to spot such clues.

My mouth went dry as I thought through the possibilities.

Pyromancer jumped to mind, but no. They tended to exude hot, pulsing energy that could be felt a mile away.

Dragon shifter, my beast side suggested hopefully.

Another no. Erin had neither the fidgety temperament nor the scent.

Witch was my second guess, but she didn't seem aware of her effect on the candles.

Relic, my dragon finally rumbled.

I went still, trying to get my head around that. A relic?

All three, maybe, if they're sisters, my dragon said.

"I know, I know." The guy beside me chuckled. "The game's that bad."

I snapped my mouth shut. It wasn't the game that astounded me. It was coming across a relic in a place like this.

Then again, Sedona had a reputation for attracting supernaturals — shifters, vampires, witches, and the like. That meant it would attract relics too — descendants of supernaturals who'd interbred with enough humans over the years to dilute or erase their powers.

Some relics were aware of their faint power and could manipulate it at will. Others had no clue. Most were harmless, party-trick types. People who could hold their breath for crazy-long periods of time, for example, often descended from mermaids. People whose fingers could fly over musical instruments to produce heavenly tunes usually had magic in a distant branch of the family tree. Most top athletes were relics too, possessing extraordinary speed, strength, or agility. Olympic gymnasts were a prime example of watered-down shifter blood — usually feline. Who else could string together four backflips on a beam just a few inches wide?

Only a tiny portion of relics caused trouble — and that's when guys like me came in. The minute I'd left the military, I'd been recruited by the government agency responsible for such things.

All the usual protocols ran through my head... until I remembered I wasn't in that line of work any more.

I stared into my drink for a while, then peeked back at Erin. Was she really a relic?

I decided to focus on Pippa instead. As the most outgoing sister, she was more likely to reveal hints of her hidden nature than the other two. Erin was more guarded, while the third sister was *way* beyond guarded. More like locked in a turret with the key thrown away.

So, Pippa it was. I focused on her reflection in the mirror, just visible between a bottle of Jim Beam and Jack Daniel's...

Pippa, I hissed to my dragon side when my eyes strayed back to Erin.

The beast grumbled, then stopped, suddenly on alert.

A motorcycle pulled into the no-parking zone in front of the bar. Then another... and another, all revving so loudly, they were impossible to ignore.

"What the...?" A guy at the bar stood for a look.

The bottom two-thirds of the front window was covered in black foil, but the top was clear. My stool was high enough for me to peer out if I sat tall. I counted as a fifth and sixth motorcycle rolled into the no-parking zone in front of the bar. Then a seventh and eighth, all revving away like they were about to zoom off instead of coming to a halt.

I lost count after a dozen.

They kept up the racket until the top dog pulled into the lot and gave his own ride a commanding rev. When they finally cut the engines, they cracked jokes and hollered to one another.

"Now would you look at that," someone murmured, though everyone already was. "Those guys sure know how to make an entrance."

My dragon snorted. *They think they're so big and bad.*

"Trouble?" someone muttered to the bartender.

My whole body tensed, sensing at least one supernatural among them.

My dragon growled. *Trouble, for sure.*

Chapter Three

NASH

The bartender laughed off the question.

"Trouble? Nah. Those guys wouldn't hurt a fly."

Superficially, he had a point. The youngest of the gang were in their late fifties. The rest were older, with gray hair worn long to compensate for the bald spots. Most were big and broad-chested, but a little creaky swinging their legs over their bikes.

But those guys didn't worry me. It was their leader I had my eye on.

Top Dog sauntered in like he owned the place. A fit, tough, sixtysomething, leather-clad guy with a big old handlebar mustache to complete the Hells Angels look. He took in the crowd with one dismissive fly-by, then lit up on spotting... Erin?

I did a double take, because she really didn't seem like a biker-babe type.

But Erin it was, and my dragon immediately went on high alert.

If that guy so much as bothers her...

Then I gaped. Not only did he point to her like an old bag he'd come back to claim, but Erin jumped up with a happy squeak. When they met two steps away from her table, the big guy picked her up, twirled her around, and puckered up for a kiss.

Gross, my dragon rumbled.

I looked away just in time, deeply disappointed. She didn't seem the type to hook up with a motorcycle dude twice her age. But, hey. There was no telling with some people.

Still, my stomach roiled, and something like jealousy slugged through my veins.

"Hey, baby," he announced.

I scowled. Baby? She was a grown woman. And yet she fawned all over the guy — one of those silver-fox types women swooned over.

Every head in the place followed Top Dog, then jumped away at his glare of warning. The rest of his gang filed in, flooding the place.

"Mike! Ted! Bones!" Erin and her sisters cheered at each of them.

Bones? Hadn't they outgrown dumb nicknames like that?

I swiveled slightly, studying Top Dog's wide shoulders from the back. Or rather, studying the space around them. Was it shimmering?

I leaned this way and that, but it was impossible to tell. Finally, I strolled toward the restroom to check from a different angle.

My breath caught. The space around his shoulders was definitely shimmering.

I sniffed the air. The man had the commanding presence of a shifter but not the scent of one. On the other hand, he didn't lack any odor at all, which would have been *really* bad news. The only beings with no scent — or, at most, the faint smell of ammonia — were vampires.

So, he wasn't a shifter or a vampire. But definitely not human.

Warlock, my dragon growled.

I coughed to cover the sound.

Clearly, Erin had no idea, because she'd cuddled up close and was hooting along with his jokes.

I stared at her, a piercing stare I wanted her to notice. When she finally did, I motioned to the restroom as subtly as I could. Which wasn't all too subtle, because she blinked in confusion. Then her eyes hardened, and she looked away. Like I was some weirdo and not one of the good guys.

I let enough of my dragon creep into my stare — powerful, insistent — to make her look again.

Restroom. Now. I mouthed the words and jerked a finger to the rear hallway.

It was a wonder half the place didn't holler to her, *He wants to meet you by the restrooms right now. But don't let that biker dude you're with notice!*

Erin furrowed her brow, considering her options.

Definitely not all human, I decided, because the average human didn't hesitate when ordered to move by a dragon.

Please, I telegraphed. Maybe *polite* would work.

Top Dog started to turn, following her gaze. I darted down the back hallway, then waited, praying she would follow. Sulfur laced the air as my dragon fought closer to the surface.

A moment later, Erin stormed around the corner, then crossed her arms.

"What the hell do you want?"

I stepped back. The woman had some serious presence when she was mad. And damn, was she mad.

After checking to make sure Top Dog hadn't followed us, I hustled her through the nearest door, then held it shut behind us.

Her hands shot up in an *I can break bricks* karate pose. "One more move, and you'll regret it."

I stuck up my free hand. "I just need to warn you."

She huffed. "In the men's toilet?"

I looked around. Oops. A good thing the urinals weren't occupied. At least there was that.

But I wasn't off to a good start, and any minute now, Top Dog might be onto us.

"Not a good choice," I admitted, then dropped my voice. "That man out there. The one at your table..."

Her eyes narrowed.

"The biker dude," I went on.

She rolled her eyes. "Oh, *that* man at my table."

I made a face. Okay, okay. He was the *only* man at her table.

"You need to stay away from him. He's trouble."

"Says the man keeping me captive in a restroom." She wrinkled her nose. "God, it smells in here. Can men not aim?"

It did smell, but I was not about to let myself get distracted by the comment...or the lavender scent of her hair or those luminous green eyes. Or were they blue?

Either way, my insides went all warm, and my dragon hummed dreamily. *One green, one blue.*

Little alarms went off in my mind, but I'd figure out why later. Right now, I had to tip her off about a warlock without sounding like a lunatic.

This was the tricky part to my job. Well, my former job, but that wasn't the point. The point was to keep humans from tangling with malicious supernaturals without revealing too much.

And, Lord. If humans had truly evolved to the top of the food chain, that had more to do with opposable digits than brains, because they rarely did what was best for them — especially in matters of the heart.

"I mean it. He's trouble."

Her arms went from *Bruce Lee* to crossed tightly over her chest. "Obviously. Was it the tattoos or motorcycle that tipped you off?"

Any minute now, we'd need a mop for that pool of sarcasm dripping from her tongue.

I shook my head. "Believe me. He's pure trouble."

"Aha. And you know this because...?"

If I could only tell it straight. *Because I'm a dragon shifter and can scent his kind. Because I did a year of top-secret FBI-style training in identifying and containing supernaturals, and I aced the "witches and warlocks" part.*

My gut roiled at the part of training I *hadn't* aced, but she didn't need to know about that.

"Because I know his type. I know his tactics."

Her laugh rose to the ceiling. "Let me guess. He sneaks into out-of-the-way bars and corrupts young, naïve women like me." She leaned in and continued in a conspiracy-theory tone. "Before you know it, he'll have his dirty boots on the table and a sweet young thing in his lap while he plots his next crime. A hit-and-run, maybe, or just running his chopper in circles through some old lady's rose garden. Then he'll leave town without paying the bills and go on to wreak havoc elsewhere. That type?"

Her voice rose in a damning crescendo, making me blink. Wow. Why was she so defensive?

And, hell. She wasn't done yet.

"And of course, we innocent young women have no chance against his type. We desperately need to be rescued by complete strangers because we're incapable of coherent thought — and certainly not capable of taking care of ourselves."

Boy, she really had a chip on her shoulder.

Her eyes — blue? green? — blazed. "Let me set you straight. I am not that woman. I did not ask for your advice. I do not *need* your advice." She stuck a finger in the middle of my chest, puncturing — er, punctuating — every word. "If I need your help or advice, I'll ask. Until then, stuff it."

She paused for a deep breath, then hammered my chest one more time. "And if you follow me out of this bathroom, I swear, your ego is not the only thing that will suffer."

A twinge went through my groin, and I turned sideways, just in case.

She slammed the door open and stomped away, nearly bowling over a trucker-type in a John Deere cap.

The guy stared at her, then me.

I shook my head wearily. "Don't ask."

He shot me one of those *I'm with you, brother* looks on his way to the urinal.

If Erin were still there, I was sure she would mutter, *Make sure you aim.*

I left. Quickly. At the corner of the hallway, I paused. Erin made a beeline back to her table — and the warlock. She sidled up to him and looped an arm defiantly over his shoulders.

My dragon sighed. *Maybe the warlock will be the one who bit off more than he can chew.*

I could only hope.

For a few minutes, I stood at the bar, warring with myself. Then I downed the rest of my drink and threw down a few bills. I headed to the door, reminding myself I was a civilian now. It wasn't my job to get involved.

But, hell. Something in me *begged* to be involved, even though it would be no use.

Outside, I scowled at the motorcycles crowding the no-parking zone directly in front of the bar.

Any warlock was suspicious as hell, but unlike vampires, they rarely hurt their victims. They simply used their magic to enthrall and seduce. In that sense, they weren't too different from humans with power or celebrity appeal, like CEOs or sports stars. Heck, many CEOs and sports stars were warlocks or relics. Either way, lots of women fell for those types. But unless that warlock was up to something much sneakier, I had no grounds to interfere.

I glanced back, fighting like a dog on the leash of my own determination. Then I growled at myself. Was I getting soft? Or were the last couple of listless, depressing months getting to me?

Maybe she's *getting to you,* my dragon murmured.

I spotted Erin through the window, throwing her head back with a laugh. Her glossy hair cascaded through the air, reflecting the firelight.

My heart beat a little faster, and my breath hitched.

Then I scowled and walked on, cursing every motorcycle in my way. Finally, I slid into my truck and started the engine with a roar, followed by the heating. Damn, was it cold. It didn't take long for the lights of town to fade behind me, leaving only the twin beams of my headlights to cut through the crisp night.

I drove, trying to think of anything but Erin. Cursing, because wasn't Arizona supposed to be warm? And, crap. How early the next morning was I supposed to be at my new job?

Things that didn't matter flitted in and out of my mind, but one thing refused to leave. The woman I wasn't interested in. Or so I kept telling myself.

Chapter Four

ERIN

"Good news or bad news first?" Henry, my boss, asked.

The cup of coffee he pressed into my hand hinted at *bad*. I took a quick sip and shut my eyes, reminding myself I could cope with anything — such as idiots lecturing me about who I kept company with, like that jerk from last night. Oh, or a ten foot tear in the balloon I was scheduled to pilot that morning — that would be *really* bad news.

I jerked my eyes to check the colorful bundle on the trailer before me. God, please, no. Not the balloon. Nothing that would disrupt my flight.

"The balloon's fine," Henry said quickly.

"Then what's the bad news?"

Henry had parked in our launch area — a clearing a few miles out of town on national forest land — and sleepy guests were piling out of the van, rubbing their hands and stomping their feet to keep warm. Henry maneuvered me away from them to speak privately. Another bad sign.

"Kenny won't be coming in today." His breath crystallized in the cold winter air and hung there, motionless.

I jutted my jaw, waiting, because something in Henry's expression said that wasn't all.

"Kenny won't be coming tomorrow either," Henry continued after a significant pause. "Or the rest of the week. Not for the rest of the month, actually. He's got some... issues to deal with."

I scowled. Kenny, like so much of the casual help in the balloon business, always seemed to be hampered by *issues* —

man-talk for problems with one's ex, run-ins with the law, or four-digit sums owed to the wrong kind of "business associate."

Henry heaved a sigh that said *Poor guy*, but I felt no such mercy.

"Issues? What kind this time?" I started, then stuck up a hand. "Forget it." It was probably better not to get on a rant, though I still rattled through one in my mind.

Wanda, the receptionist for the balloon company, had three kids, zero alimony, and a crushing mortgage. But did she complain about issues?

No, she did not.

Deirdre, Henry's accountant, had a mother with dementia, a Honda that ran on fumes, and a Schnauzer with heartworm. Yet, did she fail to turn up at work due to issues?

No, she did not.

In fact, I knew very few women who complained about *issues*. They just struggled on, because they had no choice. But when the going got tough, big-talking guys like Kenny got going and escaped their problems. Or worse, leaving those problems for other people to solve.

People like me, who found themselves at five a.m. with a short-handed ground crew, twenty-plus guests, and a job to do.

For the record, I am not a man-hater. I loved and appreciated Henry, who'd given me a chance when no one else would. I had many male friends — some with, er, *benefits* I'd thoroughly enjoyed. I loved my father dearly and would be eternally grateful for all the sacrifices he'd made for me.

It was just Kenny's type that got me riled, especially at o-dark-thirty.

I folded my arms and stared Henry down. "The good news better be that you found a replacement."

"I did!" He grinned then turned and hollered toward one of the men. "Come on over, son."

I glanced into the darkness, prepared to be let down.

"Can he drive?"

Yes, my expectations were that low. At least I didn't start with, *Does he have a pulse?*

Henry's laugh sent condensation swirling through the air. "Of course he can drive."

"I mean, does he know the back roads? Can he drive the way we need our ground crew to?"

That meant one eye on the road, one eye on the sky, and both ears tuned to the radio that allowed the ground crew to communicate with the pilot.

"He's a fast learner. Especially with you as his teacher." Henry grinned.

"Henry. . ." I growled.

"I know it's not what you hoped for," he admitted.

I snorted. Being my mother's daughter had taught me that life didn't deliver what you hoped for. But this was different.

"It's not what we agreed on," I pointed out, then lowered my voice to plead. "I need this flight, Henry."

"I know, I know. I promise we'll find you that hour soon," Henry swore.

I balled my hands into fists. I'd worked for Desert Skies Balloon Adventures for over a year, grabbing every rare opportunity to go aloft with Henry or his second pilot, Madden. But that depended on the balloon having a free spot — and having a competent ground crew chief to chase the balloons wherever the wind brought them on any given day.

Today, Desert Skies One had several free spots. But without Kenny to head the ground crew. . .

"I need this flight," I repeated, clenching my teeth before I begged.

I *really* needed it, and not just to be able to pilot solo. My whole life, I'd felt a primal, inner itch to get off the ground and defy gravity, at least for a while. But lately, that itch had intensified to an all-out craving.

The faint morning breeze toyed with my hair, teasing me.

"You'll get that hour. Soon," Henry promised. Then he grinned and raised his voice. "There you are, son. Meet Erin, our ground crew chief. She'll teach you the ropes."

The new guy moved through the predawn darkness the way a panther prowled through a forest, more shadow than substance. He stuck out his hand, and murmured a gruff, "Hello."

I reached out, then froze, spotting his jacket — a fleece-lined denim jacket with a tear in one sleeve.

When I raised my eyes higher, my hands formed fists. Him?

Strong jaw. Strong shoulders. Strong everything, all looming a few inches over me, just like the previous evening.

Our eyes collided like a couple of storm fronts.

You, I nearly hissed.

His expression hardened, echoing the sentiment.

"Erin, this is Nash, Kenny's replacement." Henry looked at me, then him. "Oh. Do you know each other?"

"No," I grunted, dropping my hand.

I did not know him, and I did not want to know him. Not after what he'd done last night.

John, one of the ground crew, walked by just then, chuckling. "Hey, Erin. I heard your father's back in town."

I shot a pointed look at the new guy. "Yes, he is. Word travels fast."

John laughed. "It does when you rock into town at the head of a motorcycle gang."

"Club," I growled.

John laughed. "Right. Club." He twisted his wrist, miming a *vroom-vroom* sound effect. "Too bad I missed him. Did you have a good time?"

I glared at Nash. "Yes, I did. With my *father.*" I emphasized the last word.

His eyes went wide. His cheeks flushed. Did he have that *I want to crawl into a hole and die* feeling? Good. He deserved it.

"Your father, huh?" he murmured, clenching his fists.

"Yep," I gloated.

Henry's confused expression said, *Are you sure you don't know each other?*

Out loud, he asked, "How long is your father in town for?"

"He's leaving later today. Just passing through this time."

All too short a visit, but I could forgive him that. My dad had sacrificed his *Easy Rider* lifestyle to raise me alone. The custom bike shop he started to support us had been wildly successful too. But the moment I'd turned eighteen and started my first steady job, Dad had hit the road. He stopped by regularly, though, and every time he said goodbye, he spent a long time wiping his eyes — from dust, or so he claimed.

So proud of you, honey.

I'm proud of you too, Dad.

I truly was — proud and grateful. My dad was the best. Unconventional, maybe, but definitely the best.

I shot Nash another killer look. *If you ever insult my father again. . .*

His brownish-green eyes briefly met mine, then dropped to the ground.

Too embarrassed to face me? Good.

"You'll have to pass on my regards to your father," Henry said amiably.

"I will," I said, forcing a smile.

"Well, back to work. . ." John said, ambling away.

Henry smacked Nash on the shoulder like a prize bull and picked up where he left off. "Nash has quite a resumé. This man is a pilot with years of experience." Henry beamed at his fine catch. "Was that Army or Marines?"

"Marines," Nash grunted, looking at no one in particular.

"Ten years," Henry announced, smacking Nash's shoulder again. A good thing the guy was built to take it.

"Marine pilot, huh?" Madden, Henry's second pilot, came over, attracted like a bug to a testosterone-fueled light. "My father was in the Marines."

I rolled my eyes, barely holding back, *And you were not.*

"Nice," Nash mumbled.

"Ten years piloting, huh? Heck, we should get you to fly one of our balloons," Madden crowed.

One of Henry's *balloons,* I wanted to snap. *And anyway, no, because those flight hours are mine, not his.*

"Happy to contribute any way I can," Nash murmured in that low, rumbly tone.

"Attaboy." Madden added his own firm smack of approval to the newcomer's back.

I was tempted to chip in with my own, just aimed at a different location. Ugh! What was it with men and their gorilla rituals?

"I bet you have war stories to tell," Madden went on eagerly. "Hey, the guests would love that."

I shook my head. What if Nash had *actual* war stories? What if he didn't want to share them?

That didn't stop Madden from enthusing, "What do you think, Henry? We have a free spot in the balloon today."

I glared at Henry. If he said yes, I would scream.

To his credit, Henry shook his head. "We need Nash to learn the ropes with the ground crew."

Madden scoffed as if that were beneath a real man.

My fingers twitched. Lucky for him, I had no talent for magic. Maybe I could hire someone who did and have him turned into a toad.

That was the thing with supernaturals in Sedona, though. It was hard to tell the wannabes from the real thing.

"Happy to contribute any way I can," Nash repeated in that same, measured tone.

But, shoot. I could see the bromance flourish already. Madden chumming up to Nash. Nash completing a fast-track ballooning certificate and using his thousands of hours of flight time to edge me out for a piloting spot — if he stuck around long enough.

Either way, my dreams would be grounded. Literally.

I slapped my work gloves against my jeans. Time to get to work. And I didn't have to like my new colleague to do that.

I pointed Nash to the bundled balloon. "We need to unroll this. Get that side. I'll take this one." Then I called Chico and John, our ground crew. Neither of whom aspired to fly, God bless them. "Ready, everyone? On three..."

Chapter Five

NASH

Crap. That motorcycle guy was Erin's father?

I'd nearly died at her mic-drop moment. Even now, my cheeks felt hot. But, hell. How was I supposed to know?

Still. . . her father was a goddamned warlock? A motorcycle-riding, gang-leading warlock?

That explained some things about Erin but raised a thousand questions too.

And, crap. She was my boss now. A boss who hated me to the core.

So much for landing an easy, low-drama job.

"That way. A little more. Good. Now, let me check it." Erin leaned in, tracing every line and hose in the dim dawn light.

I stepped back, giving her space to do her thing. And man, did she know what she was doing. Every movement was quick and efficient, every order delivered in a firm, even tone — and a glare at me.

We'd unrolled the first balloon and filled it with a huge fan, but it was still lying on its side.

"Now, we need to get it erect," John said.

Chico chuckled. I rolled my eyes.

Erin muttered without taking her eyes off the basket's steel frame. "You can borrow the fan if you need to get anything else erect, John."

"Ooh. Busted," Chico jeered.

John, to his credit, laughed too. "Good one, boss."

"Yeah, yeah," she muttered, then pointed down the length of the balloon. "The crown line is twisted."

"Got it," John said, stepping away.

Henry, the big boss, company owner, and primary pilot, was overseeing prep on the other balloon, *Desert Skies One. Desert Skies Two,* the balloon Erin was prepping, would be piloted by Madden, who was so busy chatting up female guests half his age that everything else fell to Erin.

I frowned. The Marines had technicians pre-check every flight, but every self-respecting pilot did their own check too.

Not Madden.

I stepped back, looking over the balloon, the lines, and the basket one more time.

"Boss lady won't like you admiring her ass," Chico warned in a low, laughing whisper.

I wasn't admiring her ass. I was admiring her work. But now that he mentioned it...

My gaze wandered down the curve of her jeans as she squatted before the balloon. A split second later, I jerked my eyes back to the balloon.

Not appropriate. Not respectful. And above all, not interested.

"Not that it's not a nice ass," Chico went on, using the loud jabber of guests to cover his chuckle. "Still, a little scrawny for my taste."

Scrawny? Looked pretty perfect to me. The thick flannel shirt and blue beanie clamped down over her long chestnut hair gave her a cute, tomboy look too. Not that I said as much.

"All right, everyone. Keep back, please." Erin checked the area, then pulled the burner cord.

And, *whoosh!* A four-foot flame blasted into the frigid dawn air.

I watched it, transfixed by the heat. The roar. The sheer power.

I didn't know what I was expecting, but I didn't expect it to be so...exhilarating. A little like dragon fire.

Not even close, my inner beast sniffed.

Maybe not, but my senses had been so dull lately, it was nice to be mesmerized for a change.

Our guests oohed and aahed as the balloon slowly rose until it was vertical. *Thump!* The basket followed, tipping from sideways to upright.

Whoosh! Erin released another blast of fire.

My throat warmed as my dragon side fantasized about spitting fire.

"Wow. That's amazing," one of the guests murmured.

Ha. What would they say if they knew I really could spit fire?

I glanced at Erin through the flames. The glow reflected on her cheeks, hair, and in her laser-focused eyes. Her fingers played over the burner cord as she judged exactly when to blast more fire.

Then I cocked my head, because she didn't move her fingers in any which way. Her fingers curled, and a sagging section of the balloon filled out smoothly.

Hang on. Is she directing the air? my dragon asked.

I stared, thinking of the previous night, when the candles had reacted to her. That, and the fact that her father was a warlock. Was she only a relic — or more?

Either way, she was awfully good at filling a balloon. So perfectly, the entire, massive bulb rose half an inch off the ground and hovered there. Not bad, especially on a chilly winter morning when tiny temperature shifts made for tricky handling — and especially on a balloon that big.

I glanced over to *Desert Skies One.* Henry had forty years' experience, but his balloon vacillated between scratching the ground and two feet above.

"Grab it here." Chico gestured for me to help him steady the basket as Madden climbed in.

"All right, ladies and gents," he announced. "Time to board. You and you, please."

"Oh! We're flying!" someone cried a few minutes later, once everyone was aboard and the basket floated at about my eye level.

I'd been so busy, I'd barely noticed the sun rise. But, wow. The sky was glowing orange and gold, colors echoed in the landscape and in the balloon fabric.

"It's so quiet!" someone else exclaimed.

It really was. Quieter than dragon takeoffs, even.

My inner beast scoffed. *I can be quiet. Like when I dive from a cliff.*

True, but taking off from a flat surface took powerful wing-beats that flattened every bush, flower, and blade of grass in a ten-yard radius. The balloon, on the other hand, lifted smoothly, silently.

I couldn't help grinning as it rose higher.

"Pretty cool, eh?" John murmured from my side.

I nodded. My dragon side had pooh-poohed the whole balloon/propane/basket arrangement, but I had to admit... Pretty cool was right.

∞∞∞∞

Working ground crew was a strange gig, I decided twenty minutes later in the parking lot of the Circle K convenience store. Work started at 4:30 a.m. with a flurry of activity to get the balloons aloft. Then we piled into the van, blasted the heating to full, and roared off to take up the chase — only to pull over at the Circle K.

That must have been a little ritual, judging by the *buy ten, get one free* coffee cards Chico and John pulled out to get stamped. Erin added a chocolate doughnut to her order, munching on it on her way back to the van.

"Come on, everyone." Her nostrils flared. "The wind is picking up."

I moved toward the back seat, but Erin shook her head. "You're riding shotgun, so you can watch and learn."

It was more grunt than invitation, but hell. That was fine with me.

As we drove off, John leaned into the space between the two front seats.

"So, you were in the Marines, huh?"

Good thing I'd left *Special Forces* off the resumé. But I wouldn't be mentioning that any sooner than I would mention the job I'd taken afterward.

"And a pilot, no less," John went on. "What do you fly?"

I sensed Erin stiffen. I did too. Some civilians avoided talk of military duty like the plague. Others pried too much.

What did I fly? I held back a dry, *Myself, in dragon form,* and stuck to the part he could understand. "Helicopters."

"What's a helicopter pilot doing on ground crew?" He cackled. "Did you get suspended or something?"

I clicked my jaw. Suspended? Yes. But not from that job. Not that I said that aloud.

"Just taking a little break. I'm happy for some mindless work for a while."

Erin shot me a withering look. Oops, I didn't mean to imply her job didn't take skill. Just that the rest of the ground crew could afford to kick back.

Especially me. No decisions, no responsibilities. My new mantra in life.

John chuckled. "Amen, man."

"Oh! It's beautiful!" a voice squeaked over one of the handheld radios Erin had placed in the cupholder between the front seats. Through it, we could hear both pilots as well as the guests.

"We keep that one on transmit," John explained. "That way, we can monitor them without the pilots having to call in. This second radio is set to a different channel if we need to hail them. We usually don't have to, though."

I nodded, listening to the guests rave.

"And, wow! I can feel the vortex!" the woman continued.

"No, you feel the updraft from Deer Mountain," Erin murmured.

I stifled a laugh, looking at the mesa they flew over.

About a mile outside town, Erin pulled over and cracked open the window, though she kept her eyes on the balloons.

"Kind of cold, boss." Chico shivered in the back seat.

"Sorry. I just need a minute," Erin murmured absently.

She tilted her head, letting the cold air flow over her left cheek.

Henry's voice carried over the radio. "Three-forty degrees at four point two."

Madden chimed in a moment later. "Three-forty degrees at four point four."

I looked north by northwest, drawing a mental compass as the balloons wafted slowly overhead.

Erin shook her head, murmuring, "Not for long."

I looked around. The last streaks of pink and orange were fading into a perfect blue sky. It was beautiful. Stunning, really, especially with snow dusting the spectacular rock formations. No wonder Sedona drew so many visitors. And no wonder folks forked out hundreds of dollars for a ninety-minute balloon flight.

My dragon huffed. *Poor things.*

There was no sign of a wind shift, however. What made Erin think the balloons would change course?

I rolled down the passenger-side window, letting my dragon senses sift through subtle cues in the dry desert air, from the thick, pine-scented layer closest to the ground to the thinner, blander layers higher up, each sliding over and around one another like eddies in an ocean.

My ears twitched just as my dragon said, *Over there.*

I turned northeast, focusing my senses there.

"*Three-forty… Three-thirty-five,*" Henry called over the radio. "Looks like we got ourselves a wind shift."

Erin pursed her lips.

I slid a glance at her. Lucky guess, unusual sixth sense, or magic powers?

"Oh, this is amazing!" one of the guests oohed and aahed.

"Beautiful," another agreed.

"I can feel my chakras opening up," yet another gushed.

I did a double take. Her what?

"Is that Airport Mesa?" the first asked.

"Yep. Right over there." Henry's voice came over the radio next.

"I knew it," the woman said. "I can feel the power of its vortex from here."

"So true," another chimed in. "I didn't realize how blocked my third eye was until now that it's opening up."

"Very cleansing," another agreed. "That amethyst you bought probably helped too."

John cackled. I arched an eyebrow.

He shrugged. "Some folks come to Sedona for the scenery. But lots come for the vortexes, the energy... You know." He flipped a hand. "The spiritual vibes."

Yeah, I'd picked up on that on my first drive through the town center two days earlier. Every second shop was packed with crystals, gems, dream catchers, and ads for spiritual retreats. But hearing those women talk was like overhearing a foreign language.

"Do you believe in that stuff?" I asked.

"Ha. Not me. What about you, boss?" John asked.

Erin pulled back onto the road. Her eyes, as always, darted between the asphalt and the sky.

"I believe there's something special about Sedona," she murmured.

Ha. A diplomatic answer. Was it an honest answer, though?

Maybe she knows, my dragon mused.

The world was full of things humans were ignorant of — and not just shifters like me, but witches, vampires, and demons. Beyond those were far greater forces that mystified even supernaturals at times. Fate... Destiny...

With a warlock for a father, Erin had to know about some of that. Or had he somehow kept it all a secret from her? But she seemed too down-to-earth and no-nonsense for the more spiritual stuff humans loved to speculate about.

She was quiet too. I swear, she uttered more words to herself than she did to me over the course of the next half hour. Which suited me, because I wasn't here to chat. I was here for a job — an easy job — and to tune out for a while.

Which I didn't exactly succeed in, because my senses — and my dragon — refused to snooze. My nose kept sniffing, hoping to catch a whiff of Erin's scent. Which was a lottery, given all the competing odors out there. But every time her sunny, wild flower scent filtered through, my dragon side sighed. My mind replayed little movements she'd made, from her easy slide into the van's high cab to the sway of her hair in the wind. And her eyes... were they green or blue?

I frowned. What did it matter? I wasn't interested.

Not even a little? my dragon teased.

Not even a little. Some serious shit hitting the fan over the past year had turned me into a sulky, self-absorbed bastard, and that was that.

Plus, she hated me.

Well, I'll enjoy while you sulk, my dragon murmured.

I folded my arms and watched scrub blur past the side window of the van.

Eventually, Erin exited the state highway for a dirt road. After one bouncy mile, she pulled over on the crest of a hill. Chico and John yawned and stretched, slowly gearing up for action.

"Landing point will be Angel Valley pullout," Henry announced over the open comms.

"Copy that," Madden echoed from the second balloon. "Angel Valley."

Chico looked at Erin.

She shook her head and murmured, "Lime Kiln Road."

I glanced in the direction she indicated, then back at the balloons. If Angel Valley pullout was the hollow just below our vantage point, it was a no-brainer — the balloons were heading directly for it.

But they're moving a little too quickly, my dragon observed. *And the airstream down here is more westerly than up there.*

I sniffed the air. As a dragon shifter, I couldn't see the wind any more than a human could, but I could sense different layers threading, weaving, and colliding when I really tuned in. And when I did that...

Huh. Erin was right. The wind would accelerate the balloons right over that hollow and carry them closer to the road.

Just then, Henry's curse came over the radio.

"Correction," he muttered. "Another wind shift. Plan B — Lime Kiln Road."

With that, he pulled the burner cord, releasing a roar of hot air.

Madden followed suit — so quickly, some of his guests clutched the basket edges.

"Are we supposed to lurch like that?" someone peeped.

Madden chuckled. "Don't you worry. It happens sometimes."

I snorted. Not if he'd observed what Erin had. But, heck. I had only picked up on the wind shift at the last possible moment, so I couldn't blame him. But Erin...

I glanced at her out of the corner of my eye. How had she known?

"Lime Kiln Road, here we come," she murmured, letting the van coast down the road.

Soon after, she parked and motioned everyone out of the van. We fanned out around an open area, watching the balloons waft in.

From a distance, they hardly seemed to move. But now that they were only a few yards away, they barreled toward us like elephants surfing an invisible wave.

"Just grab one of the straps on the basket and jog alongside, slowing it down," Erin warned. "Don't try to slam the brakes on all by yourself."

When the bottom of the basket swept by at eye level, I grabbed on to a leather strap. And, whoa — the balloon's momentum nearly wrenched my arm off.

"Steady," Erin ordered in the same voice you'd use on a couple of horses.

Our hips bumped, then our shoulders. My body warmed pleasantly.

The balloon dropped lower, keeping up that sideways shear. A moment later, the bottom of the basket thwacked through a bush.

I cursed, whacking through it too.

Beside me, Erin clutched another strap, all cowgirl determined to tame a wild bronco. A foot above me, someone gaped.

"Whoa. We're coming in fast."

But three jogging steps later, momentum gave up the fight, and the basket touched down with a light creak. Henry pulled a cord, dumping air. The balloon swung sideways, slowly deflating.

"There — grab the crown line." Erin pointed.

Chico and I caught it and strode away from the basket, guiding the top of the balloon until it lay neatly stretched along the ground.

A few minutes later, the guests clustered around a champagne brunch while we ground crew heaved, rolled, and muscled both balloons into neat packages.

So much easier to fly alone, my dragon muttered.

True, but a job was a job.

My eyes slid to Erin before I forced them to the ground.

Just a job, I reminded myself. *A little mindless work to help me get back on track.* Once I got my shit together, I would be on my way to greener pastures and a new direction in life.

I just had to figure out what that might be.

Chapter Six

ERIN

The problem with someone ticking you off was that it stuck with you, no matter how hard you tried to shake it away.

And boy, did I try to shake Nash away.

Which only annoyed me more. He was the annoyer. I was the annoyee. What right did he have to stick in my mind like that?

Yet there he was, sticking like glue.

Stunningly handsome glue. Especially the eyes. The shoulders. His chest. Oh, and that perfect, boxy ass — much, much preferable to Madden's pudgy crack.

But that was about all he had going for him. He'd insulted my job — Mindless? Seriously? — and maligned my dad. On top of that, he might be secretly gunning for my pilot's job. What a jerk.

I stalked through the supermarket, taking my frustration out on products I slammed into my shopping cart. A bag of wholewheat English muffins — *thump!* Half a pound of cheddar cheese — extra sharp — *bang!* A package of frozen ground turkey — *crash!*

The woman in the meat aisle looked at me, then quickly turned away.

I didn't take it out on the lady at the register, because she probably had to cope with arrogant, belittling people too. But I did take it out my grocery bags, thrusting each item in, then shoving them into the cart. Zipping up my jacket, I headed outside, where the winter sun painted the sky a startlingly clear Navajo blue. Sedona's spectacular red mesas spread below that, wrinkled by time and dusted with snow. Lower down, a deep green patchwork of pines, oaks, and junipers surrounded town, all sprinkled with a thinner layer of confectioner's powder.

I closed my eyes and took a few deep breaths, letting peace filter through my soul.

Someone bumped me, then hurried to apologize. "Oh, sorry."

"My fault." I moved aside, keeping my eyes closed.

"Not available? Are you sure?" the same man asked, his voice smooth as honey — the dark, thick kind that tempted you to dip in a spoon and lick.

I glanced over at a styled, sixtysomething man holding a phone to his ear. His sleeve slid down far enough to reveal one of those fancy watches that cost five figures and could measure barometric pressure and the time in Hong Kong — from a hundred feet underwater, no doubt. The rest of his outfit was what Pippa called Marlboro Man Chic, with a rancher's jacket by Ralph Lauren and gleaming boots that had never, ever been smeared with cow dung and never would be.

All in all, you could call him coiffed. Elegant. Worldly, too, like he had to head off to a business meeting in New York — make that, London — very soon. One of those silver foxes who made women's hearts skip, because here was a man who wouldn't get excited about inviting a date to cheap stadium seats where spilled beer and soda kept shoes half glued to the floor. A man who'd learned that birthdays were not to be forgotten and that dirty clothes belonged in a bin.

So, not necessarily my type, but a fun fantasy to indulge in from time to time.

"Nothing available at all?" he asked. I expected a corporate-rich guy like that to start hollering and threatening, but he kept his cool. "Not a single helicopter? Not even a four-seater plane?"

Two doors down the strip mall, a woman in high heels click-click-clicked out of a real estate office and pressed a manila envelope into his hands.

He flashed a stunning Colgate smile and nodded his thanks without interrupting his call.

"What a pity. But surely something can be done. I'm only in town for a few days, and I really don't want to miss the experience of seeing it from the air."

I was liking this guy more and more all the time.

"Yes, I'll stay on the line," he said, checking his watch.

And, heck. I wasn't a born hustler, but I knew an opportunity when I saw one.

I stepped closer with a little wave. He looked up — and wow. That thousand-watt smile made something flutter in my chest.

I pushed the feeling away and smiled back. "I couldn't help overhearing. Are you looking for someone to take you on a scenic flight?"

His eyes, voice, and smile all lasered into me, making my cheeks heat. "Yes, I am. Are you a pilot?"

I fell in love with him right there. Most people would have said, *Do you know a pilot?* not given me credit for being one.

"I am — at Desert Skies Balloon Adventures." I pointed at our office on the other side of the strip mall. "Have you considered a balloon ride? No engine howling in your ears, no blades chopping up the air. Just you floating peacefully through the sky."

His eyes sparkled. "You know, I hadn't thought of that. But it could fit the bill." He blinked, then spoke into the phone as the other party came back on the line. "Nothing until next week? Unfortunately, that won't work. But I believe I may have found a different solution." He winked at me, then hung up, smiling. "What are my chances of getting a private flight soon, Captain?"

My heart fluttered again.

"We'll have to ask my boss, but I'm sure he can arrange something. How many passengers?"

"Two minimum. If space allows, perhaps a few more."

"No problem. Even our smallest baskets carry eight," I said.

My heart raced for a different reason. Desert Skies Balloon Adventures was doing all right, but every booking was important. If I brought in extra business, *and* if there was a free spot, Henry would reward me by letting me copilot, right? Then I would have that last hour I needed and could pilot to my heart's content.

Marlboro Chic stuck out a hand. "Well, then, please show me the way, Miss...?"

"Sattler."

He grinned. "Harlon Greene."

We shook, and I marched him over to Henry's office.

"But your groceries..." he started.

I didn't care — not even about the double chocolate chip mint ice cream that was sure to melt. That was how much a flight meant to me. Plus, I had another reason to escort him over. If Madden was in the office when this customer came in, Madden would claim the business for himself in hopes of a big tip — and Harlon Greene had *big tipper* written all over him.

He insisted on helping me load the groceries into my car, then followed me to the office. And yay — it really was my lucky day, because Henry was at the desk, not Madden, and we had an opening in two days' time.

"I'd really appreciate it if Miss Sattler could be my pilot." Harlon lit up the room with another smile.

My lord. A smile that sunny could power all of Sedona on a cloudy day — not that we got many of those.

Even Henry beamed. "I'll make sure she is."

I smiled all the way home, my troubles forgotten. I was scheduled to fly — at last! My dream of a piloting career was about to come true.

∞∞∞∞

My spirits soared for the next thirty-six hours, and I barely slept the night before the flight. Chico and John were in their usual, half-asleep state when I picked them up. Nash was his effortlessly handsome, *Channing Tatum meets Oscar the Grouch* self. I was the Energizer Bunny on steroids, talking a mile a minute to Chico. He'd been on ground crew long enough to know the back roads, and I'd cajoled Henry into letting him drive the chase car for that one, low-wind, easy day. That freed me up to copilot with Henry and clock that last hour of flight time I so desperately needed.

"Will you slow down a little?" John protested as we hitched up the balloon trailer and triple-checked the propane tanks.

I revved the van to life and motioned them in.

"I think that means no," Chico murmured as I sped away at twice my usual speed.

But the minute I pulled up to our launch point and spotted Madden, not Henry, arriving with the guests in a second van, my mood plummeted.

I glued on a fake smile as I dragged Madden aside.

"Where's Henry?"

"Morning to you too," Madden mumbled between sips of steaming coffee. Then he yawned. "You didn't check your messages?"

No, I hadn't. Reception was crap out where I lived, and I'd been too busy giving Chico last-minute instructions to check messages when we'd passed through town.

"Henry had to go to Denver. His brother had a heart attack." Madden yawned in a manner more suited to *flat tire* than *life-threatening emergency*. "I'm filling in."

I stared, none too pleased at the prospect of flying with Madden. Then I chided myself and got my priorities straight. "Is Henry's brother all right?"

Madden shrugged. "I didn't ask."

I snorted. Of course he hadn't.

"Ah, Miss Sattler," a smooth voice greeted me.

That turned my smile genuine. "Mr. Greene. Good morning."

"Please, call me Harlon." He clasped my hand warmly, then gestured behind him. "I hope it's all right. I brought a few friends."

Friends? More like a business associate — a bald, portly guy carrying a briefcase — plus several stunning young women. His daughters?

More like groupies, I realized when one blew a kiss at him. My heart sank as I did a mental count.

"Madden assured me there was enough space..." Harlon went on.

I froze, counting again. Seven guests, plus a pilot. An eight-person balloon. Enough space for everyone... but me.

"Can we get a selfie with you?" the groupies cooed at Madden.

Madden cozied up to them to squeeze into the frame. "Anything you ladies desire."

The "ladies" struck several different poses before the one holding the phone switched to video and started to narrate.

"Here we are, ready for our flight, with our pilot..."

Madden made a hang loose sign, grinning as buxom young women crushed in around him.

"And Miss Sattler," Harlon added.

Madden stuck up a hand. "Not today, unfortunately."

Or any other day, his *sorry/not sorry* expression made clear.

"There's only space for seven, and Erin's not cleared to fly solo," Madden gloated. "She can only copilot."

But only for one more hour, I nearly barked. *One measly hour.*

"Oh, I didn't realize," Harlon said. "What a pity. I didn't know that when I invited the ladies along."

He couldn't have known, but Madden did. I glowered at him.

Harlon turned to his groupies. "I don't suppose one of you would like to bow out?"

They crushed forward like panicked sheep, petting his Ralph Lauren shearling jacket. "And miss the fun?"

Harlon looked between them and me, obviously torn.

I burned to talk one — better yet, *all* — of the young women out of flying. But business was business, and every paying customer counted in a roller-coaster business in roller-coaster times.

I stuck up my hands. "Very kind of you, but it's fine. Really," I lied.

"See?" one of the women practically jeered. "It's fine."

Harlon looked annoyed, perhaps considering the flip side of maintaining a brood of willing and eager groupies. His eyes narrowed on the woman, and his lips went hard.

Out of nowhere, a dark-cloud-sweeping-over-the-horizon feeling whooshed in, and I swear, the earth trembled. Something terrible was about to happen, and I didn't want to stick around to find out what.

"It's okay. Really," I cut in, touching Harlon's arm.

The moment I did, *zap!* Static electricity hit me so hard, I jolted.

Well, I did inside, though I managed not to let it show.

But, yikes. Harlon's eyes burned into me, and that creeping feeling went from *surrounding* me to *invading.* A strange sensation tickled at the edge of my mind, and my thoughts began to blur.

Thank goodness for Chico closing the van door with a mighty bang. I turned, stepping away from Harlon's bewitching aura.

"Really, no problem," I repeated. "And anyway, I'd better get to work. Enjoy your flight."

I moved away briskly, doing my best to channel *busy bee* instead of *fleeing dog.* Because, shit. Now I knew who Harlon reminded me of.

Smooth-talker. Hot-looker. Man-magnet with just the right touch. A *magic* touch, one might even say.

Warlock.

Just like my dad.

Chapter Seven

NASH

I hadn't known Erin long, but I could tell something was off. She'd spent a few minutes talking to Madden and the guests, then hurried back to the balloon with a pale hue to her deeply tanned skin. Normally, her focus on the details of the rig was laser-sharp, but today, her eyes kept flitting to the guests.

"Don't make her madder," Chico whispered, as if I hadn't figured that out for myself. "She's already pissed off about not being able to copilot."

Whoosh! Erin let the burner blast, creating a long, angry lick of fire.

She'd make a great dragon, my inner beast decided.

She would, and woe be the man — or beast — who crossed her.

I could picture it now — the flashing eyes, the hard set of her jaw. Then I sighed, because that anger would probably be aimed at me.

"Load tapes. Cables. Pilot light." She grunted her way through the preflight checklist in staccato, machine-gun bursts. "Fuel pressure..."

"Check," Chico murmured in his usual calm, steady manner.

Most days, guests would cluster around us, fascinated by the spectacle of a launch. But this gang was more self-absorbed than the giggly newlyweds we got from time to time.

Or rather, totally fixated on their leader, a tall, fit, silver-haired man. All five women hung on his every word like repentant sinners at a sermon. They did a lot of touching too,

45

touching him as well as hip-butting one another out of the way as they vied for pole position closest to his side.

The second guy — some kind of businessman with a brief-case — wasn't much better, imitating the leader's gestures and laughing too loudly at his own jokes, then cutting himself off self-consciously when they fell flat. If that was a bromance, it was one-way at best.

I was too busy with the balloon to study the guy, and Madden blocked my view the few times I peeked.

What was with that mystery man? And what had he said or done to put Erin off?

Maybe he warned her away from her father, my dragon grumbled.

I jutted my jaw. *Do you have to rub that in?*

When the balloon was ready, Erin signaled, then called to Madden several times. Nothing. No response. Finally, she stuck her fingers in her mouth and whistled, making the whole group turn.

"All aboard."

Madden didn't lead the group over. The head honcho did. The rising sun was high enough now to backlight them all, so I couldn't make out his face. I was more interested in the space around his shoulders anyway.

I held my breath, wondering. Worrying.

Then my body went stiff. There it was — the telltale shimmer hanging over the man's shoulders like a fur coat.

No wonder his guests seemed so enthralled. They were — literally. Because that was another warlock. The second one I'd spotted in three days.

More like the tenth, my dragon muttered.

I snorted. *Those other ones don't count.*

Third-rate witches and warlocks were a dime a dozen in Sedona, but they were mere minnows to this Great White Shark.

My jaw hardened as I wondered what he was after in Sedona. I doubted it was the views.

"Move it," Erin hissed, getting me in motion again.

We ground crew each took hold of a corner of the basket, steadying it while the guests climbed in. I kept my eyes down and away from the warlock. His kind didn't have the nose to ferret out a shifter like me, but if he gazed deep enough into my eyes, he'd get a glimpse of the beast within.

"Help me, Harlon," one of the women squeaked.

Then a pudgy hand holding a clipboard — the businessman's — slapped the basket an inch from my ear. I glanced up, annoyed.

Robert Hardy. Red Rock Vistas Real Estate, read the embossed letters at the top of the custom clipboard.

A moment later, the real estate guy — Hardy himself? — tipped me off to his boss's last name. "Can I hand you my briefcase, Mr. Greene?"

I made a mental note to call in to HQ to pull up some research on Harlon Greene.

Then I cursed, because those resources were no longer available to me.

Whoosh! Madden pulled the burner cord a minute later, and the balloon slowly lifted off.

"Oh! We're in the air!" one of the women squealed.

Erin stalked to the van. I paused with John and Chico, watching the balloon rise.

"Now, that's a man with a lot of money and power," John sighed.

"And women," Chico added.

They cackled all the way over to the van. We packed up the remaining equipment, then slid into our seats. Erin took off, her hands tight on the wheel.

"Oh! It's so pretty!" A woman's voice came over the radio.

John crossed his arms, pulled his baseball cap over his eyes, and settled in for his usual nap.

Chico stuck on his headphones, slipping into his own private world.

That left Erin and me listening in to the usual commentary from the balloon. At least, it started out in the usual way. Lots of oohs, aahs, and rediscoveries of familiar places from their bird's-eye view.

Dragon's eye view, my inner beast growled.

But then things started veering away from the normal, and I found myself tuning in instead of out.

"Bob, where's this Painted Rock Creek we were discussing?" Harlon Greene asked.

Erin's sharp intake of air made me look over. Her lips were a tight line, and the groove between her brows deepened.

"I'll just open the map..." Bob replied — the Robert Hardy of Red Rock Vistas Real Estate, I assumed.

Erin swung around a turn, looking up. When we hit a bump, her right hand popped off the steering wheel, and her fingers flicked.

"Oh! Grab it! Grab it!" Hardy cried.

Scuffling sounds ensued, and something white fluttered overhead.

One of the women laughed. "So much for your map. That gust of wind is taking it in for a landing on that bush."

It was almost comical, but Erin didn't seem amused.

"Shoot. Let me just pull it up on my phone..." Hardy tried next.

"Painted Rock Creek? It's over there," Madden replied.

"Shut it, Madden," Erin cursed under her breath.

"Fly us over it," Harlon ordered.

"Sorry, no can do," Madden said. "Not unless the wind shifts."

Harlon Greene was clearly a man used to getting what he wanted, and in the dead silence that ensued, I pictured Madden wincing and looking away.

"What a pity," Harlon grunted in a low, dangerous voice.

"I mean, I'll do my best," Madden added quickly. "But in a balloon, you can't pick your direction. You can only control up and down. The wind does the rest."

"I see," Harlon muttered, not at all pleased.

I held my breath, half expecting a roar of wind to come sluicing out of the mountains. It didn't, but the coordinates Madden read off did start to veer north.

"Three-forty degrees at four-point-two knots... Three-forty-two... Three-forty-five... Well, you might be in luck, Mr. Greene," Madden exclaimed.

Erin stared at the radio, then at the balloon.

I stared too. Only the rarest, most powerful warlocks could force natural phenomena as powerful as earth, wind, water, or fire to do their bidding. If I were still with the agency, I would definitely flag Harlon Greene, big-time. But I'd left, and now, I was on my own.

Not your *problem*, a little voice said in my head.

No, it wasn't. But it sure seemed to be a problem for Erin, who grew more agitated as the conversation continued.

"That's Painted Rock, and that green line there is the creek," Madden explained. "They say there's a fifth, hidden vortex out there."

If looks could kill, the radio would have imploded, given the glare Erin leveled at it, then at the balloon.

"You don't say," Harlon replied in an extra-smooth tone.

"The property we discussed is nestled against the rocks, right back there," Hardy threw in.

Erin's cheeks paled from the red of anger to the white of fear. Well, unease, maybe. Erin didn't seem the type to fear much.

Not even a warlock? a little voice whispered in my mind.

I frowned, remembering her father. Did she think she could handle others of his kind?

But Erin's father had left as quickly as he'd come. Harlon was snooping around. Why?

"Oh, Harlon, you must buy it," one of the women cooed over the radio. "It looks so pretty back there. You could knock down those shacks and put up a mansion!"

My eyes slid over to find Erin fuming. Was one of those cabins up at Painted Rock Creek her home?

"You could do more than that," Hardy chuckled. "It's outside the national forest, so it's just a matter of paperwork to get zoning for an entire resort."

Erin didn't actually growl, but I swore, she came close.

"Of course, you'd have to talk the owner into selling," Hardy went on.

"It's not for sale," Erin muttered, almost too quietly to catch. "It never will be."

Harlon chuckled. "I'm a very persuasive man."

The women giggled, and one chirped, "He really is. He even talked me into this balloon ride!"

And probably into his bed, my dragon grumbled.

That was the thing with warlocks. No one seduced as effortlessly as they did. I doubted he was even aware of it.

Like Top Dog, my dragon muttered. *Erin's father.*

I glanced over. She had to know about her father, right? And did she share his powers, or was she a mere relic?

She's not a mere anything, my dragon growled. *And even a relic's ancestral powers can stir to life.*

So I'd been told, but confirmed cases only came about once every hundred years.

"They say there's a whole hidden canyon farther back against the rocks," Madden went on.

Erin was already so tense, it was hard to judge what her reaction to that was.

"Tell me more about this vortex," Harlon said.

Hardy chuckled. "Well, that depends on who you ask."

Harlon cut in, unamused. "Not vortexes in general. This particular one."

Hardy didn't seem to have an answer, but Madden did. Was he bullshitting — as usual — or did he actually know the facts?

"Everyone talks about the Big Four vortexes, but I've heard folks say there's a fifth, more powerful one. It comes and goes, though. For long enough that people forget about it. Of course, that could all just be a story."

I sure hoped so. Because a powerful warlock building a private complex atop a secret vortex was the kind of scenario that made folks at the agency blanch.

Erin looked like she was ready to bang her head against the steering wheel. And that was before Hardy chimed in.

"Even if it isn't, it's a hell of a location. Big enough to build your own personal golf course on too."

Erin glared upward.

Just a relic, my dragon murmured a little mournfully. *If she had any powers, they would be obvious about now.*

True. Most of the relics I'd heard about had discovered their supernatural abilities at extreme moments when emotions ran high.

A little like now, and the balloon didn't sprout a leak or crash spectacularly to the earth.

Too bad, my dragon grumbled.

"Well, we're sliding away from it now. New heading, Three-thirty-six degrees," Madden said. "Three-thirty-three... Three-thirty. Next wind shift."

I glanced over at Erin, then quietly shook my head. If she could control the wind, she would have done so by now... Wouldn't she?

Minutes ticked by with the balloon steady on its new course, and the guests' conversation turned back to the usual things. The beauty of the mesas, the sighting of a javelina, then the oohs, aahs, and pictures snapped when someone spotted the balloon's shadow on the ground.

"Oh! Everyone wave," one of the women squeaked. "Look! Our shadows are waving back to us! Did you see that, Harlon?"

I didn't catch his answer, but I'd bet he didn't wave. Instead, I pictured him staring back at the lush green line of Painted Rock Creek.

"We'll be heading for a landing over there, past the wetlands," Madden said as the balloon slowly descended.

"Oh! I need a group picture first," one of the women cried. "Can you take it, Bob?"

I snorted as they shuffled around. Poor Hardy was definitely not in with the cool kids.

"Say cheese," he said.

The women whooped and cheered. Close enough?

Then Harlon spoke, and the chitchat stopped instantly. "What a wonderful flight this has been. Thank you, Madden."

Now that they'd been cued, the women echoed the sentiment. Would they have bothered otherwise?

"Yes, we'll all remember it for a long, long time." Harlon's voice grew slower, almost singsongy. "We'll remember the incredible views. The javelinas. How peaceful it all feels. Very, very peaceful..."

Harlon droned on, slowly and softly, like a parent reading a bedtime story at that tipping point when the child gradually fell asleep.

"The way the wind snatched Bob's hat and blew it away..." he said next.

I frowned. It wasn't a hat that had blown away. It was a map.

"We'll remember how beautiful Oak Creek looks, and the property Hardy told me about there..."

Not Oak Creek, I nearly said. *Painted Rock Creek. You're mixing everything up.*

Then it hit me. Harlon was purposely mixing everything up — and planting new memories in his audiences' heads in the process.

Mindspell, my dragon whispered.

There were hundreds of magic spells, though not every witch or warlock mastered every type. A damn good thing. But, hell. Harlon had two hugely powerful spells if he'd mastered mindspells *and* wind whispering.

Then I looked at the radio. Most shifters were resistant to magic spells, but humans — and most relics — weren't.

I glanced back. Chico was bopping his head to the tune on his headphones, so he hadn't heard a word. John was sound asleep. And as for Erin...

I peeked at her from the corner of my eye. As before, though, it was hard to tell.

I burned to know. So much, I couldn't help asking as casually as I could.

"I'm still learning the lay of the land here," I said. "Which creek was that they flew over?"

Erin pulled the van into a big clearing where the balloon would land. Then she looked over at me and blinked a few times.

"Didn't you hear? Oak Creek."

I schooled my features into an expressionless mask, making sure not to give anything away. But my heart sank. I'd *wanted* her to be immune to Harlon's magic, or to possess magic of her own.

But she was just a minor relic, it seemed. Clueless. Harmless. Like every other human.

Still, my dragon grumbled. *She's special. Someday, you'll see. And I'd bet she can cause a lot of harm. . . to foolish hearts, at least.*

I made a face, vowing that fool would never be me.

Chapter Eight

ERIN

I did my best to mimic the glassy-eyed, waking-up-from-a-dream state Madden and the other guests stumbled around in once they'd disembarked. Harlon, on the other hand, was eagle-eyed.

"Lovely flight. Just lovely," he said, quietly studying each face, including mine.

My heart raced as I shut off the propane and disengaged the rigging that connected the basket to the balloon. My thoughts raced too, though I tried to exude the same airheaded vibes Harlon's young groupies did. But gee, was that hard. His gaze was a heavy hand pressing on me, and when he finally moved it away, I gulped in relief. Then I did my own spying.

John and Chico hadn't heard Harlon over the radio, but Nash had been listening as attentively as me. Had he really fallen for Harlon's magic, or was it all a bluff?

Which creek was that they flew over?

An innocent question — or an attempt to fool me?

I watched as Nash helped John and Chico fold then roll the balloon. The guy was six feet of muscle and mystery and, as always, impossible to read.

"Come along, everyone." Madden motioned the guests to the picnic basket I'd set out by the van. "Time for breakfast and champagne."

The groupies giggled and followed Harlon like so many trained corgis. I watched as they raised champagne flutes and munched on bagels. From what I'd heard, warlocks were amazing in bed. Though, yuck — I'd always avoided that topic, given that my dad was one. Was that what attracted them to Harlon, or was it his money? Both?

Spotting Madden next, I scowled, half wishing he would choke and die. Well, not really, but I was tempted to strangle him.

That's Painted Rock, he'd told Harlon. *And that green line there is the creek. They say there's a fifth, hidden vortex out there.*

Yes, there was. Operative word, *hidden.* What the hell had Madden been thinking, spilling the beans like that?

And, shit. How did he even know when only a few locals did?

Of course, Madden might have just been spouting something he'd overheard, as he often did. It just happened to be right for a change.

Either way, this was bad, bad news.

It's just a matter of paperwork to get zoning for a whole resort.

Over my dead body. My great-aunt had fought off developers for her entire life, and my sisters and I had sworn to do the same. We'd done our best to keep our property off the radar, but with real estate prices in Sedona skyrocketing, that was hard.

I'm a very persuasive man, Harlon had said.

I snorted. That was true of all warlocks, whose magic multiplied their natural, seductive charm. It was true of my father too. But where my dad's magic was playful and benign, Harlon's was dark and preying. Plus, my father didn't go around enchanting people, and he certainly couldn't overwrite other people's memories.

Of course, that was partly because the magic he wielded was unique. *Elemental* was what my great-aunt called it. That's why Dad was always roaming the West on his motorcycle — he needed that connection to the earth, sky, and wind.

Especially wind, part of me sighed, thinking of the sandstorms he set off from time to time. Some for fun, some by accident, when he was especially mad, sad, or joyous. But even then, Dad was just the match. The kindling was already there, and once that was ignited, there was no telling when Mother Nature might get carried away and let it blow, blow, blow.

The breeze teased my hair, reminding me I had no such powers.

"Miss Sattler."

I nearly jumped. Harlon seemed to appear right beside me. Could the man jump time and space too?

I turned to him with a fake smile. "Oh, hello. Did you enjoy the flight?"

He nodded. "I'm so glad you suggested it. The views over Oak Creek were lovely."

A test, and I knew it. Luckily, the right comeback jumped to my tongue.

"Yes, there's nothing like flying over vineyards, is there?"

He nodded in satisfaction. Whew.

"My only disappointment is that you couldn't fly with us."

Boy, did the man know how to hit all the right notes. Too bad he was such scum.

I managed a regretful smile. "Maybe some other time. But didn't you say you were leaving Sedona soon?"

"Yes, I have a few meetings on my calendar. I'll be off for Chicago, then London..."

Ha. I quietly awarded myself bonus points for guessing correctly.

"...but not before hosting a small party here." He pulled a card from his pocket. "Tomorrow night. I would love it if you could attend."

His expectant air indicated I ought to throw up my hands and gush, *Wow! I'd love that.* But with all my inner alarms clanging, I was closer to *Hell no. Not a party hosted by a warlock.*

I pictured witches and vampires mingling with clueless businessmen and Harlon's groupies. Not that the witches would be sporting pointy black hats. More like designer cocktail dresses, with the only giveaways being hairdos and bustlines that defied gravity. The vampires wouldn't be flashing their teeth, but sipping Bloody Marys while quietly eyeing the necks of any sweet young thing who wandered by.

"Tomorrow night, huh?" My mind spun for plausible excuses.

"Yes, at six. I would be delighted if you could attend."

His voice took on that singsong tone he'd used on the guests, and the air around me went as warm and cozy as a blanket. If I hadn't been aware of Harlon's powers, I might have fallen into a sleepy, agreeable state.

Oh, I'd love to attend your stupid party. And, sure. Let me sell you the ranch too.

It made me sick to think I might have fallen for his tricks.

The thing was, he would be onto me if I didn't agree.

"At six?" I asked, stalling.

He nodded, and the blanket trying to blur my mind wrapped around my shoulders too. And, yikes. It was one thing to resist Harlon's magic when it came through the filter of a radio. Resisting it in person, standing face-to-face...

Deep in my pockets, I clenched my hands, determined not to give in.

"Five o'clock would be even better," he said. "I would love to tap into your knowledge of the area. Maybe we could even talk business."

Until then, the alarms in my mind had been the beeping, digital-watch kind. Now, they whooped like firehouse sirens.

"Business?" I echoed stupidly.

His warm smile was engineered to put me at ease, but the effect was the opposite. "I hope to return to Sedona regularly. It's the perfect place to relax and entertain guests."

Entertain... as in, on the resort he planned to build on my ranch if he could get his dirty hands on it?

I could picture it now, the third hole of a golf course smothering what had once been the east paddock.

Harlon grinned. "My plans are still in the earliest stages, but I like to think big. Such as keeping a balloon pilot on retainer for my guests to be able to fly whenever they wish." He chuckled. "Of course, I'd need to buy a balloon too, but I suppose you could advise me on that."

I blinked. Wow. Did he know how much balloons cost? Not to mention the expense of keeping a pilot around for the rare day guests might hanker for a last-minute, early-morning flight?

Then again, developing the brambles of a remote ranch into a lush resort had to cost millions, so why not throw in a pilot's salary and a balloon?

Admittedly, my heart skipped a few beats. What a dream job. Lots of downtime. No marketing. Just a handful of guests at a time. I even went as far as wondering if they might tip.

Then I caught myself. No, no, no. That was not a dream job. Not if that land was mine — or any of the other last parcels of unspoiled land in the area. And especially not if my boss was a scheming warlock.

I blinked. "Wow. You really do think big."

He grinned. "And I'm very persuasive."

He meant it like a joke, but I caught the threat beneath.

I forced a polite laugh. "I'm sure you are."

"So, you'll come, then?"

"I'd love to, but I doubt my closet has anything appropriate." A weak attempt, but it was all I could think of. And it was absolutely true. For me, dressing up meant decent jeans, a clean shirt, and spit-polished boots.

Harlon threw back his head, laughing. "Miss Sattler, you can come as you are now and still light up the party."

Heat rushed to my cheeks. He was just buttering me up, right? There was no way I could compete with his fashion-model groupies with their big tits, crop tops, and flat bellies. I could only imagine what they would wear to his party. Off-the-shoulder dresses with super-high leg slits? Skintight sheaths they'd have to wiggle into like worms?

The groupies moved in like restless cattle, unhappy with Harlon's attention on me, not them.

"Oh, Harlon..." Groupie Girl One called.

"More champagne?" Groupie Girl Two threw in, hefting a bottle.

Nash moved in too, looking equally alarmed. I scowled. Was he going to warn me off Harlon like he'd warned me away from my father?

And, wait. That would make Nash two for two when it came to spotting warlocks. Was he another warlock? Some kind of other supernatural, maybe?

I huffed, tempted to go to Harlon's party just to spite Nash. The man had to learn to mind his own business.

Then it hit me. *Business.* If I went to Harlon's party, I might find out what he was up to. The way he was sneaking around suggested he was keeping his plans under wraps. Heck, even Bob Hardy, the real estate guy, didn't seem to have a clear idea of what Harlon had planned.

"So, you'll come?" Harlon thrust his card at me with an unspoken command.

I looked down at the card. His contact details were embossed on the front, and a swanky Sedona address was penciled in on the back in tight, neat print.

Harlon leaned in, turning up the charm. "As I said, I'd love to chat at five."

The groupies swarmed in like Africanized honeybees. I stepped away, glad to let them reclaim the space around their sugar daddy.

"I'll be there," I assured him.

"Wonderful. And don't worry about the dress code," Harlon called with a little waggle of his eyebrows, channeling Richard Gere in *Pretty Woman.*

Well, I was no Julia Roberts about to take off on a spending spree. But I did have a plan.

"Thanks again," I called, turning back to work.

Five seconds later, Nash grabbed me by the arm, hissing, "You are not going to that snake's party."

Lucky for him, I pulled free without jabbing my elbow into his solar plexus. Did he think I was completely stupid? And who was he to tell me what to do?

Still, I flashed a sugar-sweet smile while quietly pocketing Harlon's card.

"Of course not."

At least, not without backup. But I wasn't going to spill my whole plan. A plan with a heck of a lot of details to work out in a very short time.

"On three," I told the ground crew. "One...two...three."

We tipped the basket onto its side, then slid it into the trailer. Next, we heaved the rolled-up balloon behind it and finally dusted our hands.

"Our work here is done," John joked, looking at his watch. "And it isn't even eight a.m."

Chico laughed. I pretended to. Nash pinned me with a piercing look I ignored.

Because my work might be done for the morning, but I had a lot to put in place by tomorrow. And the countdown had just begun.

Chapter Nine

ERIN

I knew Harlon's vacation rental would be an impressive piece of real estate, but I still gawked when I pulled up at the gate.

Yes, the gate. With two guards and a dozen cameras pointed in every direction. If they'd wanted to check the oil level of my vintage Chevy, they probably could. Stone walls curtained the entire exclusive community, and a sign read *Coyote Grove Ranch.*

I snorted. *Coyote Grove* implied tidy lines of trees, each sprouting canines. Or did the coyotes frolic under the trees? *Coyote Ranch,* on the other hand, conjured up images of an open range with coyotes quietly chewing their cud.

The marketing exec who'd named this development was definitely not from the Southwest.

I handed Harlon's card to the security guard. "Coyote Grove Ranch, huh?"

The guy shrugged. "You got twelve million dollars to buy a house in there, you can call it anything you like."

I laughed, then waved my thanks as he opened the automatic gate.

He pointed. "Number nine is at the top of the hill."

Of course. Nothing less for Harlon Greene.

"Thanks."

As the gate slid silently aside, I shook my head at the figure sculpted into the center. That canine's tail was so bushy, it screamed fox, not coyote. My sister Abby, the blacksmith, would not be impressed.

More gawking ensued as I followed the meandering road uphill. The houses were huge, and the smallest garage fit four cars. My mind got tangled in the math of a house with eight bedrooms and twice as many baths. That made a toilet-to-car ratio of four-to-one, right?

At the top of the hill, I tried working out a new ratio but failed. Harlon's place was twice as big as the others, with massive, twenty-five-foot windows that reflected the stunning red rock vistas. Very nice, but disorienting, because Cathedral Rock was behind me — yet there it was, reflected in the four long panes straight ahead. The windows on the right framed Bell Rock and a corner of Courthouse Butte, but their positions were flipped.

I parked, leaving a good two yards between my shabby truck and the nearest cars — a BMW and a sparkling Range Rover — then slid out and took a deep breath. The optical illusions of the windows were a good reminder of what I faced inside. Trickery, wrapped in a pretty package designed to distract.

Someone waved from a second-story balcony, and I waved back.

It was Harlon, speaking into a phone. And, wow. Now that I was aware of it, the shimmer of magic around his shoulders was obvious. How had I missed it before?

He paused long enough to call out, "Miss Sattler! Do come in. I'll be down in a minute."

It was more like fifteen, but that gave me time to get my bearings after one of the staff let me in.

Yes, *one* of the staff. Plural.

The foyer was bigger than my entire home, with an ornate staircase straight out of *Gone with the Wind*. The dining area was two stories high, just like the windows, and doors to at last six different rooms opened onto the mezzanine above. Every-thing was done in a grandiose style better suited to Tuscany than Sedona. But it was like the security guy said. If you had twelve million dollars to buy a house, you could decorate in any style you liked.

A handful of other early guests nodded in greeting, then left me alone. One woman kept peeking, though, amused by...my dress? My hair? My shoes? All of the above?

I stared straight at her until she turned meekly away. Ha. My dad had taught me that one. Proof that magic wasn't as important as attitude.

At least, that's what I liked to think.

The caterers were still setting up, so I poured half a glass of champagne and stepped back to gaze out the south windows. So many magnificent mesas and buttes...so much space...

Whack! I jumped when something bounced off the glass outside. A tiny, metallic green form flashed, then plunged to the ground. When I identified it, my heart wept. That was a hummingbird, and it had just broken its neck. Not the first victim of this villa either, judging by the tiny, crumpled bodies on the gravel outside.

I turned away, setting my champagne glass aside.

"Ah, Miss Sattler. What a pleasure."

I whirled, caught off guard. There went Harlon, sneaking up on me again.

He was as groomed and well-dressed as ever, but I saw a cat smeared with feathers and blood.

Still, I stuck on a smile. The game had begun, and I refused to be his pawn.

"Harlon. What a beautiful place you have here."

He gave one of those *Yes, I feel so grateful and privileged to be rich* shrugs. "It is, though I hope to have a place of my own soon." His eyes glinted. "Apropos...that business I wanted to discuss with you. Won't you come to my study?"

My heart pounded as I followed him upstairs. Each step brought me past another painting, though the heavy gold frames left more of an impression than the actual artwork.

"Did you have a good day?" He started with meaningless chitchat designed to put me at ease.

My eyes went to the windows, wondering how many more hummingbirds lay lifeless beneath those panes.

"It's hard not to," I bluffed. "Sedona is so beautiful at this time of year."

"It certainly is."

One of his groupies burst in, squeezed into the tightest sheath dress I'd ever seen. I added two more bonus points to my private score card.

"Help me, Harlon," she whined, holding out a silver choker while shooting me the same side-eye glance as the woman downstairs.

I glared. The sleeveless yellow dress I'd borrowed from Pippa was perfectly fine, and so were Abby's dress boots. And fine was good enough for me.

"Can you put this on, please?" She turned her back to Harlon and waited.

He looped it around her neck in the intimate gesture I was sure she'd been hoping for.

He's all yours, honey, I wanted to laugh. *I have no interest in your man — make that, your warlock. One I suspect of hatching nefarious plans. But don't worry your pretty little head about that. Just keep enjoying your sugar daddy... as long as the good times last.*

Which made me wonder... What was the average "lifespan" of one of Harlon Greene's groupies?

Longer than yours if you're not careful, an inner voice warned me.

"There." Harlon finished and dismissed her with a little pat, making corgi images prance through my mind. "I'll be down soon."

I would bet the ranch she was going to ask him to check something else next — like her earrings or possibly her bra. But a stern look from Harlon made her go glassy-eyed, and she stepped away like a woman in a trance.

I sucked in a deep breath, tightening the mental armor I'd developed through years of interactions with my dad. But my dad was a good-natured warlock, so all I'd ever had to resist were mind games aimed at early bedtimes or eating my vegetables. Would my defenses hold up against a man like Harlon?

"As I was saying..." he started, only to be cut off by another call. "Apologies. I made the mistake of telling my assistant I was available until six." Then he spoke into the phone. "Yes, Bridget?"

I pictured a stunning and highly competent assistant — a modern Moneypenny, capable of conjuring up anything her boss wanted with a few calls, from chilled champagne to hits on his enemies.

"Yes, I've gone over the numbers," Harlon said into the phone.

I wandered over to the fireplace, making a show of inspecting the stonework and definitely, definitely not snooping.

"Yes, and the prognosis..." Harlon continued.

I wandered past a dining-sized table nestled between the fireplace and the windows. Tidy stacks of paperwork covered most of the surface, all paper-clipped and marked with Post-it notes. Was that Bridget's work, or did Harlon's assistant have her own assistant who handled such things?

Brochures and folders half covered a map, and I burned to push them aside. Still, I saw enough to recognize the contours of Bear Mountain — a landmark that literally cast its shadow onto my ranch.

That, and two more items made my gut twist — a book on Native American petroglyphs marked with more Post-its, and an architectural model of a sprawling private compound. The place Harlon intended to build on my land?

Over my dead body, I nearly growled.

"Tell him I'll return his call tomorrow," Harlon continued.

I wandered to the windows, where a telescope pointed west. I didn't peer through it, but I could tell it was aimed slightly left of Bear Mountain, in the vicinity of Painted Rock Ranch.

I moved on, reminding myself not to peer down at the hummingbird graveyard outside.

Harlon went on talking, giving me time to circle his desk and note everything, though there was nothing as obvious as a manila folder marked *Top Secret: Plot to Steal Painted Rock Ranch.*

There was a second door to the office, however. I penciled it into my mental map of the house.

Eventually, Harlon thanked Bridget and hung up — just as the doorbell rang downstairs.

Grimacing, he checked his watch. "Five forty-five. Where does the time go? And since when are guests so damned punctual?"

I laughed, secretly relieved.

"So inconvenient," I joked.

He ran a hand through his thick hair — another hallmark of a warlock, or at least a man with supernatural blood. Most mere humans went bald with age.

"Then I suppose I should use our time well. I hoped to ask if you knew of any properties for sale. You know, given your local knowledge."

His expression was neutral, but I could sense his magic inching toward me.

I played dumb while raising my mental shield — slowly, subtly, lest he notice.

"Oh. Did that place along Oak Creek not work out?"

He shrugged. "I was hoping for something a little more remote. Not too far out of town, but somewhere off the beaten path would be good."

Someplace like yours. He didn't say that much, but the words slithered into my mind, and I nearly parroted them back to him.

Resisting magic was like tuning out an annoying, intermittent noise. Like when Abby used the weed whacker on my only morning to sleep in or when Roscoe barked hysterically, then stopped, only to kick back in again. Not too difficult in principle, but nigh impossible once the sound got under your skin.

"Unfortunately, every parcel of land up to the national forest has been bought up," I said, still playing dumb.

His eyes sparkled, and I cringed. Was that his Plan B — to convince town planners to carve out part of that protected land and rework the zoning? As absurd as it sounded, Harlon could probably pull it off.

"Every single parcel?" Harlon waited, letting the silence stretch.

"There is Granite Wash Ranch," I tried, mentioning the latest big-ticket property to be listed. Everyone in town was talking about it.

He shook his head. "Unfortunately, it doesn't meet my specifications."

You mean, no vortex? I nearly quipped.

"Anything else you can think of?" Harlon probed.

In the awkwardness of the long, quiet minute that ensued, my defenses slipped. Crap.

"Oh. You mean where I live?"

He nodded warmly, and his magic congratulated me on being a good girl.

I flashed a sunny, Pippa-grade smile. "Too bad it's not for sale."

His grin didn't falter. "Too bad."

His magic wormed its way around me, prodding for weak spots. *Not for sale yet,* a siren's voice whispered. *But just imagine if you sold it. You'd never have to work another day in your life.* The warmth around me intensified, like a candlelit bubble bath on a chilly night. *You could even work out a deal and live rent-free in your cabin to the end of your days.*

"Perhaps you'll reconsider." He pulled a large manila envelope from his briefcase and slid it across the desk. "Go on, open it."

As if my heart weren't already hammering away.

At a loss for words, I fiddled with the envelope. And, holy crap. When the flap opened, I caught a glimpse of a wad of greenbacks. Correction — many, many wads with lots and lots of greenbacks.

Harlon chuckled. "Go on. Have a look."

I pulled out a bundle of bills. *Hundred* dollar bills, neatly wrapped in a white paper strip with the total marked in pink numbers. A one and so many zeroes, my eyes blurred.

When I gasped, Harlon grinned the way rich people did when they were oh-so generous.

"That's just a down payment."

My brain short-circuited. Wow. I'd never seen so much money.

So much money... The words coated my mind like honey.

I knew it was Harlon's trickery, but... well... Maybe it wouldn't be so bad to be tricked.

Then I pictured a golf course and hot tubs — and, most importantly, the vortex.

I slid the envelope back over. "Unfortunately, my ranch is not for sale."

Harlon's cheek twitched as if I'd just spoken in a foreign language. And I suppose I had, because he probably didn't hear *no* too often.

"You don't know how much I'm offering."

I shrugged. "Some things don't have a price."

He scoffed. "Everything has a price."

"Granite Wash Ranch does. Seventeen million, from what I hear," I tried redirecting him. "Two hundred and fifty acres and lots of privacy."

Harlon gazed at me impassively, not saying a word.

The silence was crushing, and I hurried to fill it. "Then there's Crooked Canyon Ranch. It's much more accessible, and the water runs year-round. Our creek dries earlier and earlier each year." I shook my head sadly, stressing how unsuitable the land was.

He leaned in, gazing deep into my eyes. "To be absolutely truthful, I'm not interested in any other place. You can name your price. Say, twenty-one million?"

Technically, that was him naming my price, but I decided not to point that out.

Twenty-one million, a smooth, soft voice cooed in my mind.

I gulped. Twenty-one million was a lot of money — even divided by three. My sisters and I could buy a smaller, more manageable place on the edge of Sedona. Heck, each of us could. I could buy my own balloon and fly just because I wanted to. Abby could open her own shop and pick and choose which jobs she accepted. Ditto for Pippa — no more boring old wineglasses to create day in, day out in the hot shop. We could even find adjoining properties and open a proper animal sanctuary to add to the handful of swaybacked horses we'd already taken in. We could even breed alpacas...

Wait. Alpacas?

I frowned, catching myself. Or had I just caught Harlon weaving another mind spell?

I closed my eyes, searching desperately for some way to turn him down without revealing that I was onto him.

I gulped and stuck on what I hoped was a dumb blonde look. "I'm sorry, but it's not for sale."

His jaw went hard and his gaze piercing. But a moment later, he worked up a thin smile and turned back on the charm.

"Such a pity. It's a good thing I'm a patient man."

Subtext: *I can wait longer than you, so make a deal while you can.*

I wrestled my face into a fake grin. "I'm sure you'll find something. And this place isn't exactly bad."

I laughed, cueing him to do the same, though his chuckle had a forced edge.

Thank goodness the doorbell rang, and this time, a chorus of voices carried up the stairs.

"Harlon! You'll miss your own party!"

I flashed him an apologetic smile and made for the door. "I'd hate to keep you from your guests. But I'll keep an eye out for any property for sale."

"Very kind of you. Please stay and enjoy the party."

He followed me out of the office, and the door clicked when he shut it behind us. Locked?

My heart went into double time. I would find out soon enough.

Chapter Ten

ERIN

The party was pretty much what I'd expected — lots of schmoozing rich folks who didn't seem to know one another yet pretended they did. By seven o'clock, a line of fancy cars stretched down the side of the road, sleek SUVs alternating with classy sedans and a handful of sports cars. Conversations focused on mutual funds, real estate deals, and how thin/not thin so-and-so looked. Fancy finger food and drinks were served amid the soothing background music of a professional pianist with an impressively long name that made her sound like the great-great-granddaughter of Rachmaninoff, give or take a few syllables.

No magic on display, or even hidden magic, from what I could tell after studying each guest. Only Harlon, who charmed his way around the room.

I endured an hour of mingling and rich people jokes along the lines of "... and then he called my Rocket Espresso a coffee machine!"

Finally, Harlon was pulled aside by two balding business-men — my chance to sneak upstairs.

I made my way up slowly, pretending to admire the artwork. The door to Harlon's office opened onto the mezzanine that anyone could see from below, but that side door I'd noticed...

I tiptoed down the hallway, knocked softly, opened the door... and bingo. A marble-lined bathroom opened onto the hallway as well as the room on the other side.

Office, here I come.

With one last, furtive look around, I slipped through the bathroom and into the office, locking both doors behind me.

Let the snooping commence.

My heart was in my throat the whole time, and every few seconds, I swore I would only stay a few more. Because, shit. I *really* didn't want to be caught here.

I pictured the dead birds lying beneath the windows. Would I end up among them with my neck brutally twisted to one side? Or did Harlon have another place to dispose of burglars?

By then, the sun had set, and enough moonlight filtered into the room to see. I started at the table with the brochures and map. Using a pen to move things gently around — that's how burglars avoided leaving fingerprints, right? — I exposed more of the map. There wasn't anything as damning as a red circle around my property, but the map had been folded back to focus on that area, which was bad enough.

Then I tried the folders. It took me three tries to flip the first one open, only to find brochures with the usual tourist spiel about crystals, Jeep tours, and vortexes. A second folder held a welcome packet from the Sedona Chamber of Commerce. The third...

My breath caught.

The seal of the county assessor's office graced the top of the first page. Below that was a full report on Painted Rock Ranch, with all previous owners, estimated value, tax assessments, sales history...

The fact that those details were a matter of public record didn't ease my fears.

Laughter filtered in from downstairs. I looked up, then hurried over to check Harlon's desk.

Using the pen to pull open drawer after drawer, all I found was stationery and office supplies. Then I flipped the book on Native American rock art open to a page marked with a Post-it note. Then the next and the next. All showed black-and-white photos of rock art, and while each shot contained several adjoining symbols, the common denominator in each was a spiral.

I skimmed the text beneath a close-up from the V-Bar-V Ranch Heritage Site.

Early interpretations of the spiral symbol identified it as a snake, though others interpret it as the path of the sun. Another theory is that such spirals mark water holes, while still others suggest energy fields or even portals to another world.

My arm twitched at the memory of being pushed back by an invisible force. I doubted the portal theory, but *energy field* certainly fit.

An energy field that could do... what, exactly?

I flipped the book shut and considered Harlon's laptop. Did I dare?

Just as I let my hand hover near it, a shadow fell over the moonlight behind me.

I whirled to face the windows. A man was hauling himself over the rail of the balcony. Slowly, I backed up. Had he seen me? Could I get away?

And, wait. What was he doing climbing onto the balcony?

I frowned. So far, my fears had all focused on being discovered by Harlon or one of his guests. But this guy...

I stared. Broad shoulders. Quick, silent movements, like a cat — or an assassin. Denim jacket, worn boots...

Nash?

He froze, spotting me. Then he frowned, stalked forward, and motioned to the latch.

I huffed. This was my sneak-in job, not his, dammit.

My blood boiled. Was it not enough for him to ruin my chances of ever piloting solo? Did he have to mess around with my snooping on Harlon, too?

He motioned to the latch a second time.

I folded my arms over my chest. No. Just no.

He stared. One of those uncomprehending male stares that said, *You're not jumping to follow directions? Even when they're so simple?*

I huffed. It was like training a dog. Sometimes men had to learn the hard way.

It was only when he rattled the handle, making a racket, that I gave in and opened the door.

"What the hell are you doing here?" he hissed, stepping in with a waft of cold air.

I went back to my folded-arm pose. "Says the man sneaking in from the balcony."

"You're the one in Harlon's office with the lights off." Staring at my dress, he frowned. "Wait. You came to his party? Willingly?"

"No, he hypnotized me into coming."

Nash's eyes went wide. "I knew it! You noticed what he did to the guests yesterday."

I stuck my hands on my hips. "Of course I did."

"And yet you didn't tell me," he grunted, then paused. "Wait. Did you think I didn't notice?"

He sounded so offended, I had to snort. "Hard to tell the difference between a con man and a fool sometimes."

His eyes blazed. "You mean me?"

I shrugged. "I could add burglar to the list."

He stalked forward — so close, I had to look up. "I'm not here to steal."

"Then what are you here for?"

He started to answer, then grabbed my elbow instead, hustling me toward the balcony. "You can't be here. You have no idea what you're getting into."

I yanked my arm away. "Maybe it's you who doesn't know."

"I told you not to come here," he persisted.

"Clearly, I didn't listen. Are you starting to notice a pattern?" I jabbed my finger at his chest as I whisper-barked the next few words. "You are not my boss. You do not tell me what to do."

He shook his head as if I was the unreasonable one, then tried a new tack. "It's dangerous."

"For you, Mr. Pink Panther. I have an invitation."

He motioned around. "Into Harlon's private office?"

"I lost my way to the ladies' room."

"Ha. I've never met anyone with a better sense of direction than you."

I opened my mouth, then closed it, thrown by the indirect compliment.

Nash leaned closer. "You're here because you know what he's up to."

"I'm here because I know he's up to something, and I want to know what that is."

Nash raised his eyebrows. "Even if it gets you killed?"

Who knows how long our staring contest might have lasted if the door handle hadn't turned just then.

We whirled. Shit.

Nash hauled me toward the balcony, but not outside, because there was no time. Instead, he ducked behind the heavy floor-to-ceiling curtains, pulled me in beside him, and stuck a finger in front of his lips.

I glared, making sure he got my message. *Not stupid, remember?*

He hooked a foot around mine and pulled back so my toes wouldn't show.

I grimaced. Okay, okay. I wasn't stupid, but I hadn't thought of that. But that was because I wasn't an experienced... burglar? Assassin? What was Nash anyway? He wasn't just another guy who'd happened to drift through Sedona, that was for sure.

We stood still, listening to the office door open, then close, followed by the steps of one — no, two — people sneaking in.

I did a double take. Wait. Sneaking? What was it with this office?

That did solve one minor mystery, though — the main door hadn't been locked after all. Not that it mattered at this point.

"Oh, Josh..." a woman murmured.

I blinked. That had to be Harlon's Groupie Girl Two... or Three. I could tell by the airheaded voice and attitude.

"Cindy..." a man breathed.

"Candy," she corrected, not at all perturbed.

"Sorry, baby," the guy said.

Heavy breathing made their mission abundantly clear. A zipper zipped, and a shoe fell to the floor.

"I need you," Josh breathed. "Right here." That was followed by a low thump. Him lifting Cindy — er, Candy — to the desk?

"Right here is perfect," she cooed.

More heavy breathing. I could have screamed. Was this really happening?

Nash checked his watch. Was he on a deadline or something?

Then I cursed — very, very quietly. He might not have a deadline, but I did. Sooner or later, someone would notice I'd slipped away from the party.

Someone like Harlon. Shit.

I eyed the balcony door, which showed in the gap between the curtain and the wall. But unless the young lovers got really absorbed in their... er, hanky-panky, there was no way to slip out unnoticed.

Nash gave me a firm look. We were in for the long haul.

"Oh. Oh. Oh!" Candy moaned.

I didn't want to imagine what Josh was doing, but I couldn't help it. Not with the action just two steps away.

"Wait. This way." Josh stepped toward the curtain. I couldn't see him, but my sixth sense told me so.

Nash went flat against the wall and pulled me close, my back to his chest. Not the place I wanted to be, but we had no choice.

Another zipper unzipped — Josh's fly? — and something struck the curtain, then fell away. Candy's underwear?

"Oh, baby..." Josh groaned.

Pippa liked to joke that sex was like softball — more fun to do than to watch. And while I wasn't watching, my other senses filled me in on exactly what was going on. The rocking of hips. The muffled slap of Josh's balls. The scratch of Candy's talons — er, nails — across his back...

"Oh...Oh..." Candy moaned on.

I couldn't help wondering. Did Harlon mind sharing? Did he care? Or were these Josh's last hours of life as a man before he was turned into a toad?

That was one little corner of my mind. The rest went in a totally different direction, and I couldn't help but get a little...um...warm. Achy. Hungry — for sex. And not with Josh.

With Nash, I was appalled to realize. That was where my mind went.

What would it be like to be on a desk with Nash's corded arms braced on either side of my head? What would it be like to wrap my legs around him and buck every time he thrust?

I puffed a little air up over my cheeks. It didn't help. Especially with me pancaked up against him, my rear to his groin.

I gritted my teeth. I was not interested in anything about Nash. Especially sex.

If only my girl parts would get that message.

"Oh... Oh..." Candy went on, cueing more groans from Josh.

Apparently, they were reaching the climax of their little romp. The sooner, the better. Because another few minutes of this, and I would start twerking against Nash.

"Yes..." Josh breathed.

Nash inched sideways. Shit. It was bad enough that I was getting turned on. Him too?

Crap, crap, crap. How had it come to this?

Finally, the two banging bunnies came. But that only led to throaty sighs, light giggles, and soft touches.

I was not a giggler. And I doubted Nash was a throaty sigher. But soft touches...

Funny how much I yearned for that. My last friend-with-benefits had been quite a while ago now, and although Nash was aggravating, he was also undeniably hot. Really hot, in an off-the-charts, superhuman way.

Which was when it struck me.

Superhuman...

I didn't have space to turn, but in my mind, I examined him from head to toe. Those sparkling brownish-green eyes — really sparkling, edging over to a glowing bronze color sometimes. Strength that exceeded what even his impressive muscles ought to be able to exert. The cagey, animal-like restlessness...

What if the man I was stuck behind a curtain with wasn't all human?

An idea I'd come back to later. My brain was already processing too many inputs.

"Baby, you're beautiful," Josh murmured.

I tried not to picture Candy splayed out on Harlon's desk.

"And you're amazing," her pigeon-sized brain made her coo.

I wanted to stir the air with my hand and whisper, *Get back to the party, guys.*

"I guess we ought to get back to the party," Josh sighed.

I froze. Just a coincidence, right?

"I guess we should," Candy agreed. Then she brightened. "But this is a big house. We could sneak off again. You know, to the pool..."

"The billiards room..." Josh chimed in.

Anywhere but this office. I pushed the thought in their direction, just as an experiment.

"Anywhere but the back of a car," Candy chuckled.

I considered. Close enough?

Josh and Candy took their sweet time getting decent again.

"Now, where's your underwear?" Josh chuckled, groping around.

I went stone-still when his hand brushed my foot. Thank goodness he found the lingerie instead of my toes.

"Here you go," he said.

Candy giggled. "Only so you can take it off again later."

I tried not to gag. If I ever had sex with Nash — which I never, ever would — I would certainly not be spouting lines like that.

Josh and Candy finally slipped out the door, but Nash and I remained pressed close behind the curtain for a while.

Just in case someone else comes along, I told myself. Not for any other reason. Not at all.

Chapter Eleven

NASH

If I had stayed smashed up against the wall with Erin's perfect ass pressed against me a minute longer, I would have exploded. Or moaned, because the hard-on I'd been desperately trying to suppress hurt like hell with nowhere to go.

My dragon grumbled something about knowing exactly where it ought to go.

I ignored it. But, damn. Maybe it was time for me to get out of town. Every time I'd brushed up against Erin at work over the past few days, the little embers she'd kindled inside me on day one flared into a full-fledged fire.

On the plus side, it was good to feel alive after months of senses so muted, I was less *man* than *machine*. At first, I thought Sedona might be stimulating my mind back toward *pleasantly aware*. But maybe that wasn't Sedona. Maybe it was Erin.

Definitely Erin, my dragon breathed.

One thing was for sure. The physical attraction was getting harder and harder to ignore.

Like now. Really, really hard.

Literally, my dragon grumbled.

A damn good thing I had enough space to turn sideways and hide the bulge in my jeans.

Maybe Erin doesn't want it hidden, my dragon whispered. *Maybe she wants this as much as we do.*

I shook my head. There was no *this*. She hated me, and I wasn't interested in her. I wasn't interested in *anything*, and I hadn't been for months.

Until now. Being with Erin was the highlight of my day, every day. And since we finished work at about eight in the morning, the rest of the day was pretty much all downhill.

"The coast is clear," she whispered, stepping out from behind the curtain.

I took a few deep breaths before following her, still coaxing away that hard-on. Even then, I made sure not to look at the desk, though my dragon insisted on imagining her there with her long, toned legs wrapped around me — Erin, not Candy.

Hell no, my dragon huffed.

I cleared my throat, trying to get back to business.

"You need to get out of here," I said, picking up where we'd left off before.

"I'm the one with the invitation. You're the one who needs to get away before someone sounds the alarm."

"Like you?"

"Believe me, I'm tempted."

"Harlon is the bad guy here, not me."

She crossed her arms. "I know Harlon is the bad guy. It's you I'm still deciding about."

Ha. Me, a bad guy? I worked for the Agency for the Detection and Monitoring of Supernatural Activity. I was the one who hunted down bad guys.

Then I remembered, and my dragon murmured sadly, *Not any more.*

I swallowed hard, trying to concentrate.

"I'm on your side, Erin."

She looked deep into my eyes. Deeper than I thought the view in there could go. Then she jutted her chin. "Prove it."

I would love to, but I had to coax her out of Harlon's lair first.

I pointed toward the hallway. "All right. You make a quick exit out the front door. Tell Harlon you're tired...sick...whatever. Then we'll meet."

"Meet? Where?" She narrowed her eyes, and I nearly sighed. Did she think I was planning to lure her to some dark, quiet alley and murder her?

"Back on the main road. The first big intersection with a light. There's a quad rental place there."

Her eyes flickered with recognition, but she didn't agree — yet.

"We'll talk there," I promised. "You tell me what you know, and I'll tell you what I know."

She shook her head. "The other way around."

"Fine. Just go." I shooed her toward the door.

She made a face but finally edged out of the office and into the bathroom, then out the far door, murmuring, "Easier said than done."

I looked over her shoulder. The bathroom opened on a side hallway, but it was close enough to the mezzanine that someone at the party could see her if they glanced up at the right time. Even if she snuck out unnoticed, she couldn't just saunter down the stairs. How would she explain where she'd been?

I cursed the young lovers who'd made us waste so much time.

"Maybe that way?" I pointed the other way down the hall.

Erin shook her head, thinking. Then she pulled out her phone, squared her shoulders, and stepped boldly out into the hall. Without bothering to conceal herself, she paced to the mezzanine and back, holding her phone to her ear.

"What are you doing?" I hissed.

"Taking a very important call away from the noise of the party, of course," she muttered before pacing back to the mezzanine. She stood in plain view, intent on her fictional call, then paced to a window and gestured as if in conversation.

She pulled off the charade perfectly, even waving to someone downstairs. Harlon?

So sorry, the gesture said. *I'll be down in a minute.*

Smart woman, my dragon hummed.

Beautiful woman, I couldn't help thinking. At work, she wore jeans, a long-sleeved T-shirt, and a thick flannel shirt over that. A down-to-earth, *what you see is what you get* look that fit her perfectly. But wow. That yellow dress brought out her beauty in a whole different way.

Downstairs, someone tapped a spoon against a glass, and the guests quieted.

Erin mouthed something to her imaginary caller. Something like, *I have to go now.*

From my angle, I could only see a handful of guests in one corner of the dining area below. No one stood out, but a cold, gnawing presence crept over my soul.

The hair on the back of my neck stood, and not just because Harlon stepped into the space I could see.

Flashing his perfect, *I'm such a rich asshole* smile, Harlon motioned someone closer to his side. A woman in a tight red dress appeared, showing off her too-thin figure and the elaborate twist in her jet-black hair.

Cold sweat broke out on my brow.

God, no. Not her. Not here. Not now, my dragon half growled, half whimpered.

"Ladies and gentlemen, thank you for joining me here tonight," Harlon announced. "I'd like to take this opportunity to introduce my business associate..."

I clutched the doorjamb. *Please, no. Not Angelina.*

"Angelina Saint James," Harlon said.

Every syllable twisted a knife in my soul.

When Angelina smiled, her wine-red lips contrasted with the white blaze of her teeth. Well, her human teeth. Her pointy canines gave the barest hint at what lay hidden beneath.

Vampire.

She gave the guests a regal wave that said, *I know I'm gorgeous, so don't be shy about admiring me. I do it all the time.*

She wasn't gorgeous, though. She was far too pale and bony, and her eyes didn't take in her surroundings so much as pick through them for potential prey. Still, her commanding air made up for that in a kind of *I believe I'm gorgeous, so you will believe it too* leap of logic.

Once upon a time, I really had believed. Now, I just felt sick.

Too late, I realized my heart was pounding, my blood rushing.

Angelina's nose twitched as she surveyed the crowd.

"We'll be announcing the details of our latest project soon. A mutually beneficial partnership of our unique talents, you might say." Harlon chuckled.

A warlock and a vampire conspiring? Very bad news.

"But tonight, we're all off the clock," Harlon finished, making everyone laugh. Then he raised his glass. "Enjoy the party, everyone."

A round of applause broke out, but all I heard was the pounding of my heart.

Angelina's nostrils flared, and her eyes took on a predatory look.

Get away from the door, I screamed at my legs. *Get away from here. Get away from her.*

Harlon was bad news, but Angelina took evil to an entirely new level. And if she sensed I was here...

Not *if. When.* But despite my mind barking orders, my legs just wouldn't obey.

Out of the corner of my eye, I saw Erin frown at me.

The alarms clanging in my ears were deafening, but I couldn't move. Hell, I could scarcely think.

Angelina's obsidian eyes bounced over the guests, then rose.

Erin! I wanted to scream. *Run away. Hide.*

Erin went stiff as Angelina's eyes roved over, then past her. Luckily, she had the presence of mind not to glance in my direction and give me away.

But it was only a question of time. Angelina was a vampire, and once a vampire had tasted your blood, they could always hunt you down.

Always, her greedy eyes promised as they flitted toward the door I clutched.

Move! Hide! Step back! Erin's voice sounded in my mind.

So maybe she didn't hate me. Not enough to see me get sucked dry by a vampire, at least.

The thought wasn't comforting, especially since it could be my last.

Then something metal clattered downstairs — loud enough for every guest to whip around and gasp. Another crash followed the first.

The sound wasn't what distracted Angelina, though. It was a smell that made her spin around.

A smell that only reached me a moment later. Fresh blood.

"Oh no! I'm so sorry," someone downstairs cried. "All the spare ribs..."

Angelina's eyes practically glowed, totally focused there.

"Oh God. I hope I don't lose my job..." that same *someone* fretted.

Still, I stood dumbly, practically begging Angelina to find me.

It was only Erin's voice booming through my mind that finally shoved me into action.

Get back! Now!

With a lurch, I broke away and rushed to the balcony. It was time to exit this mansion the way I'd entered. Pronto. But, yikes. What the hell had just happened?

Angelina happened, my dragon sighed. *Some klutz from catering saved your ass.*

A catering klutz who looked strangely familiar, I decided, catching a glimpse of her through the ground-floor windows before I took off into the night. On foot, like a common criminal, because there was no way Harlon — or worse, Angelina — would miss the burst of energy that accompanied a shift.

...and you heard Erin's thoughts, my dragon finished.

Unexpected, for sure. But it did confirm my hunch about her being a relic — or more. We not-quite-humans could communicate without speaking if we tried hard enough. Especially in extreme or urgent situations.

I sprinted away from the house, replaying it all in my mind.

A few steps later, I nearly stumbled, placing the caterer.

Whatshername, my dragon murmured in shock. *Erin's sister.*

Pippa, I remembered.

I ran, keeping to the shadows. All this time, I'd been thinking Erin didn't know much. But maybe she knew more than she let on.

We have to talk, my dragon grumbled. *We definitely have to talk.*

Chapter Twelve

ERIN

It took another fifteen minutes for me to excuse myself from Harlon's party, though every second was an eternity. The guests were all buzzing about the — bewitching? beautiful? terrifying? — woman Harlon had introduced or tut-tutting about the catering disaster.

"I'm so sorry." Pippa cried over the mess she'd made. Literally.

My sister was brilliant — in action and acting. She cried so long and so pitifully, the guests forgave her mistake and even helped clean up the mess.

I would have helped too, but I couldn't risk anyone figuring out we were related. Not when Pippa had used one of her many connections to infiltrate the catering team and act as my backup.

Yep, that would be a little tricky to explain.

Besides, it was hard enough for me to wheedle my way past Harlon.

"It's been lovely, but I really have to get going. That's the downside of the balloon business," I lamented. "Four a.m. wake-ups make for very early bedtimes."

Harlon nodded as slowly as he released my hand from his possessive handshake.

"Such a pity. I wanted to introduce you to Angelina."

Thank God she was on the other side of the room.

She looked over, pinning me with a reptilian stare, then making eye contact with Harlon in a way that made me tense even more.

"Truly a pity." I did my best to sound genuine. "But thanks again for inviting me."

"Thank you for coming. I hope we can meet again soon."

He didn't mention my property, but I sensed the subtext.

"That would be very nice." Boy, was I was turning into a serial liar. "Good night."

The moment I stepped outside, I sucked in the crisp night air. Not just to steady my nerves, but to clear my foggy mind too. Was that just the stuffiness of the party or a side-effect of Harlon's subtle mind games?

I forced myself to walk, not run, to my Chevy and drive away at the speed limit, checking the rearview mirror the whole time.

The security gate took forever to open, and I eyed the cameras capturing me from four different angles. A good thing Nash wasn't with me. But, yikes. How had he gotten past security?

And, shit. What if he hadn't?

I tapped my jittery fingers on the steering wheel.

"Good night," the guard called agreeably.

"Good night," I called back as innocently as possible.

The moment I turned the first corner, I floored the gas pedal. Five minutes later, I slowed at a traffic signal and coasted into the quad rental parking. The office was locked up and dim, but bright lights illuminated the quads out front. I drove around to the back, killed the engine, and waited.

And waited...

Where was Nash? More importantly, *who* was Nash? What was his interest in Harlon — and why had he frozen at the sight of that woman?

That *vampire,* a little voice reminded me.

A good thing Pippa had realized that in time. Of we three half sisters, Pippa was the most tuned in to supernatural beings. *Other* supernatural beings, she might say, including herself in that category. Abby and I didn't, though we didn't fit in with humans either. We were the unlucky losers of a genetic lottery in which our parents' different powers had canceled each other out, leaving us with no special abilities.

I frowned as a scrap of trash stirred in a breeze. There'd been no wind a moment ago, but now that I'd idly wiggled my fingers...

Okay, *nearly* no abilities. Nothing worth mentioning anyway. Not when my dad could conjure up entire dust storms, like that huge haboob that had consumed Phoenix years ago.

I remembered him watching the news that evening, then whispering, *Oops.*

All because of a sports car driver who had cut him off, then flipped him the bird.

A good lesson about events spinning out of control... a little like now, maybe.

The bushes stirred, and I spun around. Another false alarm, but it did turn my thoughts back to Nash. Was he a warlock too?

I snorted. No, because the man had zero charisma — the most identifiable warlock trait.

What, then? A vampire?

My blood chilled, but I rejected that too. He lacked their creepy aura, not to mention their slick, polished appearance and manners. At least, that's how Pippa claimed to spot them.

A shifter, maybe?

My hand tightened around the steering wheel. Shifters came in all types, so they were hard to pin down.

My lips tightened bitterly. *A lot like Mom.*

Footsteps scuffed at the far end of the lot, and I whirled in the driver's seat. Before I had time to say *boo*, someone yanked the passenger door open and jumped in.

"Hit it," Nash ordered, pointing to the road.

I scowled. "Nice to see you too."

"Nice to see you," he grunted with zero warmth. "Hit it."

With a screech of tires, I pulled out and headed west on 89A. When Nash reached up to adjust the rearview mirror to his angle, I turned it back.

"My car, my mirror. Where's yours?"

"My car?" He made a vague gesture. "I came on foot."

I wasn't sure I bought that story, but that was the least of my worries now.

A few minutes passed in tense silence before he suddenly erupted.

"Dammit, I told you not to go to Harlon's!"

I snorted. "Sorry, boss. Oh, wait. That's me."

"This isn't about work."

"No, it isn't. It's about a warlock, a vampire, and a man who has no right to boss me around. Or wait. Are you even a man? As in, human?"

He stared.

I drove through another three lights, close to crushing the steering wheel in my tight grip. Then I cracked.

"Boy, you really think I'm stupid, don't you?"

He shook his head quickly. "Not stupid. I thought you were human. . . or close enough."

"Gee, thanks for underestimating me."

The worn tires of my pickup hummed over another mile of road before he finally murmured, "Sorry."

I made a face. Let him apologize. I didn't have to accept it gracefully.

He went on a little lamely. "I thought Harlon's spell worked on you yesterday, during the flight."

I shrugged. "I'm a good pretender."

"Or a good liar."

I shrugged. "You lied too. Who are you? *What* are you?"

A grim purse of the lips was his only answer.

By then, we'd nearly passed the exit for Paige Springs, but I hit the brakes and turned at the last minute. Nash braced himself as we careened off the highway. He still had both arms against the dashboard when I pulled over and faced him.

"I'll say it again. Who are you? *What* are you? And what are you up to?"

"I'm not up to anything."

"No, you're just happy being mindless," I barked, echoing his own words. Then I shook my head impatiently. "You show up at my job. You show up at Buffalo Bill's the night my sisters and I went there—" Suddenly suspicious, I grabbed him by the collar, growling, "If you're after one of my sisters. . ."

He stuck up his hands. "I'm not after anyone. I swear."

I kept my hands twisted in the fabric of his shirt a moment longer, then released him with a little shove.

"No, you just happen to keep appearing in my life. Including at Harlon's party. All just coincidence?"

His eyes sparkled at the accusation and not in a good way. But then he frowned, considering.

I killed the engine and switched off the headlights, plunging the view from starkly contrasting shadows to a softer, undulating outline of the landscape.

"Fine," I grumbled. "Let me keep it simple for you. Who do you work for?"

"Desert Skies Balloon Adventures."

I scoffed. "Who do you *really* work for?"

A roadrunner scurried across the dirt road, and we watched as it disappeared into the bushes. Nash kept his eyes there a long time before answering.

"I don't work for anyone other than Henry. Not any more. But I used to work for the ADMSA."

He watched my reaction. Did he actually expect me to recognize that jumble of letters?

I didn't, so I got creative. "ADMSA...Association of Dimwits Making Stupid Assumptions?"

His eyebrows popped up. "Uh, no. The Agency for the Detection and Monitoring of Supernatural Activity."

"I like mine better," I muttered, but then his words sank in. "Wait. The agency for *what*?"

He peered around as if the next roadrunner might report him for spilling state secrets. "The Agency for the Detection and Monitoring of Supernatural Activity. We—" He grimaced, correcting himself. "*They* keep an eye on the likes of Harlon...Angelina..."

I bared my teeth. "My father?"

He shook his head. "No. Yes. I mean, warlocks in general. Not your father in particular."

I studied his face for a lie but didn't detect one.

"Are they keeping an eye on Harlon?" I tried next.

Nash made a face. "If they aren't, they ought to be. He's up to no good."

I huffed. "Like it takes a special agency to figure that out." Then I stopped. "Whose jurisdiction is this agency under?"

He hesitated, then murmured, "The government's."

I rolled my eyes. *No shit, Sherlock.* "I mean, what branch?"

"That's classified. I shouldn't even be telling you it exists."

"Because I'm likely to announce it to everyone at Buffalo Bill's?" I laughed without humor. "Like anyone would believe me."

He didn't say anything.

I mulled it all over. "You don't work for this agency any more, and yet here you are, snooping on me."

"I'm not snooping on anyone."

"No, you were just joining the party very quietly through the second-floor balcony when no one was looking."

He made a face, but I had him there, and he knew it.

"Even though I don't work for the agency, I can still report suspicious activity. But I need more than a hunch to do that."

"Harlon rewriting the memories of seven balloon passengers doesn't count as evidence?"

"Evidence of malicious wrongdoing, I mean."

I cackled. "Malicious? Why don't you report that Angelina woman, then?"

He paled. Clearly, I'd struck a nerve there.

"Vampires weren't what I trained for." His eyes dulled, hinting at a lie — or a stretch in the truth, at least.

"How do you train for vampires?" I pictured a 007-style lab equipped with wooden stakes, cloves of garlic, and booby-trapped coffins.

"Good question," Nash murmured bitterly.

Was that bitterness aimed at all vampires or Angelina in particular? And, yikes. Did he and she have a history?

Jealousy stabbed my gut, which was weird. Jealousy was when you wanted the guy, and that wasn't the case here. Not even remotely.

"Can you report her — and Harlon?" I tried.

"I could." His flat tone didn't exactly inspire.

"Why wouldn't you?"

He looked at his feet for a long time before replying. "I left for...several reasons..."

I bit back the impulse to fill in his pause with some guesses. *Inability to cooperate? Poor communication? Insubordination?*

Angelina? the back of my mind added.

Finally, he continued. "One reason I left was a hunch that we'd been infiltrated and that someone was leaking information."

"Leaking information to whom? Harlon?"

He shrugged. "Possibly. I never got to the bottom of it. But entire investigations were compromised, and agents were endangered. I reported my suspicions, but no one took it seriously. Maybe the higher-ups I reported to were guilty." He ran his fingers through his hair and sighed. "Who knows."

I resisted the urge to smooth his hair back into place, because a lock had fallen over his eye, giving him that tortured bad-boy look women found irresistible.

Other women, I mean.

I forced my focus to a different topic. "How is an agent supposed to protect him or herself against a warlock, anyway?"

"You tell me." He held my gaze stubbornly. "You're the one who took on Harlon."

"I didn't take him on. I was just...just..."

"Snooping?"

I sighed. "Yes, snooping. But he snooped first."

Not a good argument, but I was in no mood to brush up my logic.

"He was snooping around your property, you mean," Nash said.

I nodded slowly, wondering how much to tell him.

"A property with a secret vortex," Nash continued.

I glared. I was the one questioning *him*, dammit.

But I was getting tired of arguing, and I had no idea what to do about Harlon.

I eyed Nash warily, considering. "What was that agency again? The BDSM?"

And, oops. The unintended innuendo made my cheeks heat. But now that my dirty mind started moving in that direction...

"ADMSA," he grumbled.

"Whatever." I glowered at the steering wheel. "Here's the thing, James Bond. This is not a one-way street. If I tell you what I know, you have to do the same."

He shook his head. "Too dangerous."

I scoffed. "For me or for you? Because I wasn't the one racing away from Harlon's party like I'd seen a ghost."

His eyes flashed with resentment, and his voice dropped to an ominous growl. "You have no idea the fire you're playing with."

Ha. Did he mean Angelina, Harlon, or himself?

I shrugged. "Maybe not. But maybe Harlon is the one biting off more than he can chew." I leaned in. "We both know he's up to something. So let's talk — openly. No lies. Because this goes too deep and there might not be anyone but us to stop it. Not if your agency can't be trusted."

"Not my agency," he muttered.

"Whatever. Are you with me on this, or aren't you?"

His eyes bored into mine. I glared back, refusing to give in.

Usually, I avoided trouble. But I had a hunch this trouble was coming no matter what, so I might as well take the initiative while I could.

"Well? What do you say?" I asked, growing impatient. "It's gonna be a hell of a long walk back to town if I leave you way out here, you know."

He made a face. "Threats are not a good way to win trust."

"Not a threat. A warning. If I trust you, you have to trust me."

His expression made it clear what a hurdle that would be. A hurdle that would take more than words to overcome. For him *and* for me.

He thought it over for another long, quiet minute, then nodded slightly. "Okay. I'm in. Tell me what you know — starting with your property. Why is Harlon so interested?"

Chapter Thirteen

NASH

Boy, did this woman drive a hard bargain.

As hard as my dick after that BSDM comment she'd made. Not that I was into bondage. But, hell. If Erin was, I could try being open-minded.

Only if we *get to tie* her *up,* my dragon rumbled.

I nearly snorted. Yeah, like she was ever going to let that happen.

Any way she likes it would be perfect, my dragon added.

I did my best to focus. But my mind — and heart — was a jumble of emotions and ugly memories.

Angelina. The Agency. The sinking realization that fate might be screwing with me. Because, as Erin had pointed out, I'd shown up at her job — and also at the bar the night before that, when her father had come to visit.

Which you handled so beautifully, my dragon muttered.

I jutted my jaw. How was I supposed to know he was her goddamn father?

And anyway, this wasn't about him. It was about Harlon. How did he fit into this picture?

My throat heated with the first stirrings of fire. Fate had messed with me before, and it probably would again. But I'd be damned if it played its ugly games with Erin.

Not on my watch, dammit, my dragon vowed. *Not on my watch.*

Technically, this wasn't my watch. I wasn't with the agency any more, and I hadn't been assigned to investigate — or protect — Erin. And yet, here I was, feeling more duty-driven than I had been in years.

"Why is Harlon interested in my property?" Erin echoed glumly. "I wish I knew."

"Madden sure seems to know about it — especially that vortex."

She shot me a cutting look. "Madden *thinks* he knows, but he doesn't. And he certainly doesn't understand."

"What is there to understand about a vortex?"

She cackled. "Where do I begin?"

I held my tongue. Pushing would only get me smartass replies, and Erin had already proven what a quick thinker she was.

She'd make a great dragon, my inner beast hummed happily.

For a long, silent minute, Erin stared at the moonlit valley. Somewhere down there was a creek, judging by the faint trickle of water and a crooked line of cottonwoods.

"Different people say different things about the vortexes," she finally whispered. "Probably because they feel different things. And most folks feel nothing."

I waited. If there was one thing I'd learned about Erin, it was that she wasn't *most folks.*

"When I first went up Cathedral Rock, I waited and waited, trying to feel something," she continued. "But there was nothing. Nothing but the majesty of the place, I mean. No magic, no mystical powers. Just the sheer natural beauty." She motioned at the moonlit landscape before us. "The second and third times I went, still nothing. But the fourth time..." Her throat bobbed. "My great-aunt took us up there — all three of us — saying the vortex was open. And that time, I felt it."

Working at the agency had taught me a lot about supernatural phenomena, but that didn't stop goose bumps from prickling along my skin.

Erin wiggled her fingers. "A disturbance, like air moving. Pushing. Twisting, like a tiny tornado. Another time we went, it was more like a pulsing feeling, as if pressure deep underground was trying to find a way out. My sisters and I combed the whole area, and we couldn't trace it to any particular point. It was more like a general feeling." Then she looked left, over the wall of the valley. "Airport Mesa was similar. One time, I felt it. Another time, nothing." Then she sucked in a deep breath and whispered, "But the vortex at our ranch is different."

I waited and waited, then finally cued her. "Different, how?"

She studied me, hesitating, then finally explaining. "It has a smaller outlet." She curled a hand into a fist and tapped the top, where her thumb wrapped around her fingers. "Like this. And it's much, much more powerful."

I raised an eyebrow. "How powerful?"

She bit her lip, then motioned for me to hold out my hand vertically, palm facing her.

"The other vortexes are like this." She blew softly at my hand.

It tickled, making the caveman part of my soul all hot and horny.

"At most, you feel this." She placed her hand flat over mine, pressing gently. So gently, I dreamed of her doing the same with her other hand. Or better yet, pressing against me with her whole body.

I coughed before Erin caught the sound of my dragon humming enthusiastically.

"But the vortex at the ranch is like this." Erin rammed my hand back so abruptly, it nearly smacked my shoulder.

I whipped it aside, then smoothed the sting away. "Okay, okay. I get the picture."

She frowned. "I don't think you do. It's terrifying."

I would have chalked that up to exaggeration, because Erin wasn't terrified of anything — not Harlon, nor Angelina.

But the crack in her voice indicated, *I mean it. Truly terrifying.*

"Terrifying because. . . ?" I finally ventured.

"Because I don't know where it's coming from or what it wants. Because there's no off switch. The best you can do is keep away from it." She rubbed the center of her hand.

"Terrifying because I fear what Harlon could do if he tapped into it."

I frowned. "Could he?"

"You tell me."

I scratched my head. "My training didn't cover vortexes."

She laughed dryly. "What a pity."

I studied her closely. "What does your father say?" When her eyes flashed, I stuck up my hands. "Just a question, not an accusation."

Still, she kept up that *evil eye* thing. "He's more in touch with air than earth."

The words might as well have been capitalized and underlined like key terms in a warlock's dictionary. Come to think of it, the grizzled old eagle shifter who'd taught *Introduction to Witches and Warlocks* at the academy really did capitalize and underline them.

Witches and warlocks often have an affinity for one of the four core elements, he'd said, tapping away at the chalkboard. *Earth, Air, Fire, Water. However, it's rare for a witch or warlock to really master them. Those who do are the most powerful.*

Like Harlon.

"It doesn't matter what I think Harlon is capable of," Erin said grimly. "What matters is that *he* thinks he can use the vortex. And that's what scares me."

I nodded slowly. As a shifter, I was immune to any magic a warlock might turn on me directly — like mindspells, for example. But warlocks could use their magic to turn objects — even living beings — into weapons. In my time with the agency, I'd been bombarded by everything from cars to boulders, and I'd had to fight humans, animals, and even swarms of killer bees that had been turned against me.

But, crap. A warlock with access to a vortex would be like a doped-up athlete. Invincible — at least to anyone playing by the rules.

So, we'll have to fight dirty, my dragon huffed.

Something told me it wasn't that simple.

"What can *you* do with the vortex?" I asked Erin.

She snorted. "I can stay the hell away, that's what. And keep others away."

"Using what powers?"

She shook her head. "No powers. Nothing to speak of anyway."

"And yet, your father is a warlock."

"I don't take after that side of the family."

I pounced on that opening. "What about your mother? Is she a witch?"

Erin's features went hard. "What she is doesn't matter."

"Maybe it does."

"Nothing about her is relevant." Erin's fiery reply practically slammed me backward. "She's barely even a mother."

Ouch. Definitely a sore point.

I went on more gently. "I'm just trying to understand how this all fits together. You said it yourself — if we're going to stop Harlon, we have to share what we know."

She shook her head firmly. "We share what's relevant. And my mother is no more relevant to this than the color of my underwear."

And, *whoosh!* Off went my dragon with his own sultry fantasies.

Ivory, with beige trim.

"Color of your underwear, huh?"

"Just a random example." She crossed her arms, putting a firm end to that subject. "There. I've shared what I know. Your turn."

I blinked, trying to get my mind off her panties. "Me?"

"Yes, you. Who are you? *What* are you?"

I scratched my chin, buying time. How much could I afford to reveal?

She huffed, impatient. "Okay, let me narrow it down for you. You're not human. Not a warlock. Not a vampire. That leaves shifter. The question is, what kind?"

I went very, very still, half hoping she would guess, half hoping to protect my secret. One of them anyway.

"How much do you know about shifters?" I ventured.

She squared her jaw. "Enough."

A bluff, and I knew it. Well, I could bluff too.

"If I said *wolf...*" I suggested, watching her carefully.

My dragon grumbled. *You must be joking.*

"And wolves are somehow immune to warlocks?" She wrinkled her nose as if to test my scent, then nodded, cutting me to the bone. Did she really take me for a lowly canine?

I instantly regretted my words, sensing they could come back to bite me — no pun intended. But it was too late now, so I nodded. "With training, yes."

"What about vampires?" She leaned closer. "You know, like whatshername. Angelina. Are you immune to them?"

And, ouch. If the *canine* part stung, the reminder of Angelina was a full-body slam against a brick wall.

"No. Not immune," I admitted through clenched teeth.

Erin let an awkward moment tick by. Was she graciously giving me time to collect myself or enjoying the sight of me wallowing in self-pity?

"Too bad," she finally murmured. Another few seconds passed before she went on. "How do you know Angelina?"

Not *Do you know her,* but *How.* God, was it that obvious?

I stalled. In one sense, I knew Angelina intimately. We hadn't actually had sex, but we'd gotten close. Close enough for her to fog my senses with her vampire allure and—

I practically gasped for fresh air, shoving away the hazy memories.

Biggest mistake of your life. My dragon, as always, made it perfectly clear who was to blame.

I cleared my throat. "The agency is a top-secret group of humans and supernaturals who keep tabs on other supernaturals that are deemed a threat. Angelina led the vampire-resistance part of the training program."

The part I'd flunked — spectacularly. Not that I planned to elaborate on that detail.

"I specialized in warlocks," I finished, edging away from the subject.

Erin studied me long and hard. Most folks learned about you from what you said. But Erin paid equal attention to what you *didn't* say, and I had the uneasy feeling she saw right into me.

At least she had the grace to let me off fairly gently.

"Is Angelina still with the agency?"

I shook my head. "From what I hear, she left a few months ago."

"And now she's hanging out with Harlon?" Erin shook her head. "Maybe someone should be investigating *her*."

I nearly snorted, picturing the skeletons waiting to be discovered in Angelina's closets — literally. She was far too devious to get caught, though.

Erin tapped her fingers. "Look, I hate to pry, but if you two have some history, and it could be related to her turning up now..."

My face went stony. I'd been wondering the same thing. Was that coincidence, or had Angelina tracked me here? On the other hand, she hadn't made a move to hunt me down since our disastrous tryst the previous spring. Why would she want to now?

"Her turning up now has nothing to do with me," I said. "I'm sure of it."

"She did seem awfully interested in you at Harlon's party. And the way she homed in on you, despite all those other people there..."

Bile rose in my throat. Angelina could pick me out from a crowd of a thousand men — unless she'd also tasted the blood of the other 999 of them.

"Nothing to do with me," I repeated in a tight, flat tone.

Erin stuck up her hands. "Just asking. We said we'd share what we know."

"We share what's relevant," I grunted. "Like you said."

"*Touché*," she muttered. "*Touché*."

I cursed myself, because we were back where we'd started — each in our opposite corners of the boxing ring, studying the other for an opening.

Finally, I puffed out my cheeks and gave in. "Sorry. It's a touchy subject. No offense."

"None taken," she said, all calm and businesslike.

Yep, we really were back where we'd started, with Erin eyeing me closely.

"What?" I finally demanded.

She shrugged. "Maybe whatever happened between you and Angelina isn't relevant. But the fact that she's working with Harlon is. So, here's the million-dollar question. You think you can take on Harlon. But can you take on Angelina?"

I opened my mouth, ready to swear I could. But once my brain caught up...

A long, awkward silence stretched in which Erin's eyes bored into me.

"Great," she finally muttered, turning her glare upon the landscape.

My cheeks burned, and I ground my teeth, wishing I could go back in time and undo all those mistakes.

An owl hooted, telling me, *Fat chance, buster.*

"Look," I gritted out. "If I turn out to be a liability, I swear, I will leave this to you. But right now, I'm all you've got."

"I have my sisters," she shot back fiercely.

I stuck up my hands. "You do. And I'm sure they're as badass as you..."

Damn right, we are, Erin's expression said.

"...but unless they're trained in identifying and containing supernaturals, I'm your best bet. For now, at least."

Erin's dour look said she wasn't convinced.

I shook my head, trying to get the conversation back on track. "Look, you and I aren't enemies. Harlon is the enemy."

"And Angelina," Erin added.

I sighed. "And Angelina."

For the next few minutes, crickets chirped while we studied the stars.

Finally, Erin sighed, as if resigned to her fate — and to me, her not-good-enough ally.

"So, where do we go from here?" she asked.

Part of me swelled a little, because that implied she trusted me — at least enough to get us started. Another part of me sank. What if her trust was misplaced?

"Harlon is scheduled to leave town tomorrow, right?"

"We can only hope," Erin muttered.

"That gives us some time to investigate. I could put out some feelers with guys I know in the agency — trustworthy guys."

She nodded slowly. "I can look into things here in town. Like exactly what Harlon is up to. Maybe I can track down the architect who drafted the plans in his office."

I nodded, then touched her arm. And, *zing!* There they went again — those hopeful crackles of energy, like we were on a first date instead of embarking on a potentially lethal venture.

"We have to be careful. *You* have to be careful," I warned.

Her eyes flashed, and she bared her teeth, making me glad she was on my side. "I'll make sure Harlon's the one who has to be careful."

With that, she stared into the night, wondering, perhaps, what she had just gotten herself into.

Chapter Fourteen

ERIN

A week passed. Quietly enough to lull a girl into a false sense of security if she wasn't on guard.

And, boy, was I on guard. I jumped at every shadow and scrutinized every unfamiliar face for any sign of trouble. I watched Nash like a hawk and kept a shotgun by my bedside. I'd even been tempted to research silver bullets. Not something I could pick up at the local ammo supplier.

I'd talked it all over with Pippa and Abby, and they were on high alert too. Well, once they'd gotten over the shock of it all. My ears still rang with Abby's screech.

"You turned down twenty million dollars?"

Twenty-one, actually, but I'd rounded down a little.

Luckily, Abby had come around once I explained Harlon's devious actions.

"Arrogant son of bitch," she'd muttered.

So, Abby was on board. Pippa, too. It helped that she was fresh off her triumph at Harlon's party.

"You were brilliant," I'd told her. "I would never have thought of distracting a vampire with spareribs."

Pippa had shrugged smugly. "I knew the minute she waltzed in on those thousand-dollar stilettos that she was up to no good."

The stilettos weren't what had put me off. More like the vampire fangs Angelina had been hiding — and her connection to Nash.

I ground my teeth, just thinking of it. They'd definitely been an item. What on earth had he seen in her?

It made me feel sick, though I couldn't understand why I cared, or why the air sizzled every time he and I bumped or made extended eye contact. On the other hand, maybe that caveman-level physical attraction was to be expected. Nash was a strapping shifter in his prime. I was... well, just me, but hey. Maybe he dug women who didn't have time for perfect hair, nails, or makeup.

Anyway, the important thing was to save our ranch — and possibly my skin — from the likes of Harlon.

All three of us sisters had put out feelers around town, though Pippa's network was by far the biggest. Abby and I mostly kept to ourselves, while Pippa was best friends with just about everyone in Sedona, from the cute guy who drove the garbage truck to park rangers to the cackling old fortune-teller from the little shop on Main Street.

"If there's any dirt to dig up on Harlon, we'll find it," Pippa promised as the three of us took our weekly ride across the ranch.

Apache, her pinto, shook his mane, emphasizing her point.

"No way is Harlon getting his hands on this ranch," Abby growled. "No way."

She rode Lucky, a sweet, good-natured palomino — her polar opposite, in other words — while I rode Buckeye, my favorite roan.

Two of the three were holdovers from my great-aunt's time; the other, and the additional four horses grazing in the east paddock, were rescues, along with a pair of scruffy miniature ponies and one colicky donkey. They all had Abby to thank for their lives. She was tough on the outside but all heart inside — especially when it came to orphans and outcasts.

The ranch stretched out all around us, sweeping across flatlands, snaking into canyons, and wrapping around mesas. I'd grown up in Albuquerque, but no place had ever felt more like home than Painted Rock Ranch.

And no place I'd ever cared about had ever been as threatened. I pictured resort buildings in place of our beautiful cottonwoods. Groomed golf greens standing in for prickly pears and gnarled junipers. Our overgrown natural spring would be tamed and transformed into an infinity pool, and the purple and green dragonflies that hovered over it would be nothing more than a memory.

Over my dead body, I nearly grunted.

The question was, how to outtrick a warlock and a scheming vampire?

Abby and Pippa rode ahead while I stared off in the direction of the petroglyphs. My fingers went tight around the reins as I pictured the spiral.

Buckeye snorted and pawed the ground, anxious to move on.

"You coming, Erin?" Pippa called.

I looked up, then nudged Buckeye into motion.

"Coming," I whispered.

∞∞∞∞

Nash had been doing his own snooping. Where he went after work each morning, I wasn't sure, but we'd agreed to check in with each other in town every afternoon at three.

"Anything new?" I asked, taking a seat beside him on Friday.

The food court in the center of town sported a huge back patio, and Nash was in the far corner, soaking in the winter sun and gazing at the spectacularly colored bands of Wilson Mountain.

Nodding in greeting, he pushed out the chair next to his and slid over his platter of nachos. Which was actually pretty thoughtful. Go figure.

I took a chip, dipped it in guacamole, and crunched away.

Nash leaned in with his side of our daily report. "A friend at the agency checked the records for Harlon but hasn't found anything."

I frowned. "Nothing? Not even a mention?"

Nash shook his head. "Not even a mention."

Not the news I'd been hoping for. "How comprehensive are the agency's records?"

"Not very. There are supernaturals everywhere, and they like to keep a low profile. Hell, one of the most powerful wolf packs in the West is only a few miles away from here, and they're barely listed." When I tilted my head, Nash waved his hand curtly. "Twin Moon Pack."

"Never heard of them."

"That's the way they like it."

"Like Harlon," I muttered, stabbing another chip into the sour cream. "Is your friend sure? Harlon's not even on their radar?"

"Not even a blip, or..." He trailed off, thinking.

"Or?" I prompted.

Nash dropped his voice. "Or he's had himself erased from the records."

I mulled over the implications in silence before Nash leaned back with a sigh. "Either way, that's a dead end. What did you find?"

"Not much. But Pippa's hairdresser's dog groomer knows the cleaner at the—"

Nash cut in. "Pippa's *what*?"

"Pippa's hairdresser's dog groomer. She knows the woman who cleans the architect's office — the architect who made that mock-up we saw in Harlon's office." I shrugged at his expression. "Never underestimate the power of a cleaner. See?" I pulled out my phone and swiped through the images the Pippa had forwarded, pausing at each for Nash to see. "The model we saw corresponds to these plans. It looks like Harlon is planning a big spread, but not a commercial one. Space enough for all the luxuries for himself and about ten guests."

The plans were so detailed, Nash had to lean in close to see them. Our shoulders touched, and I didn't catch myself inhaling his leather-and-lavender aftershave until it was too late.

My girl parts sighed longingly.

I ordered myself to hand the phone over and give Nash his own space. But somehow, I failed to achieve that, and Nash stayed nice and close.

"I don't see a tennis court." Nash pretended not to be impressed. When I swiped to the next picture, he snorted. "Oh. There it is."

"And there's my balloon shed..." I quipped, swiping again.

Nash chuckled, making my body go all warm. "What would Henry say about that?"

I sighed. Henry was still in Denver, and his brother was recovering, thank goodness. But I still hadn't had a chance to pilot one of the balloons.

"Henry would tell me to follow the money," I said, then put away my phone. "Not that I would, especially not in this case."

Nash nudged the nacho platter, and I helped myself to another chip. I'd hoped our investigation would reveal more, but even if it had, what would I do with the information? Confront Harlon? Call in the agency? Find an indigenous shaman who could tell me something about the vortex?

Nash grabbed his empty soda bottle and stood. "I'm getting another drink. Would you like one?"

I nodded.

"Ginger ale?" he asked.

I had to give it to the guy. He actually remembered my preferences. But maybe that was something he'd learned at the agency — memorizing details that could be useful to his case.

I wasn't his case, though. Harlon was.

And, oops. Technically, Harlon wasn't his case either, because Nash had left the agency.

I did my best not to wonder what exactly had led to that...and failed miserably.

"With a slice of lemon?" he went on.

God, were we turning into an old couple. Too bad we'd skipped over many happy, horny years of courtship to get there.

"Yes, please."

On the first day of our uneasy alliance, simple questions like that had turned into major negotiations. Who would fetch what? One bill or two? And so forth and so on. By now, we'd started going with the flow. And gee, was that easier.

As Nash walked away, my eyes followed his perfect ass.

The woman sitting two tables over watched just as closely, then shot me a look that said, *Lucky you.*

I wanted to tell her it wasn't like that between us — God, no! But when I glanced back at Nash, my mind went blank. It was only when he turned the corner that I focused on Sedona's second-best sight: the red rocky outcrops. I zipped my jacket high, turtled my chin into the collar, and stuck my hands into my pockets, feeling the cold for the first time. Hadn't it been warmer a moment earlier?

I stared off into the distance, thinking. When footsteps sounded behind me, I almost stuck out a hand for my drink. Then the hair on the back of my neck stood in warning.

That wasn't the familiar stomp of Nash's work boots. More like the light click of a woman's heels.

"Well, well. Who do we have here?" a haughty voice snipped.

I whirled, then froze at the sight of a too-thin, too-pale woman with strangely dark lips, black hair, and an outfit better suited to Beverly Hills than Sedona.

Angelina.

Her outfit was rounded out by a silk scarf and a pair of huge, movie-star sunglasses, so as not to leave too much skin exposed. Because, you know. Vampires. The sun didn't fry them instantly — that was an urban legend — but it did hurt enough that they preferred the indoors and nighttime.

"We?" I glanced behind her, searching for her evil twin or reinforcements.

God, please, no, I prayed quietly. *No twin, no reinforcements. This vampire alone is bad enough.*

Luckily, it was a royal we. So, whew. Just one vampire to deal with, though that was still one too many.

I glanced again. The table, chairs, and my body all threw shadows. Not Angelina, though.

Angelina's cheek twitched. "You're the balloon pilot, aren't you?"

I did my best not to show my unease. Harlon hadn't introduced us, but clearly, they'd talked.

"And you're a friend of Harlon's," I said flatly.

She flashed a shark-attack smile, all teeth and gums. "Business associate."

Her eyes swept over the table, and her nostrils twitched as if to locate someone.

Shit. She was after Nash, wasn't she?

When she half turned to check the entrance, I snatched away the sole evidence of his presence — a crumpled napkin. Boy, did I hope Nash would spot her in time to stay away.

"Angela..." I started.

Her voice turned to pure ice. "Angelina. Angelina Saint James."

I didn't offer my name, figuring Harlon had mentioned that too.

Which was just plain creepy — the idea that a warlock and a vampire had been discussing me.

Angelina looked around a moment longer, then took the chair opposite mine. "Well, seeing as I've bumped into you, we might as well talk business."

Bumped into? I doubted it. And as for business...

Alarms rang through my mind.

"Business?"

Placing her purse on the seat beside her, she rested her elbows on the table and folded her gloved hands. "Yes, business. Apparently, you own the Painted Rock property."

My throat went dry, but I managed to shrug. "One of the properties out there."

Angelina's hawk eyes said, *The only one that matters.*

"Have you considered Harlon's offer?" she snipped.

Ha. I'd considered it plenty, though not in the way she meant.

I shook my head slowly. "Not really. It's not for sale."

With her lips pursed that tightly, Angelina looked like a fish. The really pale, creepy kind that lived in the deepest parts of the ocean.

"No? Well, Harlon asked me to remind you of his offer. Twenty-five million dollars."

My eyes nearly bugged out, and I squeaked, "Twenty-five million?"

She nodded, amused, the way one might with a child content with a trifle, like a lollipop or a balloon. "Twenty-five million."

My mind spun. The ranch wasn't worth anywhere near that. Was Harlon desperate to close the deal before anyone else could? Or did the price reflect what he thought he could gain from harnessing the power of the vortex?

I gulped and checked the door to the food court.

Angelina lifted one eyebrow, following my gaze. "Are you expecting someone?"

I laughed as if to say, *Of course not. Especially not a former agent of the BSDM — er, ADMSA.*

"Just checking the time," I bluffed.

"You should be checking with the co-owners of the property. Your two half sisters, I mean."

Crap. She'd done her homework.

"Oh, and that adorable niece of yours..." she added.

My gut lurched. She knew about Claire, Abby's eight-year-old daughter?

Angelina leaned in like we were besties. "I like you, Miss Sattler. I really do."

Ha. More like, *I despise you.* The feeling was mutual.

"So much, it would pain me to find myself at odds with you," she continued.

Her tone told me the consequences would pain me too.

I did my best to keep cool. "I'm not at odds with you or Harlon. It's just that I'm not interested in selling. The ranch goes way back in the family, and we promised to keep it that way."

Her eyes were a storm with my name on it. "Shouldn't make promises you can't keep."

"Is that a threat?"

She laughed. "Finally, you're getting the idea."

There was more coming — I was sure of it — but she stopped suddenly, turning to the door. In the space of one heartbeat, her expression went from vengeful to coy.

"Why, there you are, Nash," she practically purred.

And, *whoosh!* The wave of anger creeping through me became a tsunami, roaring in my ears. Because that was Nash in the doorway, and the drinks he held were his and mine.

Mine, dammit. Not hers.

But Angelina's expression said, *Mine. All mine.*

Chapter Fifteen

NASH

When I'd spotted Angelina in the food court a few minutes earlier, I froze. Luckily, a waitress had walked by with a platter of juicy hamburgers, making Angelina turn. I'd ducked behind a drink machine, then cursed myself. Was I hiding?

Yes, I was. Because any second now, my blood would start calling to her, no matter how much my soul resisted. Me, the mighty dragon, who'd spent his whole life impervious to lesser beings.

So I hid like a goddamn coward, hoping that Angelina would magically disappear. She didn't, but the waitress had given me a reprieve, and this was my chance to run.

Then I spotted Angelina stalking toward the back deck. A tornado of emotions tore through me, and it was all I could do not to sway on my feet.

Stay away from Erin, my inner dragon roared. *Stay away, or I will kill you.*

I'd never, ever hated with such a passion. And I'd never, ever been so crystal-clear about what I vowed to defend.

Erin. I would give my life for her.

Er — justice. I would give my life for justice.

I stormed toward the door, ready to tear apart the vampire in plain view of humans, if that's what it took. The idea appealed more and more with every step I took.

Kill Angelina. Free myself from the power she held over my soul. Power I'd given her, unsuspecting fool that I'd been.

Of course, killing Angelina meant my own death, because vampires benefited from a safety clause, so to speak. If they were killed by someone they'd bitten, that person died too. But, hell. At least I would be free.

Kill Angelina! my dragon took up the battle cry as I raced for the door.

Outside, the cold air hit me, but that was nothing compared to the force of Angelina's stare. All the blood rushed to the front of my body in a sick race to offer itself to her.

Why, there you are, Nash. Her words locked my limbs. It didn't matter what my mind vowed. My body was at her beck and call and always would be.

Then I found Erin's eyes, and they were twin beams of a lighthouse, guiding me away from dangerous shoals.

I've got this under control, her eyes declared. *Now, you get yourself under control too.*

I took a deep breath, then another. With each breath, Angelina's grip on my soul loosened, a boa constrictor pried away from my core. Faintly at first, then more noticeably.

I strode over to Erin's side of the table, practically baring my teeth.

"Angelina here was just leaving," Erin grunted, crossing her arms.

Angelina raised one penciled-in eyebrow. "Was I?"

I put a hand on Erin's shoulder and growled. "Yes, you were."

Angelina laughed, and that boa squeezed. But when Erin reached up and covered my hand with hers, a warmer, kinder force sparked to life, chasing away that invader.

Hope filled my heart — enough to make me wonder. Maybe there was another way of freeing myself of this vampire's spell. One they didn't teach at the agency.

Angelina flashed her teeth, letting her canines extend in case we didn't get the hint.

"Oh, I don't think so." Her eyes slid up my chest, then lingered on my neck.

Cold seeped into my skin.

Angelina grinned and addressed Erin without bothering to look at her. "Give us a minute, won't you?"

Her words were a deliberate echo of those she'd uttered months earlier, in her office at the agency on a Friday afternoon when everything had been winding down. I'd had the stupid ambition to become the first agent to master warlock *and* vampire training, and Angelina was an instructor in the latter. She'd called me in on a pretense I no longer recalled and cooed to the agent who'd come with me.

Give us a minute, won't you?

Ingo had warned me with his eyes, but it was too late.

The next thing I remembered was coming to hours later on a red velvet couch in a totally different place, dizzy and weak. Blood crusted the left side of my body, and when I stumbled over to a sink to wash, I found two puncture marks on my wrist. The ones that still scarred my skin.

I'd rushed to the door, bumping into furniture all the way. Blurry visions plagued my mind. Visions of Angelina, getting closer and more seductive. Visions of myself, knowing I had to resist, but falling for it anyway. Visions of her fangs sinking into my flesh and—

I tightened my grip on Erin's shoulder and grunted back. "She stays. You're the one who's leaving."

It was laughable, really — a powerful dragon shifter desperately clinging to a woman for help. But, hell. Touching Erin muted Angelina's power, like hearing a noisy disco from outside a thick door instead of standing next to a speaker.

Angelina smirked. "Oh, this will be fun."

Maybe in your sick mind, my dragon grumbled.

"What exactly is your plan here, Angelina?" Erin demanded. "Are you going to try to get Nash to sell you my property? It's not his to sell."

"No, she'll just try to get me to sell my soul to the devil," I growled.

Angelina's smug smile said, *You already did.*

I shook my head, refusing to take the bait. Whatever hold Angelina had over me stemmed from her trickery, not my consent. And for the first time ever, I was ready to fight back.

Too bad we were in downtown Sedona in the middle of the day. Here and now was not the place.

Someday, somehow. . . my dragon vowed.

Erin munched down the last nacho, then declared, "Well, I have nothing more to say to you. Nash has nothing more to say. Also, we're out of nachos. So, it's time for you to tootle along, don't you think?"

Angelina shook her head. "Not before I get what I came for."

Erin snorted. "What Harlon sent you for, you mean?"

Angelina's nostrils flared, and her voice was pure ice. "Harlon has his business interests. I have mine."

I stiffened, because the only thing worse than a scheming supernatural was a second schemer behind them.

"So, the twenty million you offered for my land is your money? Or is it Harlon's?" Erin waited a split second, then went on. "Oh, wait. Twenty-five million."

"Harlon's money," I grunted.

That was one of the few secrets I'd dug up on Angelina. She came from old money, but her family had squandered most of it. That was why she'd had to stoop so low as to work for the agency.

Angelina's canines extended another quarter-inch, but Erin spoke first, cutting her off.

"In any case, it's a moot point. My property is not for sale."

Vampires weren't witches, with the ability to play with people's minds. But a vampire glare could still make even the strongest human tremble in fear. But, wow. Erin stubbornly held Angelina's gaze.

She's not just a relic, my dragon whispered.

No, Erin was more than that. Much more, though I doubted she knew it.

A zephyr of wind wafted over the deck just then, blowing a loose napkin into the air. Erin and Angelina grabbed for it at the same time. Erin immediately snatched her hand away.

"Watch it!" She rubbed the scratch on the back of her hand, inflicted by one of Angelina's two-inch nails.

An innocent-enough accident, though with Angelina, you never knew.

At first, Angelina looked annoyed. But the moment she spotted a drop of Erin's blood on those talons of hers, her eyes sparkled.

No! I wanted to yell as Angelina brought her hand to her mouth.

A taste of human blood — even a tiny drop — allowed a vampire to track the source anywhere, anytime. For all eternity.

Angelina's smile grew as she brought her hand toward her lips. I lunged to stop her, but the table stood in the way.

Erin muttered, making a shooing motion, and all hell broke loose.

Plastic chairs scraped across the deck. The canvas of a sun umbrella rattled, and more napkins flipped by as an out-of-nowhere microburst ripped across the deck. Angelina's long, loose hair whipped around her head, and she ducked against an onslaught of napkins the wind yanked from a dispenser on the next table.

"What the...?" she yelped, throwing up her hands.

For the next few seconds, it was all I could do to brace myself against the stinging slaps of airborne objects. Napkins...plastic cups...coasters...

"Dammit..." Angelina clawed a paper place mat from her face.

An empty can rolled across the deck and fell into the parking space below with a loud clank. The wind followed it, and a moment later, the deck calmed. My pounding heart didn't. Not with Angelina licking the blood off her finger with a look of triumph.

An instant later, she frowned and licked again. Then she looked at her hand, perplexed.

Whew. The blood had been wiped away by the windborne debris.

"Now, where were we?" Erin patted her hair back into place, totally unperturbed. "Oh, yes. I was making it clear to you my property is not — and will never be — for sale. You got that? Good," she concluded before Angelina could so much as peep. "Then we'll stop wasting your time — and mine." She stood, grabbed my hand, and marched me toward the door. There, she turned and flashed Angelina a fake smile. "Oh, and one more thing. You might want to check your hair on the way out."

She didn't finish with *bitch*, but her intonation left exactly enough space to fill that part in.

Chapter Sixteen

ERIN

I strutted away from Angelina with my heart hammering, though I did my best not to let it show. Because, whew. I'd just told off a vampire. Maybe not the wisest thing, but still. What a bitch!

"Good job," Nash murmured as we bustled across the food court and out to the street.

I stood a little straighter. An agent of the BDSM — er, ADMSA — thought I'd handled a vampire well. Bonus points for me.

The triumphant feeling didn't last long, though, because, yikes. How had I ever gotten involved with the likes of Angelina?

"Aren't vampires supposed to be allergic to sunlight?" I muttered.

Nash shook his head. "Popular myth. They're just like anyone else."

I snorted. "Except for a few minor differences, like drinking blood."

His lips formed a tight line, and it finally dawned on me. Shit. Angelina had drunk his blood, hadn't she?

My stomach churned with disappointment and disgust. Nash had had a fling with Angelina, and he'd let her drink his blood? Did he really have such bad taste in women?

Maybe he didn't let her, my better half argued. *Maybe she forced him.*

I snorted. A strong, hardy wolf shifter like him, forced? Not likely.

Then a really sickening thought hit me, and I took a full minute to phrase my question carefully.

"Doesn't a vampire's bite make the victim a vampire too?"

Nash jerked his head in a vehement no. "Only if they drain the victim to the last drop of their blood, then give just enough back to turn them."

The nachos in my stomach threatened to make an encore appearance.

I stomped down the street toward my car, then paused. "Where are you parked?"

Nash shook his head. "Not important. Let's go."

For once, I was happy to comply. We slid into my Chevy. As I drove off, I glanced in the rearview mirror.

"What do you think she'll get up to next?"

"She'll wait for Harlon," Nash said.

"What if she doesn't?"

He thought it over before answering. "I think they've both realized you're not an easy target."

Somehow, that didn't make me feel better.

"If I were them," Nash continued, "I would take me out first, then come for you." He stuck his hands up before I could protest. "That's what *they* would do, not what I think."

Still, I glowered. "Maybe they'll try to kill two birds with one stone. A stubborn landowner and a pesky BDSM agent too."

"Former agent," he grumbled, not bothering to correct the acronym. We were definitely turning into an old couple. "And anyway, no. Divide and conquer is always better."

I turned right at the Y intersection, heading west, still bristling. "Is that what they taught you at the agency?"

"No, that was in the Marines."

Oh. Right. I gulped, reminding myself how out of my league I was — with him and Harlon and Angelina.

"Nice truck, by the way," he said, a long, quiet minute later. Changing the subject?

Good. My mood could use it.

I patted the dashboard. "1978 Chevy Silverado. My great-aunt bought it new, way back when."

He grinned. "She has good taste."

I chuckled, picturing her in it with us kids crowded in beside her and several dogs in the back, their ears flopping in the breeze. "That, she does."

Then, whoa. Another image came to me — this time with me, an uncharacteristically carefree Nash, and a cheerful little boy between us — Nash's spitting image — plus Roscoe in the back, ears flopping in the breeze. Roscoe's ears, that is. Not Nash's, or the little boy's...

I gulped. Now, where the heck had that come from?

By then, we'd passed the strip mall and the Desert Skies office, though neither of us spoke for another mile.

"Okay, let's say they go after you first," I conceded, getting back to business. "Probably at a time and place you'd least expect it or with the fewest witnesses." Then I paled. "Wait. What if they come after you out at the cabin you're renting on Henry's property? We can't let him get drawn into this."

There were times when my boss drove me crazy, and I was still waiting for a chance to get that last hour of piloting. But Henry had given me a chance when no one else had, and he was a decent, law-abiding citizen.

Nash grimaced. "Where else could I stay that wouldn't involve innocent people?"

I tightened my hands around the steering wheel, biting back the first answer that came to mind. But when I couldn't find an alternative, I let it out, very quietly.

"You could come to the ranch."

And just like that, my foolish heart thumped harder.

He shook his head. "I said, a place that doesn't involve innocent people. You have sisters, right?"

My shoulders slumped. I did. And a niece — Abby's daughter, Claire.

Nash shook his head. "Forget it."

I couldn't, though, because they were already involved, because we all shared the property.

"What if Angelina or Harlon come for me first?" I asked. "Like you said, they would want to divide us. It would be better if we circled the wagons, if you know what I mean."

His jaw hardened. "I don't like it."

I huffed. "What's to like about any of this?"

I didn't mention the one aspect I did like — the prospect of keeping Nash close.

He didn't say anything for a while. But when I paused at the red light at the turnoff to Henry's place, Nash's eyes bored into mine. Finally, he nodded.

"All right, then. Your place."

∞∞∞

Twenty-five minutes later, we were back at the intersection, having grabbed a few things from Nash's cabin. From there, I drove another mile down the highway, then turned off on a dirt road. My heart pitter-pattered the whole way, as if I were bringing Nash to my home for fun and games rather than perfectly rational, practical, and entirely platonic reasons.

So, no. No reason for jittery nerves at all.

The only sound was the roll of the tires over asphalt, then gravel. When I slowed and took the final turn for home, Nash did a double take, as if he hadn't seen the fork in the road.

Interesting. I'd been wondering if he would be like most folks, who were blind to our particular turnoff. Now, I had my answer. My great-aunt had always claimed that spot had been spelled to blur in the eyes of the average passerby — and apparently, that worked on shifters too.

I pursed my lips. Would it fool Harlon and Angelina?

We rattled over a cattle grid, slalomed around a couple of potholes, then came to the rise with a view of the ranch — the main house, barn, corral, and a handful of other buildings, including my cabin way off to one side. Dusty paths connected the buildings, but those quickly gave way to scrub and trees that ran all the way to the rocky outcrops that hemmed in the ranch. Nash swiveled his head, taking it all in.

"Nice," he murmured. His tone was genuine, and something in me warmed.

"It is," I agreed, feeling lucky for the hundredth time that my great-aunt had entrusted the ranch to my sisters and me.

126

"That part ends in a box canyon." I pointed. "And over there is the creek."

Nash nodded quietly.

He opened his mouth with a question, then thought better of it.

"What?" I asked.

He gazed off into the distance. "Nothing."

I could guess, though — and kudos to him for not asking about the vortex. Still, I tensed a little as we cruised up to the main house. The low winter sun glared from straight ahead, making me squint, then glance sideways at Nash. Was I right to trust him?

Roscoe rose from the porch, barking and wagging his tail in his usual set of mixed messages. A small, strawberry-blond girl shot out of the house, meeting me with a cheer.

"Erin! Erin!"

I slid out of my car to greet my niece — a reminder of everything I held most dear and everything I risked.

"Claire!" I kneeled for a hug. A really big, really long one during which I closed my eyes and swore a thousand oaths.

Will not let the bad guys take this ranch. Will not let them harm those I love.

Roscoe slobbered on both of us, adding his own vow.

Claire extracted herself and smiled at Nash. "Hello. Who are you?"

His gulp indicated he wasn't the doting uncle of a half dozen kids. In fact, he'd never mentioned family at all. On the other hand, we hadn't discussed much besides work and Harlon.

Damn shame, a little voice in the back of my mind said.

"I'm Nash. Nice to meet you." He stuck out a hand awkwardly.

Definitely no practice with kids. No problem for Claire, though. She grabbed his hand and shook enthusiastically, then made him shake the paw of her stuffed animal, a pink bunny.

"This is Hopper. Do you want to see my horses?"

"Um..." Nash looked at me.

My sisters stepped outside next — Abby, with a grim, *What the Fuck* look, and Pippa, with a huge, mischievous grin.

"Hi there," Pippa called. "Nash, right?"

He nodded, sticking his hands into his pockets.

I bent to Claire's level. "I think Nash would love to see your horses. Can you show him?"

Bouncing in glee, she grabbed his hand and towed him into the house. Well, she tried, but Abby blocked the door, glaring at Nash.

I sighed, shooting her a look that said, *I'm not happy with this either, but if you give me a minute, I'll explain.*

"Mom." Claire nudged her.

Finally, Abby relented a teensy-tiny bit. "I think your horses need some exercise. Why don't you bring them out and show Nash here on the porch?"

Ah, my dear sister. Never one to trust a man farther than she could jiu-jitsu-throw him.

"I'll be right back." Claire shoved Hopper at Nash, ducked under Abby's arm, and zoomed inside. Seconds later, she reappeared with an armful of toy horses. We sisters had collected them as kids, and Claire had inherited the whole herd.

"Here." She thrust them into Nash's arms and rushed inside for more.

"Meanwhile, we'll take a little walk," I said, motioning my sisters to follow.

Pippa bounded along eagerly, and Abby reluctantly followed. We were barely out of earshot when she hissed, "What the hell is he doing here?"

∞∞∞∞

It took thirty minutes of explaining, arguing, and cajoling, but I finally filled my sisters in on everything that had transpired. They went from displeased to angry to gravely concerned but agreed it was best for Nash to stay with us while we figured out what to do.

Afterward, I rescued Nash from Claire and the horses, though that took some convincing too.

"He hasn't seen Black Beauty yet!"

"After dinner, sweetie," I promised. "I need to show him around."

Funny enough, Nash wasn't in a rush to escape Claire's tutorial. He looked more relaxed than I'd ever seen him, with his long legs hanging over the edge of the porch and his hands busy making the horses gallop.

Had he played cowboy as a kid, once upon a time? Did he have a mom as strict as Abby — or aunts as doting as Pippa and I? Had his father been as dedicated as mine, or had the man been as absent as my mother? And what about Nash himself? Would he make as good of a father as the image I'd had made him out to be?

I rubbed the bridge of my nose, pushing away stirring emotions.

"Hey, Claire." Pippa lured our niece away. "I need help making dinner — and dessert. Can you and Black Beauty help?"

Claire giggled. "Black Beauty has hooves, not hands."

"Well, she can supervise," Pippa said, then waggled her eyebrows at Nash and me. "Have fun, you two."

Fun was not on the agenda. I wanted to show Nash the lay of the land in case we needed help protecting the ranch. But Lord, I hoped it wouldn't come to that.

"Your niece, huh?" he asked once we were a few steps away.

I nodded. "Abby's daughter."

He studied the sky warily. Did he expect enemy forces to helicopter in? Or, worse — dragons?

Slowly, he turned in a circle, then stopped, staring at our dragon-shaped weather vane.

"That was one of Abby's first projects in the smithy," I explained. "It came out really well, didn't it?"

Sadly, our mother hadn't noticed, but Pippa and I loved it.

Nash nodded, genuinely impressed. "Very realistic."

"Come on. I'll show you around."

I gave him a quick tour of the ranch, warring with myself the whole time. Should I show him the vortex?

If he had pushed to see it, I would have probably refused. But seeing as he didn't... I glanced over, then made up my mind. Nash wasn't one of the bad guys. On the contrary, he had a lot going for him — a lot more than I'd originally given him credit for.

He respected that I was the boss at work.

He hated Harlon as much as I did.

And he shared nachos.

So, there. Lots of admirable characteristics.

"Now, the vortex..." I said, then hesitated.

"You want to blindfold me?" he offered with a little grin.

I bit back a bad BDSM joke.

"I hope it's not necessary," I said.

"I promise it isn't," he said, dead serious.

I nodded, then led him to the base of the cliffs by the head of the canyon.

Nash looked up at the figures etched into the stone by an ancient hand. The way he stroked his chin convinced me he must have had training in such things at that agency of his. The air went still, and a faint hum registered in my ears, like a live wire crackling with energy.

"Um...interesting," Nash finally said. "But what about the vortex?"

I blinked. Wait. What?

I waved at the wall. "You don't feel it?"

He frowned. "Feel what?"

I crossed my arms. Was he kidding?

"The vortex." I didn't finish with, *you idiot,* but I was tempted to.

"It's here?"

I pointed to the spiral, and he reached for it. I yelped in warning, but—

I stared as he moved his hand over, then around the spiral. The whole time, his expression didn't change.

I reached out, wondering if the vortex had cut out.

"Whoa," Nash said as my hand was thrust back, nearly smacking his nose.

"It's blasting out of the rock," I said. "You don't feel it?"

He tried again — carefully at first, then less so. Finally, he tilted his head. "You're not kidding me, are you?"

"No, I am not kidding you." Grabbing his hand, I held it toward the spiral, interlacing my fingers with his.

And, *bang!* I yelped again, because this blast was even more powerful — enough to make me stumble. Nash nearly toppled over, and I ended up smacked against his chest. He braced his legs and wrapped his arms around my shoulders, balancing us both.

A split second of embarrassment ensued, followed by a silent, all-body sigh. Gee, did that feel good. Scary-good, like we'd been made to fit that way.

I stayed there many, many seconds longer than I had to, relishing the feeling. Nash didn't seem in any hurry to move either, and time slowed to a crawl. My zone of focus shrank, blurring out the cliff, the breeze, and the deepening hues of evening. All I felt was the warmth of his body and the soft puff of his breath on my shoulder.

And, heck. We might have stayed there all night if Roscoe hadn't come by, crashing through the bushes after a jackrabbit.

Clearing my throat, I stepped away from Nash and the vortex.

"You seriously didn't feel that?" I asked. Then I turned pink. I'd meant the vortex, but the words could just as easily refer to touching — and that feeling of *You belong to me, with me.*

He faced the rock wall. Out of genuine interest, or was he avoiding my gaze?

"I didn't feel a thing."

I swear, my feelings weren't hurt.

Then it hit me. If he meant the vortex...

I frowned. "Am I the only one who can feel it, or am I imagining things?"

"What about your sisters?" he asked.

I thought it over, then shrugged. "Honestly, we never talk about it. But we all know it's here, because my great-aunt brought us over to warn us not to get close."

Nash studied the rock art a moment longer, then turned his gaze on me. "Well, that proves one thing."

I was afraid to ask, but I did. "What?"

"You're no relic, Erin. You're a lot more."

For years, I'd assumed that's all I was — the offspring of two supernaturals with no powers of my own. But now... Well, yikes. What if Nash was right? And what exactly did that make me?

Chapter Seventeen

NASH

Technically, I'd already met Erin's sisters — sort of — that first night in the bar. Dinner at their ranch started off just as awkwardly, and every word, gesture, and look was as loaded as before. To my surprise, though, things thawed quickly.

Pippa was the fun one, and her comments were all chipper, jokey, or playful. Abby was the broody one, and every look she shot me was a barb. Erin was somewhere in between.

Thank goodness for little Claire, the only person around the dinner table free of attitude or agenda.

"Who do you think was faster, Seabiscuit or Man o' War?" she quizzed us.

A good thing I'd "met" both horses in her collection earlier that day.

"Definitely Seabiscuit," Pippa replied.

"He was small, but fast," Abby agreed.

Pippa snorted. "Like they say — it's not the size of the dog in the fight but the size of the fight in the dog."

"Mark Twain," Erin murmured to Claire.

"Was he a horse too?"

I grinned and swirled the last strands of spaghetti around my fork. As, um — Unusual? Interesting? — as this family was, it was nice to share this time with them. It would be even nicer if Abby let some of the ice around her soul thaw.

My dragon snorted. *There's the pot calling the kettle black.*

I frowned into my glass of water.

In any case, I hadn't sat down to a family dinner in a long, long time, and it was nice. Logs crackled in the fireplace, and candles flickered softly on the table. Country music drifted in from the radio in the kitchen, and Roscoe's tail steadily thumped the rug. His eyes were locked on Claire, his best hope for snacks.

"I think Seabiscuit and Man o' War would tie," Claire decided, then switched to draft horses. "Who can pull more — a Percheron or a Clydesdale?"

Horses and dogs were definitely high on that girl's list — and probably the entire family's. I'd spotted half a dozen horses on the way in — mostly rescues, according to Erin. Roscoe was the only dog allowed in the main house, but there were several more who'd greeted Erin — and growled at me — around the ranch.

Pippa, as usual, had the most to say about Claire's latest question. As they chattered away, I looked around. Dinner was served on colorful glass plates handmade by Pippa — she was a glass artist, apparently — but the plates displayed in the cupboard to one side were all antiques. A worn braided rug cushioned my feet. A rocking chair stood in a corner near a window, with a shawl carefully folded over the back. The aunt's?

Everything about this house and these people spoke of love, painstaking work, and hardiness. My eyes swept over it all, then met Erin's as Claire chatted on.

"Mommy says Percherons are so big, they're hard to ride bareback, but I think I could..."

Now, do you understand? Erin's eyes asked. *Do you understand how much this place means to us, and how much stands at risk?*

I took a deep breath. Yes. Yes, I did.

A shotgun old enough to be my grandfather's hung over the fireplace. Did they keep it loaded? Did they have what it took to use it?

Yes, I decided. Every one of these women was that tough, that protective.

"Are Percherons big enough for me, Roscoe, and Mommy to all ride bareback at the same time?" Claire went on.

For the first time that evening, Abby cracked a smile. "You and me, for sure. But Roscoe would probably prefer to keep his feet on the ground."

It was a cute scene to imagine — mother and daughter riding bareback on a big, docile horse, with Roscoe running ahead. The lack of men in the image did strike me, though, and not for the first time. Other than Roscoe, I was the only male on the property. Was that by design or coincidence?

Even Claire noticed it. "You and Roscoe are the only boys on the ranch," she giggled.

"Don't forget the cattle, horses, and pigs. But they're all castrated," Abby observed dryly.

The candles on the table flickered, and I crossed my legs under the table. Tightly.

"Dessert, anyone?" Pippa asked, standing.

"Yay! Brownies!" Claire cheered, moving to the kitchen with Pippa.

Erin smiled, and even Abby gave a hearty thumbs-up. She didn't seem too pleased to have to share with me, but hey. I wouldn't stick around to bother her for long.

My eyes wandered over to Erin, then jerked away when she glanced up.

What if she wants us to? my dragon whispered. *Stay longer, I mean?*

I folded and refolded my napkin, avoiding her eyes.

"Voilà. Chocolate chunk fudge brownies." Pippa set the pan on the table with a flourish.

Was it that motion that made the candles flicker, or was it something else? The fire crackled at the same time, sharing Pippa's glee. And I was sure the candles brightened a little when Claire wiggled back into her seat and started on her brownie.

Pippa dabbed hers with Nutella, ignoring her sisters' pointed looks.

"It's not like I'm ruining a super-healthy dessert here," she pointed out.

Erin frowned. "Yes, you are."

Abby stuck her hand in front of Claire's eyes. "This is one of those things you shouldn't learn from Aunt Pippa."

"*Another* thing?" Pippa protested. "What else is on that list?"

"Where do I begin?" Abby sighed.

Claire giggled, while Erin shook her head in exasperation, but her love for her sister still shone through.

Every tease, every reprimand, and every laugh they shared came with a merry wobble of candlelight, and any tension that crept into the conversation came with an ominous crackle from the fireplace.

I looked at Roscoe, then around the room. What was it with this family? Or was it something about the place?

"Seconds, anyone?" Pippa offered.

"I probably shouldn't," Erin sighed, though she held out her plate.

"Break it into pieces. Fewer calories that way." Pippa winked, invoking one of those special laws of chemistry they didn't teach in school.

"Delicious," Abby announced when she finished her second portion.

"You can thank me, Claire, and Betty Crocker." Pippa grinned.

"Roscoe helped too," Claire insisted.

I looked at my brownie. God, I hoped not.

My offer to do the dishes afterward was enthusiastically accepted, and I was glad to help — and avoid any awkward after-dinner talk. But awkward was probably inevitable, I decided once everyone broke up for the night. Abby and Claire lived in the main house, with Pippa in a converted barn and Erin in her cabin a good quarter-mile away.

"Well, good night, everyone," she announced.

"Good night," I echoed, ignoring Pippa's amused look.

I was sure Erin had made it clear to her sisters it wasn't like *that,* but Pippa had no mercy.

"Good night," she said in a sultry purr.

"Oh! Are you having a sleepover?" Claire clapped. "Can I come?"

Abby's dark look said *Hell no,* a sentiment Erin expressed a little more diplomatically.

"Not this time, sweetie. Nash gets the couch. I get the bed." That point was aimed squarely at Pippa and her smirk. "So, my little house will be pretty full."

"When I do sleepovers, we all pile into one bed. It's fun," Claire said.

Pippa chortled. I kept my expression perfectly neutral.

Erin hid a smile. "I promise that you, Pippa, and I will have a sleepover soon."

"Maybe we can invite Grandpa and Grandpa," Claire said.

So, there were a lucky few men who were welcome on the ranch.

Erin waved, and I followed her outside, where the cold night snatched us away from the cozy confines of the house. It was nice, though — all those stars, all that space. Another reason this ranch was so special. The lights of Sedona were a faint glow in the distance, but the only man-made sound was the crunch of our boots over frosty ground.

Two more dogs rushed up to join us for part of the walk, then ran to the barn when Pippa called out to them. "Calvin! Hobbes!"

I looked at Erin, and she shrugged. "Claire's a fan of the cartoon. Abby too. Well, all of us, actually."

It was easy to picture her, Pippa, or Abby reading to Claire before tucking her in for the night. Family was big for these sisters, even if the structure of theirs was a little unique.

"Has this ranch been in your family a long time?" I asked quietly.

Erin nodded. "Seven generations. It was my aunt's. Well, great-aunt." A second or two went by before Erin quietly added, "We three spent every summer here. If it weren't for my aunt, I would hardly know Pippa or Abby."

I didn't ask, but I did wonder. How could three sisters not know one another?

Erin must have picked up on that, because she explained. "We each grew up with our dads. Well, Pippa and I did. Abby grew up with her other relatives."

Abby's relatives were different from Erin's? Did that mean three different fathers?

Wow. And I thought my family was a little mixed up.

"I see," I said, though I didn't.

Erin laughed, not all too humorously. "Nice of you not to ask about my mother."

I shrugged. In truth, I'd been burning to ask. "You said it wasn't relevant."

I almost missed her whispered, "I'm starting to think it might be."

I kept my lips sealed, thinking about the candles at dinner…the vortex…the microburst at the food court…

Erin led me around a patch of prickly pear and beyond the paddock, heading toward the dim outline of her cabin.

Out of nowhere, she heaved a deep, conflicted sigh. "My mom is a wanderer. A renegade. A heartbreaker."

Yes, I suppose she would have to be to leave three daughters behind with three different fathers. Then again, some men did the same and weren't judged half as harshly.

"My great-aunt said that came from the other side of the family," Erin added.

"The witch side?" I murmured.

Erin shook her head. "No. The dragon shifter side."

I stared — and stared, and stared — while inside, my dragon practically started tap-dancing.

I told you we were meant for each other.

"Dragon shifter?" I echoed stupidly.

Erin nodded, then motioned in the air. "I doubt that matters, though."

My mouth hung open. Hell, yes. It mattered. To me, anyway.

Dragon shifter! my inner beast cheered. *Just like me!*

"Maybe it's the warlock side that makes me feel the vortex when you can't," Erin continued. "And that's the scary thing — if I can feel it, what about Harlon?"

My throat went dry. Not a good scenario, and we both knew it.

"Maybe you can feel the vortex because it's connected to your family," I said.

She shook her head. "Those petroglyphs were carved centuries ago by the Sinagua, long before outsiders settled in this area. Before they were pushed out, I should say — maybe even by my own ancestors." She shook her head sadly. "So, they're not connected to my family."

"I don't know. Magic is magic," I murmured.

Erin didn't look convinced.

By then, we'd reached the stairs to her porch, and each creaked under our feet. She paused, turning to gaze at the cliffs on the far side of the ranch. I read a dozen unspoken questions on her lips.

She glanced over expectantly, so I let her down gently. "They didn't cover that at the agency." Then I tried to lighten things a little. "But maybe when this is all over, you could teach a whole new unit."

That, at least, got a little laugh out of her. "You and I, you mean. I wouldn't know where to begin."

You and I. I smiled at her, and she smiled back. Long enough that my chest warmed — and not just because the cabin blocked the chilly breeze.

Erin turned to the door abruptly. "Anyway..."

I swallowed hard. Right. We had to focus on Harlon and Angelina, not on any, er...feelings that might be developing between us.

Inside, Erin set me up for the night the way she prepared for a balloon flight — all cool, quick, and efficient. It was ridiculously early, but so was starting time for work the next day. Erin was in and out of the bathroom in three minutes flat. Afterward, she climbed a steep ladder to the open loft and turned off the lights. A few seconds later, I heard her toss something light to the floor — her clothes?

My throat went dry, and my dragon's ears perked.

"Fair warning — I set an alarm for three forty-five," she called, out of sight but still all too close. "Should I wake you up then?"

Ha. Like I was going to get any sleep.

"Fine with me." I stripped to my boxers and lay down on the couch, tucking myself in under a worn quilt.

A moment later, she called out in a forced, *this is all perfectly normal* tone, "Goodnight."

"Goodnight," I echoed in a much scratchier voice.

The next few seconds ticked by in artificial silence. But, hey. That was preferable to the awkward silence of a morning-after full of regret.

Who says we would regret it? my dragon hummed, sending dirty images into my mind.

I turned to my side, ordering myself to sleep.

Closing my eyes was easy, but that didn't work with ears, and my dragon tuned in to the faintest sound from the loft. The rustle of sheets...that had to be Erin stretching those long, toned legs. The soft, even pace of her breath, too faint for human ears, but not for me.

She's not sleeping, the beast rumbled, not at all helpfully.

Yeah, well, neither was I.

Doesn't make sense, my dragon complained. *You sleeping here, wishing you could be with her, while she's up there, doing the same.*

Was she? And anyway, some things weren't that simple.

No, it's just you making them complicated, my inner beast grumbled. *Humans make no sense,*

Maybe not, but Erin was supremely sensible — and staying away from me was a smart decision. For both of us.

Doing my best to clear my mind, I settled in for a long, sleepless night.

Chapter Eighteen

NASH

At some point, I woke — proof that I had actually fallen asleep — though not to the sound of Erin's alarm. Something else. I rolled to my side and peered around. It was still dark — around midnight, maybe, when even the crickets had turned in for the night. Erin hadn't drawn the curtains on the front windows — no need to in a place this remote — and I could make out a couple of bright stars.

I sniffed the air, because I'd been woken by a noise. What?

A high, warbling howl broke out in the distance. Then another, and another in an off-pitch chorus that carried through the night.

Coyotes. I sank back, listening. What were they singing about? Love, life, and longing, or something less profound?

Whatever the subject, the rising and falling tune drew me out of bed and onto the front porch. I pulled on my jeans on the way and threw the blanket over my shoulders. Then I stood quietly, carving peace out of the night the way a miner extracted gems from solid rock. That was a new habit of mine, ever since...

I frowned. Ever since Angelina.

Every breath I puffed crystalized in the cold night air. I raised my arms, tempted to shift, fly, and revel in a perfect night. I closed my eyes, picturing myself soaring over mesas, slaloming between rock formations, and skimming over the creek. Erin could fly with me, and—

The door creaked behind me, and I whirled, dropping my arms.

"Hi," Erin murmured, blinking like a sleepy cat.

Joy, then inexplicable sadness hit me as the fantasy evaporated. Erin couldn't fly. Not as a dragon, at least, and not on nights like these. She would never know the thrill of a barrel roll or the tickle of wind under her wings. She would never glide at my side...

I gulped, forcing the sorrow away. "Nice night."

Her feet were bare, her body wrapped in a flannel robe. Together, we gazed out over the landscape, neither uttering a word.

After a while, she gestured toward the cliffs. "Even without magic, it would still feel magical out here."

I knew what she meant. Vortex and Harlon aside, there were a hundred reasons not to sell this place.

"Oh," she exclaimed. "Were you, er...getting ready to go for a run?"

No, I'd been thinking of flying. But, shoot. Erin thought I was a wolf shifter. Why the hell had I let her believe that?

Let me show her, my dragon begged. *Right here, right now. She'd like me. She likes flying, right?*

Yes, but she'd hate me for lying.

You didn't lie. You just didn't correct her when she assumed.

Something told me Erin wouldn't see it that way.

"Just looking at the stars," I bluffed.

Erin chuckled. "When we were little, we thought the stars were closer here than anywhere else in the world."

I pictured her, Pippa, and Abby wrapped in blankets, gazing at the stars from the porch of the main house. But she'd only mentioned summers at the ranch, right?

"We spent Christmas here a few times, and it was just like this," she said.

I held my breath. Coincidence, or had my thoughts drifted into her mind?

Most supernaturals could communicate without speaking, but it usually took concerted effort — or urgency, like at Harlon's party. But to casually pick up on each other's thoughts as readily as if they'd been uttered...

No coincidence, my dragon growled. *It's destiny.*

If it was, I wasn't ready to admit it. I did inch a little closer, though.

"Orion. . . Canis Major. . . Gemini. . ." Erin pointed out constellations like old friends. When she turned to locate Taurus, we bumped, but for once, we didn't jump apart.

"Taurus," she murmured, turning slowly to follow the Milky Way — all the way around until we were inches apart and face-to-face. She blinked, readjusting her focus to me. I could tell the exact moment she did, because her lip wobbled.

"Your eyes. . ."

Were they glowing? I turned away, but she cupped my face and turned me back gently.

"Wow."

I wasn't sure what that meant, but I didn't look away. I *couldn't* look away.

The space between us warmed, and her lips moved again.

I pulled in a sharp breath, and she tilted her head. "What?"

"Don't do that," I murmured.

Keep doing that, my dragon countered. *Please, don't stop.*

"Don't do what?"

I gulped. "That. . . that thing with your lips. Your eyes. . ."

I could have added *your body*, because she'd leaned forward, coming nice and close.

"What about my eyes?" she whispered.

I struggled for words, because her eyes held an entire universe, with bright flecks of emerald and gold. Those highlights had always been always there but tonight, they flared in brilliant bursts of energy.

I tucked a lock of her hair behind her ear and kept my fingers in that silky goodness a little too long.

"It's like the Milky Way snuck into them," I said.

She laughed. "Well, your eyes are like a bonfire. Two bonfires."

The midnight breeze wound its way around us, ruffling her hair. I sniffed, catching her scent — and so many other details. For the past months, my senses had been strangely dulled. Now, they all piqued. I felt the silky texture of her hair...inhaled her wild flower scent...registered her body heat.

I turned away. The longer I stood close to Erin, the more I lost my grip on myself. She was losing her grip too.

In a good way, my dragon insisted.

Was it? I only had the vaguest memories of my encounter with Angelina — the lone silver lining in that hellish storm cloud — but I was pretty sure it had started like this.

Totally different, my dragon huffed.

That was the thing, though — telling the difference between deception and genuine desire.

Erin cupped my face, keeping her gaze locked on mine.

No deception there, my dragon insisted.

I nearly groaned at the contact. Wait, I did groan. The jeans I'd pulled on usually fit comfortably, but they were getting tight fast.

I slid my hands to her wrists and tugged them gently away.

"You know what they say about playing with fire..." I rasped.

She grinned slyly. "Oh, I know all about fire."

Whoosh! My inner furnace jumped up another ten degrees.

"What about 'don't mix business and pleasure'?" I tried.

She raised an eyebrow. "Since when do you do what other people say? I don't."

I didn't have time to answer, because Erin brushed her lips over mine. Just a tiny brush but flames erupted throughout my body.

The Milky Way in her eyes turned into comets, and she did it again. And again and again. Then, just as my eyes were glazing over and my hands sneaking to her waist, she pulled back a little and gazed directly into my eyes.

My feet were firm on the ground, but inside, I teetered. Or maybe the earth had started spinning faster, around and around like one of those merry-go-round spinners that got kids all dizzy and excited.

Yeah, that was how I felt. Dizzy. Excited.

Erin ran her thumb slowly over my chin, then my lips.

"Every time I get close to you, this happens," she mumbled.

This was the pull, the need to get close. To touch. To kiss.

"Not my fault," I tried.

Destiny, my dragon whispered.

Erin chuckled. "Yes, it is."

My mind spun. Yes, it was my fault, or yes, it was destiny?

My heart hammered. Any second now, Erin would turn pink, whisper a hasty *sorry,* and disappear into the house. We would go back to bed quietly, separately, and lonelier than ever before. Then, we would get up in the morning and pretend nothing had happened.

I don't want to pretend, my dragon growled. *I don't want to—*

Erin cut off those protests with another brush of the lips. Then she slid her arms around my neck and kissed me hard. So hard, I stifled a groan. It was that good.

She paused, and when she met my eyes, she did a double take.

"Wow again."

I gulped. "What are they doing now?"

She stared a minute longer, then shook her head and closed in for another kiss. "Hard to explain. But I like it."

Which pretty much summed up the chemistry between us. Hard to explain, but boy, did I like it.

Those first few kisses were the kind that scouted the territory ahead. The next few went deeper and longer.

"I keep trying to resist this, but I can't," Erin whispered between shaky breaths. "I don't want to."

A damn good thing, because I'd just backed her against a porch column and pressed close. The blanket was draped around us both by then, and my hands slipped, tracing her ribs. Higher, higher...

Erin tipped her head back, freeing the way for me to kiss her neck. To nip. Her hands tightened around my neck, pulling me closer.

Drunk on her scent, I slid my hands higher, cupping the underside of her breasts. No bra, because she'd worn a T-shirt and boxers to bed. A huge plus, because the soft flesh fell right into my hands. Her nipples peaked, and when I swiped a thumb over one, she arched, fighting for control. . . but losing it.

Like me.

Chapter Nineteen

ERIN

Nash ran his teeth along my neck, making me shiver. Up to that point, my hands had been locked around his neck, but now, I slid one over his ass and pressed him close.

My heart pounded, and inside, I screamed, *Yes, yes, yes!*

This instinctive drive, this unquenchable desire... It had to be the shifter thing, right? Warlocks were renowned for their powers of seduction, but shifters had a reputation for sheer, physical magnetism. No trickery involved, unlike warlocks, because shifters were as powerless in love's games as the objects of their desire.

"Mmm," I mumbled into yet another kiss.

The breeze that ought to have cooled my body only fanned my desire, and the dirty side of my imagination went wild. If Nash held me a little higher, I could wrap my legs around his waist and...

Every cell in my body rushed toward that idea. Never mind our clothes or the cold or the fact that we were upright. We could do this. We could do anything. Anything we wanted, needed, or craved.

Nash pressed closer, clearly on board with that plan. Standing sex on my porch at midnight? Yes. Why the hell not?

The coyotes' howls kept rising and falling, background noise to the rush in my ears. Then they all broke off at the same time.

Nash froze, listening. I tensed, turning to look.

Tick. Tick. Tick. The next few seconds passed in unsettling silence.

Then, *Arooo...* The coyotes started howling again. False alarm. The world could go on.

But they'd hit a pause button at exactly the wrong — or right — time. Nash and I looked at each other, breathing hard.

His eyes blazed. Would we do the smart thing and stop while we could? Or would we throw caution to the wind and dive back in?

A split second later, Nash crushed into a hard, deep kiss, and we both careened over the edge.

I clawed at his jeans. He tugged at my clothes. The blanket slipped halfway off his shoulders.

This, I wanted to order Nash. *That. Now.* But my thoughts were a jumble, and all I could do was pull him inside. He shoved the door closed behind him, but it caught on the blanket.

"Dammit," he muttered, trying again.

I laughed, though it came out more like a yowl.

"Over here," I ordered, tugging him.

He slammed the door a second time and stalked toward me, eyes ablaze.

The next few seconds were a blur, though it would be easy to reconstruct events later, given the trail we left behind. My robe... His jeans... My shirt... His boxers...

Every layer lost was an acre gained of hard, straining muscle and smooth, warm skin. Hard edges on his body, soft curves on mine. I found a scar on his chest and another on his side, but I was too intent on another destination to spend much time there.

I wrapped my fingers around his hard shaft, making Nash hiss.

I considered the loft, but beds were for civilized sex, and there was nothing tame about the instincts driving us now.

"Here," I panted, tugging him down to the floor.

The rag rug was plenty thick, and — small miracle — I'd recently vacuumed. On the other hand, I wouldn't have noticed if we'd sprawled out on bales of hay.

The fireplace was dark and empty, but I could have sworn we had a blaze roaring in there. Outside, the breeze increased, making the scrub around the cabin sway.

Nash trailed fiery kisses to my nipple and, *whoosh!* Embers swirled in my mind. When he worked his way south and put his tongue to work, those embers crackled and danced.

Yes, yes, yes! the deepest, animal part of my soul cheered. "Nash..."

I tugged him up into a deep, sloppy kiss, then wound my legs around his waist, lining up my achy core with his.

Nash braced himself on his elbows and dipped his hips.

If he'd teased, I would have screamed. But he was just as consumed by this inferno as I was, and a heartbeat later—

He thrust deep. I gasped, tilting my head back. Then I hitched my legs a little higher, and we were off.

These days, the ranch was down to a handful of horses, but my great-aunt used to keep an entire herd. Something had once spooked them into a stampede, and it was a lot like this. The earth shaking under my feet. The thunder in my ears. The unbridled commotion. The sheer, pounding power.

"Yes..." Reaching my hands overhead, I found the edge of the couch and held on.

When Nash paused, I nearly screamed. Surely he wasn't going to stop now? We hadn't bothered with protection, but he was a shifter, and I had enough magic in my genes to protect me. And as for getting knocked up... Abby might have yelled at me in warning, because she'd learned that lesson the hard way, but I was pretty sure it wasn't that time of month. Good enough?

My hazy mind nodded immediately. Not smart, but then again, I wasn't thinking all too clearly.

"Hang on," Nash murmured, pulling me close enough to hook my knees over his shoulders.

Oh yes. This was definitely going to be good.

He plunged back in, driving deep.

I didn't know how many times I cried out or what I said. I didn't know how often we rocked against each other or how deep our bodies sank into that rug. I only knew that I was stampeding along with those mustangs, feeling ragged, wild, and free. Across the open desert, then up and over the mesas at a dizzying pace, chased by a whipping wind.

Then, with one final push, Nash drove me right over the edge, and those mustangs sprouted wings and took me soaring through the air.

I sensed Nash gritting his teeth, pouring out his release. I felt myself shudder around him, inside and out. But mostly, I soared. At first, on impossibly light Pegasus wings. But those morphed gradually until I was soaring on broad, leathery dragon wings.

Outside, the shutters creaked under an increasingly powerful wind.

"Oh!" I cried out, clutching Nash through an aftershock of ecstasy.

He held me close, then gradually relaxed over me, panting hard.

I wound my arms around his shoulders and held him tightly. There was no need for words, and what would I say anyway?

Amazing didn't begin to capture what I'd just experienced. And, oops. As a wolf shifter, Nash might not be too pleased to know my imagination had taken me soaring away with dragons instead of a four-footed lover. A detail I would have to keep to myself.

Gradually, my breaths leveled out, as did his, along with that out-of-nowhere wind that had blown through the ranch.

Nash stroked my hair, keeping his face tucked against my shoulder for a long time. I wasn't quite ready to face him either. Hell, I wasn't ready to face myself. Sex always inspired a certain amount of soul-searching. Sex with the annoying guy from work, even more so. And then there was the whole bossy, secret-agent thing. . .

Except Nash wasn't annoying. Not any more — or maybe he had really never been. And as for bossy and secretive. . . well, sort of, but he'd revealed a lot too. And, hey. He was on my side, right?

Slowly, he turned, and I held my breath. Was he disappointed? Regretful? Was I? Or was this somehow going to be okay?

Then our eyes met, and I exhaled. The light in his eyes was clear, bright, and happy. A playful breeze whipped around the cabin, and my imaginary fire crackled merrily.

I looked closer. Wow. Nash's eyes were *really* clear and *really* bright, without that haunted look I sometimes caught.

Without word or signal, we settled into a long, gentle kiss. Reaching around blindly, Nash found the Mexican blanket that covered my worn couch, then pulled it over his shoulders, covering us both.

Ha. As if I were cold. But it did create a comfy nest. So comfy, I never wanted to leave.

"Nice," I whispered, risking one word.

His lips curved into a smile. "Nice."

We lay quietly, me listening to his heart thump, him gently stroking my skin. Minutes later, a coyote yipped in the distance, and I chuckled. "You sure you're not tempted to run out and join them?"

I'd never seen a shifter change forms — not directly anyway. I'd only ever caught fleeting glimpses of my father's shifter friends — or my mother leaving after upending my life with one of her rare, unannounced visits.

Nash's eyes clouded. "Not tempted, no."

I rubbed my cheek against his, then sighed. "Pippa is going to love this."

He shrugged. "Let her."

"Ha. You have no idea how annoying my sister can be."

Of course, Pippa would tease me just as mercilessly if nothing had happened between Nash and me. At least this way, I came out ahead.

Nash held me quietly, and I closed my eyes. In the morning, I would have to face up to what we'd just done. But for now...

I considered for a moment, then kissed him. Once. Twice.

Mm. My body was already warming up for a second round.

"I'm thinking about a new location for this sleepover," I announced.

Nash arched an eyebrow in a sinfully hot look. "Oh yes?"

I pointed toward the loft. "Like Claire said. Everyone piled into one bed. As long as *everyone* is only us two," I added quickly.

He laughed, rolling to his side, then getting to his feet.

The blanket fell away, and oh my goodness. Lots of goodness. Very big goodness—

I yanked my eyes back to his face. "There's not a lot of headroom, so I might have to take the top..."

He smiled, pulling me to my feet. Our bodies pressed against each other comfortably, like we'd been together for many happy years.

I forced the thought away. This was just one night, not a lifetime.

"Lead the way, boss," he murmured, following me to the loft. "Lead the way."

Chapter Twenty

NASH

I'd spent all my adult years consumed by work — first in the military, then at the agency. Both were big on rules, and mostly, those rules were fine with me.

Kind of ironic, then, to find myself breaking so many of them these days. Tonight especially.

I followed Erin up to the loft and sank down on the deep mattress.

Mmm, my dragon sighed dreamily as she pressed over me.

One kiss melted into another as our bodies heated.

Control your emotions. That was one rule the Marines and the agency stressed. But that was impossible with Erin, who'd stirred all kinds of emotions from day one. A different one for every hour, sometimes, with everything from frustration to fascination and awe.

And now that we were in bed...

Bliss. Anticipation. Trust.

That last one was the best — my trust in her, her trust in me.

Erin shifted her weight, straddling me. Still kissing, she dragged her body up an inch, then down. Flesh rubbed against flesh, soft in some places, hard in others.

I groaned. Bliss. Desire. Peace. It had been a long, long time since I'd felt any of those.

A nice change, my dragon crooned.

When Erin reared up, her hair tickled my skin, then swayed around her shoulders. Leaving her hands on my chest, she teased me with long, lazy drags of her body. Soon, her breaths came faster, as did mine. Then she sank down, taking me in, inch by burning inch.

"Oh," she murmured, tipping her head back.

If my teeth hadn't been gritted against fiery pleasure, I would have echoed that.

My vision went a little hazy as she started to dance over me. Pert breasts peeked out from the curtain of her hair, and her lips moved in silent moans. I gripped her hips, gently at first, then harder, driving up when she came down.

Don't get involved with a subject of interest.

Another rule I was breaking, and not just through sex. Getting involved was washing the dishes after dinner with her family. Playing horses with her niece. Itching for Erin to get her chance to pilot, because she deserved it.

"Oh. . ." she moaned, rocking harder and harder.

Outside, the wind picked up again, humming over the roof.

The mattress lay on a sturdy platform — and a good thing too. Another good thing was the distance to the main house because. . . Well, privacy.

Which brought me to the third rule I was breaking — *confidentiality.* There were some things you just didn't share. Like your soul, your heart, or what made you tick. Plus, no one was supposed to know the agency existed. I still had to tell Erin what type of shifter I was, but otherwise, she knew more about me than men I'd worked with for years. If I didn't watch myself, I'd be spilling my childhood secrets to her next.

But tonight, there were no rules. No limits.

We rocked harder, faster, deeper. Thrilling in that angle, then trying out a different one. Erin leaned right. . . left. . . back. So far back, her hair cascaded away, opening a view to the underside of her chin.

My dragon roared. *If we rolled now and took the top. . .*

My eyes fixed on the smooth skin of her neck, and images danced through my head. My teeth extending. Scraping that creamy surface, then sinking deep in a bite. A bite that would connect us forever.

So, so tempting.

But so wrong too. That was too close to what Angelina had done to me — not just the biting part, but the *binding you to me forever* aspect. With both parties consenting and understanding exactly what they were getting into, that could be a gift. But without... it was more like a crime.

My dragon growled, and I bared my teeth, slipping back toward anger.

"Nash—" Erin broke off.

My eyes popped open, and I smoothed my thumbs over her hips.

Dammit. I couldn't have *forever* with Erin, because that would make her a target to the vampire I abhorred. But we could have tonight, and I sure as hell wasn't going to ruin it.

"Sorry." I tugged her hips gently, desperate for her to continue.

Her eyes searched mine for a moment, and I nearly begged.

Please, please don't stop. Don't let me — or that bitch, Angelina — ruin this.

Thank goodness Erin was Erin and never, ever left things half finished. After five long seconds of reset time — and a look that asked, *okay?* — she plunged into a deep, hungry kiss. A few heartbeats later, we were panting... grinding... unraveling. Erin leaned farther and farther back, trusting her balance to my grip.

In the distance, thousands of cottonwood leaves rustled in the wind.

Then, *bam.* I exploded, and Erin cried out in her own racking orgasm.

We hung on and on, riding a wave of pleasure into a world of hot, achy bliss. When we finally eased apart, panting, Erin crumpled over me. I looped my arms around her and closed my eyes, basking in the remnants of our high.

All those rules broken, yet I'd never felt so honest. All those limits crossed, but I'd never felt so free.

Well, maybe not one hundred percent, but ninety, at least.

I frowned. Free of what?

Angelina, my dragon grumbled.

That's when it finally hit me. Ever since she'd tasted my blood, her presence had followed me like a shadow. Now, the shadow was more like a cloud — still there, but farther away. Thinner, too, with streaks of sunlight breaking through it.

Hesitantly, I peeked at my wrist. The puncture marks were still there, but they seemed fainter. Or was that wishful thinking?

Erin sighed and melted in my arms, curling in as perfectly as yang to yin.

I rubbed my chin along her shoulder, then touched the scars on my wrist. No sting. No warning burn. Nothing but a faint, ominous throb.

Huh. *Once bitten, forever chained* was one of those hard-set vampire rules.

I stared a little longer. Was that another rule that could be broken?

"Mm..." Erin snuggled up like a koala.

I smoothed her hair back and kissed her, pushing every other thought away.

∞∞∞

We stayed intertwined for a long, long time and eventually dropped off to sleep. A damn good thing, too, with that early alarm setting. But nature's call woke me first, and I had no choice but to feel my way down the ladder sometime later.

I headed back to the ladder when I was done, but something made me detour to the porch for the second time that night. Opening the door quietly, I sucked in a lungful of air. Cold as it was, the stars were amazing, and the wind was back to a whisper.

I spent a minute there, peeking back every few seconds in hopes that Erin might wake and join me. But her breaths remained soft and slow with slumber.

Stepping to the edge of the porch, I looked around. To the left, cliffs zigzagged away from the house in a long line that reached for the stars. The creek was straight ahead, marked by a line of trees. The main house was way over to the right, along with the paddock and barn.

I sniffed, suddenly tempted to shift and fly, if only for a short time. It had been a while, and the crisp winter air promised a beautiful flight. Plus, I was already naked, so there'd be no clothes to bother with.

I glanced back toward the loft. Maybe just a short flight...

I hesitated a minute longer, then made up my mind. I took off right from the porch in the kind of showboating shift I hadn't been inspired to try for a long time. That meant leaping up and away in human form, arms wide. Needles of winter air freeze-burned my skin, but a heartbeat later, I was protected by thick dragon hide, and my arms had morphed into huge, powerful wings. My ears and nose stretched into streamlined dragon form, and flesh and bone groaned. It hurt, but it was exhilarating too. A little like sex, I supposed.

My dragon grinned. *Both feel really, really good.*

The porch was only a couple of feet off the ground, so my belly nearly scraped the brush for the first few body lengths of flight. But bending to the back edge of my wings provided lift, and soon, I was soaring above the roof...above the cottonwoods...above the mesa at the west edge of the ranch.

Racing along, I circled to the far side of the mesa. Then I turned sideways, skimming the cliff in another of those hot-dog moves I'd loved as a kid — one wing pointed straight down, the other up.

Ha. Haven't lost my touch, my dragon preened.

I grinned. God, was it nice to feel good.

Circling back to the ranch, I peered at Erin's cabin. I had her to thank for this playful energy. I had her to thank for so much.

My heart squeezed, and I looked down, yearning for her company. Not just down there, but up here, flying with me.

Maybe someday she can, my dragon whispered. *She could, if she was our mate.*

The majority of the guys — and they were mostly guys — in the Marines and at the agency were single, but every once in a while, the love bug would hit, turning a perfectly rational soldier into a goofy, love-sick mess. Everyone would tease, roll their eyes, and swear that would never be them — until their turn came.

To a man, we'd all sworn it would never happen to us. We couldn't let it happen, because who wanted such an entangled, complicated life?

But suddenly, I found myself yearning for *entangled* and *complicated.*

As long as it's with Erin, my dragon added quickly.

The sentiment came with a rush of joy, and I nearly roared in glee. I flew on, picturing all kinds of blissful scenarios while ticking off local landmarks. Bear Mountain was just around the corner from Painted Rock Ranch. So was Deer Mountain — though it was more mesa than mountain. Then came the deep indents of Boynton and Fay Canyons, followed by the high plateau of Soldier's Pass. At Mescal Mountain, I curled my tail left, ruddering my body in the opposite direction. Peering down, I searched for the next landmark.

There! my dragon announced, rocketing toward a tear in the landscape.

I pictured Erin flying beside me, then yelling, *Whoa! Wait!*

Most of the time, I was more responsible than reckless. But at that moment, I was a teenager desperate to impress on a first date.

I flattened my ears, yelling, *Watch this!* in my imagination.

Devil's Bridge was right down there, and if I timed it just right. . .

Zoom! I zipped under the natural rock arch, then twisted into an impossibly tight turn to emerge before slamming into the next rock face.

I cleared it — barely — and raced on, looking back. Holy shit, that had been close.

Still, I broke into a massive grin. Close, but fun.

I glanced around, half expecting to find Erin. But there was no one, just the harsh desert and lonely, wrinkled mountains. Turning my head east, I glimpsed the lights of town — a reminder of the real world and all the troubles in it. Troubles that all started — and ended — with Angelina.

My mood plummeted. That vengeful, malicious vampire could track me anywhere, anytime. Getting involved with Erin meant endangering her and the ranch. Her sisters and her niece too.

I roared, releasing a huge plume of fire.

Let Angelina try, my dragon hissed. *I will end her. Then, when this is all over...*

I glided on grimly. The only way to end this was killing Angelina, and that would end me too.

My dragon huffed, but it didn't disagree.

Well, at least we'd die free, I reasoned.

Not much consolation. Not now that I'd tasted how good life could be.

Sapped of all that giddy energy, I flew back to the ranch, cursing the slight headwind. I came in for a landing along the dirt road and touched down smoothly, then stalked to Erin's cabin, shifting to human form as I went.

On the porch, I paused for a deep breath. Tonight was my forever, so I couldn't afford to spoil it with negative energy.

The thought made me chuckle a little. Were the New Age types in Sedona rubbing off on me?

A minute later, I crawled back into bed. Erin groped around in her sleep, found my arm, and pulled me close.

That, at least, drew a genuine smile out of me. I kissed the top of her head and stared off into the darkness, wondering where destiny might take us next.

Chapter Twenty-One

ERIN

Somehow, I managed to keep my hands off Nash for the rest of the night. Then again, I was pretty wiped out — in good ways and bad. *Good* was the blissful exhaustion that came from the best sex of my life. *Bad* was my constant worry about Harlon. Being with Nash had helped drive that out of my mind for a while, but the moment my alarm rang—

I jerked upright, picturing the worst.

I whacked the alarm off, then sank back down. No Harlon. Whew. Right now, all I had to face was work.

Nash was asleep, but his arms were still looped around me. He smelled as good as ever — like pines and a fresh breeze. I stroked his arm, staring off into the darkness for a while, thinking. Would this change things between us? Did I want it to?

The digits on my clock blinked, changing to three forty-six. I gave myself until three fifty, then quietly slipped out of bed and looked at Nash.

His arms protected the space I'd vacated, and he looked uncharacteristically carefree. A little younger, a little happier. A lot calmer.

A good look, especially with the background being my bed.

My heart panged. I really wouldn't mind keeping things that way.

I felt my way down the ladder, found my robe, and made coffee for two in the dark. Then I climbed to the top rung and tapped on Nash's leg.

"Nash. Time to get up."

He pulled his leg away and tightened his arms around my empty space.

My heart warmed, and I wished I could let him sleep. But it really was time to get going.

"Nash..."

When his arms closed over nothing, he stirred, then shot upright, fists balled.

I gave him a wave to say, *I'm right here, everything is okay, and yes, we really did have raging sex last night. I loved it, by the way.*

Well, one little wave might not have captured all that, but he got the drift. His body relaxed, and his eyes sparkled at me. Then he rubbed his face, still drowsy.

"Coming."

Our clothes were strewn all over the floor, which meant that any minute now, six feet of naked, rippled man-flesh would step into view. I licked my lips, imaging that. Then I blushed, because I didn't have to imagine it. Not now that I'd seen — *and* kissed *and* touched — just about every inch of him.

Still, my heart did a little cha-cha when he came down.

Heat shot to my cheeks, and after five spellbound seconds of gazing into his eyes, I avoided the inevitable awkwardness of a morning-after by pecking his lips — then racing to the bathroom.

"Just taking a quick shower..."

I took my coffee with me, chugging half down before setting it on the bathroom sink. The shower, as usual, ran cold for a painfully long time before going lukewarm. But, heck. Maybe a cold shower was just what I needed to focus on the day ahead.

The door creaked, and the shower curtain billowed outward. It was translucent but printed with enough constellations to distract the eye. Well, most of the time. Now, my eyes went right to Nash's...um, star attractions.

He set his mug next to mine. "Mind if I join you? Seeing as time is short, I mean."

Cheap excuse, but a welcome one.

"Sure. Come in," I said, turning away.

I might have looked and sounded casual, but my heart rate tripled.

The curtain rings rasped over the rod, and the shower heated right up. Not the water. Just the mood.

I passed the bar of soap over my shoulder, then lathered shampoo into my hair.

Nash stepped closer, making water ricochet between my body and his. I held my breath. What would he do? Say? Touch?

Without a word, he pressed a kiss to my shoulder. Then he ran the soap over my back and gently spread the lather with both hands.

My eyelids drooped. God, that felt good. Not at all as awkward as I'd feared, though not as casual as I'd pretended. *Natural* was a better word, like we were right where we belonged.

Nash did his front after finishing my back, then handed me the soap and turned, waiting. I took a deep breath before scrubbing his back, determined to keep my hands away from the danger zones. Which was hard as hell, given all those tempting contours.

I ran my hands over his shoulders, then his ribs. Too bad he'd washed his front already. But a second rinse never hurt...

I started sneaking my hands forward, then retreated, muttering, "I deserve a goddamn medal."

"For...?"

I poked the soap into a spot just above his sculpted ass. "For resisting temptation."

He chuckled. "Smart decision. I'd love a rain check, though."

I patted his ass. Or rather, I tapped my hand against those buns of steel. I bounced back.

"You got it," I promised. "A rain check for a shower with more time for...er...dirty thoughts."

"Promise?"

"Bet your ass, I do." I patted the area in question.

Nash laughed. "I'll look forward to that."

I conditioned my hair in double time and stepped out of the shower, dripping. Nash followed a minute later, and we managed to resist temptation from there on. A damn shame, but duty called. After a quick, companionable breakfast, we set off for work, bouncing down the dirt road in my pickup.

The kind of morning I could get used to.

Without thinking, I reached for Nash's hand and squeezed. Then I caught myself, wondering how he would react.

Nash brought my hand to his lips, kissed it, then released it with a squeeze.

My heart squeezed too. I could *definitely* get used to this.

The roads were silent, the town asleep as we early birds went through our usual routine — picking up the company van, hooking up the trailer, meeting Chico and John, and driving out to the launch spot. There, we found Madden and the guests, who stood yawning around a second van they had shuttled over with.

I did a quick head count — then stopped and counted again. Six guests. Only six.

My breath caught. Could this be my chance?

Hustling over to Madden, I practically snatched the clipboard out of his hands. "How many guests today?"

He gave a foul-breathed yawn and scratched his belly.

"Um... seven?"

I counted again, then called them over. A bachelor party, by the looks of it — all big football-player types in their late-twenties.

"Good morning, everyone. Just a quick head count, please." I tapped a pen over the list as I called out names. "Switalski... Naylor... Richard Smith... Nate Smith..."

One after another, they replied.

"Yo."

"That's me."

"Right here."

But at the fifth name, they shook their heads.

"Joe's still in bed," Richard said.

"Too much partying last night," Nate snickered.

My heart leaped. "Oh, a cancelation? What a shame."

Nash grinned. John and Chico gave me two thumbs up.

I went through the rest of the list, worried they might have a late addition — like a cheerleader-type named Mindy one of them had picked up at a bar the previous evening. Hopefully someone other than the groom.

But no. No Mindy. No late additions at all. Just an inflatable sex doll with giant lips shaped for a blow-job — without the blowing, I supposed, unless the doll had an air cartridge wedged between those huge tits.

"Can Lola come?" Switalski asked, patting the doll on the ass.

I shoved the clipboard back at Madden. "Absolutely not."

Then I hurried over to finish preparing the balloon. The sooner it was ready, the sooner I could get aloft — as copilot, clocking that last hour I needed. Ideally, before their buddy Joe decided to turn up after all.

"Can you drive the van today?" I asked Nash.

He grinned and thumped me on the back. "Absolutely."

I nearly did a happy dance. For months, I'd dreamed about this day. Hooray!

But now that it was here, my elation was punctured with a thousand concerns. "Are you sure?"

He nodded. "We got this."

Chico and John nodded. "This is your chance, boss!"

It was, and I couldn't believe it. Still, I hesitated. What if they got lost? What if they misjudged the landing and the basket was damaged? What if—

"Go," Chico ordered with a huge smile.

I dashed back to Madden. "One less guest means you have space for a copilot."

"Awesome." He grinned and called out to Nash. "Your chance to fly, buddy." Then he turned to the guests with a knowing grin. "Nash flew helicopters for the Marines, you know."

He managed to make it sound as if he'd been on the front lines with Nash.

The guests looked suitably impressed, but Nash looked ready to kill Madden... unless I got to that rat first.

"I'm flying," I hissed. "Not him. Got it?"

Madden ignored me. "Aw, come on, Nash."

The guests called out too. "Yeah, man. We'd love to hear your stories."

Nash's eyes flashed, but he handled it well. "Ear infection. I'm grounded for two weeks."

Total bull — and we wouldn't ascend high enough for it to matter even if it were true. Madden ought to have known better, but he just shrugged.

"Whatever."

Punching Madden wouldn't accomplish anything, but I was sorely tempted. My dream coming true was not *whatever*. It was everything.

I checked every inch of the balloon, then met with Nash, Chico, and John. After a quick sniff of the wind, I drew a map in the dirt.

"Remember, the forestry road looks like it dead ends after the bridge, but you can get through if you take it slow. But if we end up landing at the Chute Canyon overlook, don't park the trailer too close to the edge. It's more crumbly than it looks. And if we land at Haunted Hollow—"

Nash cut me off. "We'll figure it out. Now, go." He gave me a gentle shove.

I stopped, tempted to hug him. To kiss him, too, and dance him around. I settled for a huge, happy smile that Nash returned, then ran over to where Madden was delivering the safety brief.

As he spoke in his slow, lazy drawl, I checked the sky. Dawn colors lit the horizon, and everything looked fine. But the hair on the back of my neck tickled, so I sniffed the air again — and frowned. Had that cloud bank been there before?

It wasn't much — just a dark smudge against the yellow of dawn. But it hadn't been there minutes earlier.

"Nothing to worry about," Madden said when I pointed it out. "Besides, look at the forecast." He tapped a second page on the clipboard. "All clear. See?"

For the second time that morning, I grabbed the clipboard. The forecast called for light, stable winds out of the northeast at five to seven miles per hour. Perfect — on paper.

"Aw, that's nothing," John echoed, following my eyes to the horizon.

My eyes agreed, but my gut wouldn't settle down.

I checked the lines, then tested the burner. *Whoosh!* Flames shot into the balloon, lifting it off the ground. My heart lifted with it. Any minute now, I would be flying the way I did in my dreams. But that niggling feeling persisted.

I continued filling the balloon with quick bursts, punctuated by concerned looks at the sky.

Still nothing. Nothing to put a finger on anyway.

Nash came up beside me, looking in the same direction. "What?"

"Just checking," I bluffed.

Nash studied me so closely, I swear he could read my mind.

I grabbed my phone and checked the more recent airport weather report I'd downloaded on the drive. The fact that it failed to mention that incoming system did little to settle me down.

Nash helped Chico put away the fan, then came over and stood by my side.

"You know what they say about trusting your instincts..." he murmured.

I did. Well, usually. But given the complete lack of evidence...

"Especially *your* instincts," he added, dead serious.

I stood a little taller, prouder. But that nagging *something* refused to back down.

"All right, everyone," Madden called out. "You can leave your things in the van. We're about to take off."

The guests high-fived one another — except Nate, who was peeing in the bushes.

I studied the sky a few seconds longer, then tugged Madden's sleeve and pointed again. "Look at that."

He scoffed. "The forecast says—"

"Forecasts can be wrong," I hissed, keeping my voice down.

Madden snorted. "You scared?"

I nearly stamped my foot — and if it landed on his, all the better.

"No. I'm thinking about safety. I know that cloud is small, but if that's not in the forecast, the forecast could be wrong about other things too."

"There's safety, and there's paranoia," Madden said.

"No, there's safety and more safety," Nash emphasized. "Seriously. I don't like the look of that cloud."

Then Madden looked, but he just shrugged again. "We'll keep an eye on it."

"Keep an eye on it or be *caught* in it?" I barked.

Madden huffed. "Caught in what? That's tiny."

It was. But as Pippa liked to say, *It's not the size of the dog in the fight...*

When Madden leaned in, I wrinkled my nose at his stale breath.

"If we don't fly, we'll have to refund everyone," he reminded me. "What would Henry say about that?"

"Henry would err on the side of caution. We have a perfect record—"

"*I* have a perfect record," Madden emphasized, cutting me off.

Nash put a hand on my arm before I socked the man.

"I've seen the Marines ground all units based on a tiny wind shift," Nash warned.

I appreciated his help, but I resented the need for it. Why would Madden listen to Nash and not to me?

Okay, easy answer. Because Nash was a man, and Madden was a misogynistic ass.

Madden wavered for a few seconds, and I didn't know whether to hope or not. Staying grounded ruined my chances of piloting my own flights, but going aloft might prove irresponsible.

Finally, Madden shook his head. "The wind could just as easily shift in our favor." He shoved the clipboard back at me and climbed into the basket. "It'll be fine." Then he raised his voice. "All right, guys. Climb in one at a time, from different sides."

The hair on the back of my neck signaled *Danger. Danger. Don't go.*

"Do you sense anything?" I asked Nash. "Any weather shift, I mean?"

"No, but if you do..."

I warmed at his trust. But, hell. I'd been wrong in the past. What if I was wrong again?

Nash shook his head. "Forget it. Don't go."

I weighed my choices. Madden was going to fly, no matter what I did. And if that weather system proved insignificant, I would have forfeited my chance to fly for no reason.

I gritted my teeth, looking between the balloon and the clouds.

Nash's whisper went all gritty. "What if it's Harlon?"

I stared at the sky, thinking of the out-of-nowhere wind shifts during Harlon's flight with Madden. But those were minor, and Harlon was currently out of town, so...

I stepped toward the basket, finally resolute. "Worst case, we'll keep it short. We could land as close as Deer Mountain if necessary."

A quick up-and-down trip, I figured, trying to convince myself.

Nash frowned. "I don't like this."

Neither did I. But now that I'd convinced myself it would be all right...

"Erin," Nash warned as I reached for the edge of the basket.

After a last glance back, I climbed in, hoping he would understand.

Madden pulled the burner cord, making the balloon lurch off the ground. "All right, everyone. Get ready for the flight of your life!"

Chapter Twenty-Two

ERIN

The balloon rose quickly, though the churning in my gut came from watching Nash shrink into the distance below us. What if he was right? And, shoot. He looked upset. Not how I hoped the day would develop after such a blissful night.

"Desert Skies One, radio check." I spoke into the radio, something we'd forgotten to do before lift-off.

Not a good omen. What else might I have forgotten?

The radio crackled. "Desert Skies Support, reading you loud and clear." Nash's voice was tight and curt.

I cursed myself again, but there wasn't much I could do now.

"Two-eighty at three point one," I reported, then returned the radio to its cradle in transmit mode.

See? Madden's smug look told me. *All fine.*

Yes, we were moving at a smooth, pedestrian pace, but I still couldn't shake the feeling of something amiss. I checked the eastern sky. Were those clouds thickening, or was that just a trick of the dawn light?

The guests didn't know enough to notice, and Madden was too busy showing off his knowledge of the landscape — and spinning tall tales — to pay attention to the weather.

"They say there's ghosts down there at Phantom Ranch. And you see that cliff over there? A mountain biker missed a turn and flew right off the edge. They had to helicopter his body out."

Two of the guests snapped pictures, suitably impressed.

There'd been no such accident — thank goodness — although a story had gotten around about a couple of bikers who had cut it close.

"Hey, check out the quad rental," one of the guys said.

For the next twenty minutes, they tried to locate trails they'd explored the previous day, which suited me fine. I could concentrate on monitoring Madden's flying *and* the weather.

The wind slowly backed to the southeast, and our speed increased. That cloud bank was getting bigger. I was sure of it now.

"Two-seventy-two at four point five," I reported, picturing Nash drumming his fingers on the steering wheel in concern.

Over the next few minutes, our speed crept up to six miles per hour, and even Madden stopped rambling long enough to eye the storm.

"Yahoo! We're finally moving!" one of the guests hooted. "Can you make this thing go even faster?"

"We move at the speed of the wind." I looked Madden in the eye to telegraph the second, unspoken part. *And the wind is getting faster.*

Madden checked the instruments, then looked back at the clouds. Finally, he scratched his head. "Now, where did that come from?"

I refrained from pointing out the obvious. *They were there before we took off, and I told you so.*

Then again, I couldn't exactly gloat, because there I was, up in the air with him.

The wind increased, pushing the cloud bank. It churned like a wave, rolling ever closer and closer.

Madden reached for the clipboard again. "But the forecast said—"

I nearly smacked it out of his hands. "There are forecasts, and there's real life. Just look!"

After a glacial thought process, Madden clicked his jaw and studied the ground.

"We could make Heart Rock pullout if we start descending now," I murmured.

"Descend?" one of the guests said. "Already?"

"No way, man," another grumbled. "We paid a lot of money for this!"

Madden hesitated so long, I nearly reached over and pulled the cord that dumped hot air from the top of the balloon. We had to land — and soon.

"Your safety is our top priority," I said in my flattest, *you will not argue with me* voice. "As for money, Desert Skies will refund proportionally for any flight under an hour."

Five of the guests grumbled, but the sixth — Nate? — gaped at the black clouds steamrolling toward us. "Maybe it's better not to get caught in that."

"Nah. It would be cool," another declared, taking pictures. "Can we get closer?"

How he expected us to do that without a motor, I had no clue. *Why* he would want to was even harder to fathom.

I signaled to Madden, who started dumping air. Whew.

"Heading for Heart Rock pullout," I informed the ground crew over the radio. Then I cursed, because it was too late. The wind was sweeping us along faster and faster. "Correction..." I glanced around.

"Nolan Point," Madden threw in.

Good to know he'd turned on that brain cell of his. "Nolan Point," I echoed, making sure the ground crew heard.

The question was, would they find that rarely used clearing? I searched for the dusty white van and nearly cheered when I saw that it had already U-turned and set off in the correct direction.

Boy, that Nash was nearly as good at reading the wind as I was. Not bad for a wolf shifter. I supposed he'd learned in his years as a pilot.

The clouds were compacting and growing even darker. Not just gray but charcoal streaked with bluish-purple, all of it churning in an angry mass that consumed the landscape.

"Wow. Have you ever seen anything like it?" one of the guests asked.

"Reminds me of that dust storm that hit Phoenix a while back," another answered. "What did they call it? A haboob?"

Three of the guys laughed, but I just gulped. If only they knew.

But the face I pictured at the reins of this storm was Harlon's, not my father's. Was Harlon back in Sedona? Was he even capable of conjuring a storm of such power?

Well, I would have to figure that out later. Right now, I had a balloon to land — the sooner, the better.

Having finally gotten the memo, Madden continued dumping hot air in bursts to bring us to lower altitude.

"Uh, where's Nolan Point?" asked the one guest who'd caught on.

I pointed grimly. It was right under us, but the wind was sweeping us onward.

"No problem, though," I assured him. "We can land anywhere — on a road, even on private property. We just need a flat area clear of obstructions."

He nodded slowly, and I saw him grip one of the basket's handles. Smart man, because when we did land, it wouldn't be gentle.

Whoosh! The wind gusted to what felt like Mach 1, sweeping us ever faster over the landscape.

"Whoa." One of the guests watched the scrub rush under us. "Aren't we going a little fast?"

"No problem," Madden bluffed. "The west fork of Red Canyon Road will be perfect."

Perfect would not have been my word choice, but it did make sense. We just had to make sure we were well clear of the power lines before making our final descent.

I turned to the passengers. "All right, everybody. Let's go over the landing procedure. The ground crew will be there to meet us, but we'll have to anticipate a hard landing."

"How hard?" they asked, alarmed.

"Hard. But we'll be safe inside the basket. It's likely to drag over the ground for a while, and that could be bumpy, so I'll need everyone to crouch down inside until I give the okay. Not the time for pictures, folks. It's a serious situation, but everything will be fine."

I made sure my voice communicated calm and certainty. Madden, on the other hand. . .

"Shit!" he cursed, giving the balloon a burst of hot air.

I whirled. What the hell was he doing?

"Fence," he grumbled.

"Power lines," I hissed, pointing.

Madden started dumping air again. "We have plenty of space before them."

My jaw dropped, and ugly statistics ran through my mind. Balloon accidents were rare, but when they happened, they often involved power lines. The balloon could get tangled, or the power lines could ignite an onboard fire — every pilot's nightmare.

"After the power lines. We have to land *after* the power lines," I barked. "Otherwise, we risk the wind pushing us into them."

"There's no road to land on back there," he countered. "We'll damage the basket."

We would damage a lot more than the basket if we hit the power lines — a fact I made clear with the evil eye and a very quiet, "Too risky."

Madden pointed to the storm, which was almost on top of us. "We need to land before that hits." Then he turned, jutting an elbow to keep me away from the burner. "All right, everyone. The minute we land, bail out and move clear of the basket."

I fumed — and fretted, because he was risking all our lives. But short of tackling him and taking over the controls, there was nothing I could do except make sure everyone was prepared.

My only consolation was the van racing toward our position, kicking up a plume of dust. I trusted Nash, Chico, and even John more than I trusted Madden — and we would need their manpower to land the balloon upright. They sped ahead, jumped out of the vehicle, and fanned out.

Nash made an urgent, no-go motion, telling Madden not to risk it.

For once, I wouldn't have minded Madden listening to Nash rather than me. Unfortunately, he didn't and continued the risky maneuver.

To his credit, Madden did get the balloon on a low, steady line two or three yards off the ground. But we were sweeping along so fast, it would be hard to land without tipping and ejecting the passengers.

"Shit," one of the guests muttered, ducking into the shelter of the basket.

The rest followed suit. Finally, they'd grasped the severity of the situation.

"I told you we should have brought Lola," one of them muttered.

Yeah, a blow-up doll would make a handy cushion for a crash landing. But I would rather die than stoop that low.

"Now, Madden. Now!" I yelled.

Still, we swept onward. Nash, Chico, and John converged on us, but we were still too high.

"Madden!" I yelled. "Dump air!"

"Hurry!" Nash roared.

But Madden was frozen, staring at the power lines, his face twisted in panic.

"Dammit…" I reached over and pulled the valve, dumping hot air. "Everyone, get down. Brace yourselves!"

Everyone did — including Madden, who ducked down, leaving me to handle things alone.

The balloon scraped the ground, throwing everyone sideways.

Nash, Chico, and John grabbed the basket, but their combined weight wasn't enough to ground it. We scraped and bounced along, pushed by the wind.

"Okay, go!" I yelled. "Everyone out. Now!"

I meant the guests, but Madden was the first to bail out. Two guests vaulted out after him, while the rest climbed to the edge of the basket more clumsily. Not their fault, with the basket skidding along, hitting rocks and bushes. My hip banged into the propane tank, and my knee smacked into the stiff weave of the basket.

"Oof." John tripped, and that side of the basket jerked upward.

The motion flung the two guys on the lower side of the basket to the ground, while the other two toppled back in.

"Everyone out!" I yelled, doing my best to keep the balloon steady. "That side."

Having lost several hundred pounds of human ballast, the balloon rose clear of the ground. That made the motion smoother — other than the swatting and crashing of bushes. It also meant the last two guests faced a seven-foot drop to the ground. Intimidating, but not deadly.

"Go! Now!" I yelled.

Finally, they ditched, landing hard, then running clear.

"Erin!" Nash yelled.

I glanced over the edge of the basket. The balloon had risen higher, lifting Nash and Chico off the ground in their efforts to control it.

"Get out!" Nash yelled as Chico fell to the ground.

The balloon rose even higher. And, shit. The balloon continued hurtling toward the power lines, and I hadn't considered the change in ballast. Now, I was ten feet off the ground. Fifteen... Twenty...

My mind spun with a whole new set of calculations. My first priority was to keep the guests safe, and we'd accomplished that — aside from a few bruises. My second priority was the balloon. If I bailed out now and let it hit the power lines, it would be a total write-off. Worse, we could be sued for damage by the power company. Even if we weren't, the bad publicity would be a blow to the entire industry.

Of course, I had to keep myself safe too. But when I weighed it all up...

I made a split-second decision, then pulled the burner cord hard.

Flames burst out, and the balloon jumped higher.

Terrifying as it was, something primal in me cheered. A crazy, untapped section of my soul that had always yearned to fly free.

"Erin!" Nash yelled.

"Let go!" I yelled. It was too late to land before the power lines. My only option was to climb high enough to clear them.

Standard procedure for making a balloon climb was to heat the air in short bursts. But since this wasn't exactly standard procedure... I yanked on the burner cord and held it, making the balloon surge upward. That came with a risk of burning the fabric of the balloon, but that seemed the lesser of two evils.

"Erin!" Nash yelled again.

Huh. Why did he sound so close?

A glance back showed Chico, John, and several of the guests running, pointing, yelling. As if I hadn't noticed the power lines. I huffed. Men!

I turned back to the power lines, because that was all that mattered. My heart leaped to my throat, because it would be close. Very close.

Unconsciously, I rose to my toes and raised my chin as if that would somehow help the balloon scrape over.

And, whew. The air pressure changed, and we rose an extra foot or two — high enough for the balloon to clear the power lines. But not the basket.

I gave the burner a quick break, then pulled again, praying for an inch of clearance.

Seconds later, the power lines disappeared under one side of the balloon. I braced myself, waiting for disaster.

The power lines reappeared on the other side, and my pulse leaped. Was I clear? And why were the guys on the ground still running and yelling?

When Nash yelled again, I froze. Where was he?

I released the burner cord long enough to lean over the side.

"Nash!" I gasped.

He was hanging from the leather handles on the lower edge of the basket — a basket that was at least a hundred feet off the ground.

"Are you crazy?" I yelled, reaching for him.

But he was too far, and the wicker basket didn't offer any handholds for him to climb up on.

"You're the one who's crazy. Why didn't you get out while you could?" he hollered.

"Because I had a chance of saving the balloon!"

Then I stopped. Oops. Not the time to argue.

"Just land this thing already," Nash grumbled.

Oh. My. God. He really was crazy if he planned to hang from the balloon long enough for me to land.

Worse still, the wind blew with new ferocity, and rain started pelting down.

I glanced over the terrain, overwhelmed by so many objectives. Saving Nash. Landing the balloon. Saving it, if possible — not to mention myself.

I took a couple of deep breaths, then settled on my first priority — Nash. Leaving the controls, I knotted several big loops into a spare line and lowered it over the side.

"Just give me a second to secure it," I said, ducking back into the basket.

When the basket lurched, I screamed, thinking Nash had fallen. I looked again, terrified that I would see him plunging to his death.

But, whew. Nash was still there, hanging on by one hand. The other gripped a leather handle that had just torn free.

"Uh...hurry," he mumbled.

My heart hammered as I secured the rope to the frame of the basket. Then I leaned out and swung it closer to Nash.

The leather of the remaining handle creaked ominously. His legs flailed for an eternity. Finally, he got a foot into one of the loops and grabbed for another with his free hand. I reached down, grabbing the back of his shirt.

"Not helping," he grunted as he scraped along the wicker basket.

I stopped pulling, but I didn't loosen my grip. One slip now, and he would plummet to the ground.

The moment his face cleared the top edge of the basket seared into my memory forever. Then he worked his foot into another loop, and I heaved, bringing him crashing onto me inside the basket. We sprawled there for a few heart-stopping moments, clutching each other.

"Are you okay?" I asked.

"Perfect."

I didn't know whether to smack him or kiss him.

"Perfect, my ass..." I grumbled, climbing to my feet and grabbing the controls. When Nash came to his feet beside me, I lost it.

"Are you crazy? Why didn't you let go of the basket when it started climbing?"

"Because you were in it."

And just like that, my heart melted.

I caught him in a half hug, one hand clutching his shoulder, the other on the burner cord.

"Never, ever scare me like that again," I mumbled into his shirt.

He locked his arms around me. "I promise if you promise."

I nearly laughed, but it was cut off by a *whoosh* — the next gust of wind.

We broke apart, because it wasn't over. We were still hundreds of feet in the air — and the storm raged on.

Chapter Twenty-Three

NASH

Over the past few days, I'd dreamed of flying with Erin many times. But not like this.

I wanted to shake a fist and yell that at destiny. *Not like this, dammit!*

Not in a basket in a storm suspended by flimsy material instead of strong, leathery wings. Hell, even in dragon form, I wouldn't brave a storm like this.

Just wait till we get our claws on Harlon, my inner beast growled.

That was item two on my agenda. Number one was getting Erin out of this alive.

"So, what's the plan, Captain?" I asked.

"Landing," she grunted, studying the storm.

That much was obvious. So why wasn't she bringing the balloon down? We were a good mile past the power lines now.

"Why not there?" I pointed at a clearing.

She shook her head. "Too exposed."

I gestured over the wide-open landscape. "The whole damn county is exposed — other than the canyons." I stopped and stared. "Wait. Don't tell me you're going to try to maneuver into one."

She glanced north, murmuring, "Interesting idea."

My eyes went wide. No, it wasn't. More like suicide.

Not that that stopped Erin. She studied the twisted, broken hills. "The wind eddies around the mouth of Boynton Canyon. Maybe it will do the same here..." A moment later, she shook her head. "Maybe not, though. I'll stick to Plan A."

My pulse only settled slightly. "What's Plan A?"

She pointed to a low, rocky ridge and dropped her voice. "There's a hollow just beyond those rocks. It's not big enough to land in..."

My heart rate spiked. So the allure was...what, exactly?

"...but it's big enough to drop into and stay put, if I get the timing right," she finished.

For all my faith in Erin, that sounded like a big *if*. Also, nuances. Did *drop into* mean *crash*?

I pointed to the clearing. "Wouldn't over there be better?" It looked a hundred times better to me — but I was a dragon, not a balloon pilot. I could stop on a dime, fold my wings, and take shelter. A balloon remained at the mercy of the wind throughout its entire, sluggish landing.

"No. We'll get dragged along. Mauled, practically." She rolled her hands over each other, illustrating what the basket would do — with us in it — if she tried landing there. "The balloon would be wrecked, and we would be lucky to get out alive."

At that point, the dark, rolling clouds weren't chasing us any more. They surrounded us like a pack of hungry lions. The dark, swirling masses were so dense, they blotted out everything behind us.

"Desert Skies One, Desert Skies One..." John's voice came over the radio.

Erin nodded for me to grab it.

"Desert Skies One, over," I replied.

"Holy crap!" John blurted. So much for maintaining radio etiquette. "You're crazy. Both of you."

My dragon grinned. *Makes us perfect for each other.*

"Ask him if the guests are all right," Erin said, still focusing on the clouds.

If Madden had still been in the basket, he would have been a blubbering mess. But Erin was cool and calm. Professional, in a word. If we survived this—

When we survive this, my dragon corrected.

—I would make damn sure Henry knew it was Erin who'd salvaged what she could.

"A little bruised, but okay," John confirmed. "Where are you headed?"

"To the holl—"

Erin cut me off, grabbing the mike. "To the wetlands. No time to talk now. Desert Skies One out." With that, she clicked off the radio.

"Um..." I started, confused.

She huddled closer, whispering. "No need to announce our intention. Just in case the walls have ears."

I glanced around the basket. Did she think Harlon had it bugged?

Erin shook her head, pointing to the clouds. "My dad says the wind carries sounds to him. So, just in case..."

I nodded, more uneasy than ever. The average warlock couldn't mess with things like wind and weather — not on this scale anyway. But there was nothing average about Harlon.

I glanced at Erin, wondering about her father — and her own, subtle power.

She'd started to descend, I noticed. Not by dumping air in big bursts, however. Instead, she'd stopped the flow of hot air, letting the balloon descend gradually. Did she hope the wind wouldn't notice?

The jagged line of rocks drew swiftly closer, though our path was a zigzag. Dark, cloudy tendrils buffeted the balloon from both sides, toying with us like a cat with its prey.

"Dammit..." Erin murmured, waving a hand to swat an insect away... or coaxing the wind into a more favorable direction?

I tried not to stare, because I doubted she was even aware of it. But the more I watched, the more I was sure she'd inherited some of her father's powers. Not enough to extinguish the blasts that attacked us from all directions, but enough to nudge them. The balloon's zigzag turns grew less abrupt as we steadily approached the rise.

"The minute we touch down, jump," she whispered.

I tapped her shoulder, making her look at me. "Only if you do." I wasn't going to try that hanging-off-the-balloon stunt again, and I sure wasn't going to let Erin's heroics carry her away again.

And, whoa. Her eyes were glittering. Was that determination or a trace of magic?

She nodded firmly. "Believe me, I'm bailing out this time." Then she spoke loud and clear, bluffing in case Harlon was listening. "Another mile and we'll reach the landing point near the wetlands. I'll stay low to avoid the worst wind."

Whoosh! The balloon zipped along even faster.

I gulped, looking around. Maybe Harlon really could hear us.

We were so low, the basket scraped over bushes. So low, I feared we wouldn't clear the rocky outcrop rushing up at us, concealing whatever lay beyond it.

Erin signaled for me to brace for impact.

A few feet later, the ridge dropped away to a deep, crater-like depression I would never have seen coming. Erin yanked the dump cord, then yelped as the wind whipped over the flap, flattening it. I hung on with her, wrestling to keep the flap open.

"Come on..." Erin murmured.

The basket dropped far enough into the hollow to glimpse walls on either side of us. But the balloon rose high above, still exposed to the wind. If we couldn't dump the hot air fast enough, we would crash against the far side of the crater.

Whack! Every bone in my body felt the impact when we hit bottom. But the shock wave was transmitted to the balloon, which wavered, then toppled sideways.

The space around us was eerily quiet, though the wind howled overhead. Erin was a goddamn genius. But we still had to get the balloon down.

"Hurry! Get it!" she yelled.

In one quick sequence, she twisted the propane valve off, vaulted out of the basket, and started clawing her way up the crater slope to where the balloon wafted. It was starting to fold in on itself, but enough of the fabric remained aloft to act as a sail.

Erin grabbed a handful of fabric and hauled.

"What are you doing?" I yelled.

"We might be able to salvage the balloon," she grunted, grabbing another handful.

Duck and cover seemed like a safer plan, but hey. Erin was a woman on a mission.

For the next minute, I stumbled, cursed, and yanked, half stuffing, half rolling the balloon into the bottom of the hollow. All that time, the wind blasted by, not yet catching on to our evasive maneuver. Then, with an angry whoosh, the clouds swirled, backtracking to search for us.

"Hurry. Get some rocks to hold it down," Erin hollered.

Normally, she was a stickler for neat, tidy rolling, insisting we ground crew re-do our work if it was less than perfect. Now, she settled for a bumpy mess — thank goodness.

I moved as quickly as possible, conscious of the swirling wind. Any minute now, it would find us, and I didn't want to picture the havoc that would follow. Finally, I grabbed Erin's hand and pulled her away.

"A little more," she protested, grabbing another rock.

"Not that one—" I started.

Too late. That stone had been holding back several others, and moving it set off a rockslide.

"Shit." Erin gaped as a huge boulder creaked toward us.

We both froze. The boulder was the size of one of those rideable lawnmowers — and *mow down* was exactly what it would do to Erin and me.

My mind spun for something in Marine or agency training that could solve this one, because brute force couldn't fight that kind of momentum.

And, damn. I only came up with one option. One taught by a grizzled, old, crazy-ass badger shifter at the agency. The guy was a mixed martial arts master — the kind who could break three bricks with his pinkie — who loved lecturing us on redirecting an opponent's energy rather than fighting force with force. I'd seen it work too — once, when he'd tossed a bear shifter twice his size across the room using those principles.

Once. And that had been him demonstrating. The rest of us tried but failed miserably.

All that flashed through my mind in a nanosecond. No time for a better idea. Only action.

I raised my arms. Braced my legs. Sucked in a breath. The rolling boulder blocked out the sky above me while pebbles tumbling ahead of it pinged off my legs and chest.

Ow, ow, ow, and *oof!*

I reached out, slapping one hand against the boulder before the other.

Absorb the energy. The badger's voice echoed through my mind. *Redirect it.*

I was sure the boulder would redirect *me*, but hell. I tried anyway.

Don't try, my dragon gritted. *Succeed.*

I pictured Erin, then Angelina and Harlon, and channeled all those mixed emotions — love, hate, resentment — into my arms, shoving with everything I had.

Correction — *redirecting.*

And, whoa. If a camera had freeze-framed on that particular moment, it would have caught me as Atlas holding up the globe. At least, that's what it felt like. Just as heavy, and just as crushing.

But in the next frame, the boulder inched sideways, and farther still in the next. And the next and the next, until I glimpsed sky overhead. The sky was still stormy, but I would take that over staring straight up at a boulder. One last shove with the left side of my body sent the boulder careening to the bottom of the crater. The force nearly sent me sprawling, but Erin grabbed my arm, and I fell beside her.

Rain pelted us as we stared down at the boulder.

"Well, that ought to hold the balloon down," Erin quipped, though her hands were shaking.

I gulped, then grabbed her hand. "Let's get out of here."

We crawled up a gravelly slope. It gave way under us, pushing us back one step for every two in the right direction. Finally, we made it to the top and crouched in the lee of the rocks that had hidden the crater. I feared what might come next. A goddamn tornado?

"This way." Erin pulled me along that natural rock wall.

We ran at a crouch, a lot like I'd done a couple of times in war zones. The wind continued to roar, and tumbleweeds rushed past. But every step took us farther from the epicenter of the storm.

Thunder boomed in an angry explosion. We dropped flat, though no lightning followed — that, or the clouds were so thick, even lightning couldn't pierce them. A moment later, we raced off again.

"Great," Erin muttered as rain started pattering down.

In seconds, it went from a drizzle to all-out, pelting rainstorm. Every drop was a painful projectile. I threw my arm up, protecting my face, squinting to follow Erin. The storm, having failed to locate us, seemed intent on drowning us instead.

"Not far now!" Erin hollered over the wind and rain.

Every step I took sent up a cold splash, and when we turned into a gully and headed uphill, the red soil grew slick and muddy. Still, Erin pushed onward, climbing a steep, rocky slope.

"We're nearly there." Heaving for breath, she pointed to a narrow ledge traversing the cliff.

"Are you nuts?" She wanted to head back into the open on a path as treacherous as that?

Yep. She did.

She set off, flattening herself against the cliff while sidestepping along the ledge. Cursing, I followed. The cliff became steeper, higher, and even more exposed. Rain hammered my back, and the wind whipped at my soaked shirt.

After edging along for a good fifty feet, I was ready to give up. But the ledge gradually widened, swung around a bend, and—

I stumbled into a huge cave, nearly barreling into Erin.

"Over here." She pulled me to the far wall, where we stopped, staring at the storm that raged outside. Water dripped from our bodies to the floor of the cave, pooling around our feet.

"What is this place?" I whispered, looking around.

"Robber's Roost."

Whether the name was fact or folklore, it fit. The cave was a huge scoop in the cliff, big enough to house a whole family of dragons. Traces of an ancient cliff dwelling stood against the back wall. The front opened onto a huge, natural window high over the desert, where sheets of rain blew past on a howling wind.

Erin pointed into the gray-on-gray sky, getting me oriented. "On a clear day, you can see Sedona. The highway's over there."

I took her word for it, but we might as well have been on a distant planet. Some place like Mars where storms constantly whipped an otherworldly landscape.

We stared out for a while, catching our breath and assuring ourselves we were finally safe. Then we hunkered down behind the ruins to wait.

"Holy shit," Erin muttered a few minutes later, hugging herself.

I couldn't agree more.

"You okay?" she mumbled.

I nodded.

She patted my arm. "Nice move with that boulder."

My chest swelled just a little.

"Nice move with that landing. And finding your way here. And outtricking Harlon..."

I could have gone on for a while there. The woman was amazing.

I pressed close and looped an arm around her shoulders. We were soaked, and the chilly air cut deep. In no time, Erin was shivering.

We huddled as well as we could, sharing our body heat. Even then, it was freezing, especially with our hair plastered to our skulls and wet clothes clinging to our skin.

"I wish I had some matches." Erin pointed a shaky finger at a fire pit against the back wall — a ring of stones left behind by campers. And, good news — they'd left a few sticks of firewood.

I stood, rearranged the wood, and crouched before it, blocking Erin's view as best I could. Then I cleared my throat, inhaled, and coaxed up some fire.

More, my dragon insisted, greedy to show off.

I cut off the stream of flames as soon as the fire crackled to life, searing my lips in the process.

Erin's teeth chattered when she spoke. "Wait. How did you do that?"

I gulped against the sulfury taste in my throat. Spitting fire was much easier in dragon form, dammit.

"Um..." I huddled behind her, partly to avoid her gaze and partly for the warmth. Then I did what every man did when confronted with an uncomfortable topic — I changed the subject.

"Why the hell didn't you get out of the balloon when you could?"

"Because I had a chance to save the rig," she said, still shivering.

I held her closer. "You have some crazy priorities, you know that?"

She interlaced her fingers with mine. "You're the one who hung on to the basket when it took off. What if you fell?"

I'd asked myself the same question during that heart-stopping flight. I could have opened my wings, of course. But with that wind and at such low altitude, I would probably have crashed into the ground.

So, why had I done it?

I closed my eyes, breathing in Erin's scent.

You know why, my dragon hummed.

Okay, maybe I did. But how would I go about explaining that to Erin? I couldn't just come out and say, *I'm a dragon shifter, not a wolf, and I suspect destiny thinks we're mates.*

My dragon huffed. *Who cares what destiny thinks? I know we're mates.*

An extra-strong gust of wind roared outside, and the fire flickered. Erin tensed. "This is Harlon's doing, isn't it?"

I nodded slowly. "That would be a safe guess."

The storm was dissipating, though, or at least moving on. At least there was that — and the warmth of the fire slowly seeping into our bones.

"Sanity check," Erin finally said. "Should I give Harlon the benefit of the doubt?"

I gave her a look, and she sighed.

"Okay, maybe not. But still... What if Harlon was after one of the passengers?"

"He was after you," I said as gently as I could. "Or us."

"Maybe he just wants the balloon company out of business..." she tried, then slumped at my hard look. "Okay, probably not. But, geez. Is he trying to kill us or warn us?"

My money was on *kill*, but I held my tongue.

"And is he so ruthless, he's willing to take out a half dozen guests at the same time?" Erin went on. "Plus, what good does it do him to kill me? I only own a third of the ranch. Is he going to come after us one by one?" Then she froze, gripping my arm. "Oh my God. What if he goes after Pippa and Abby next? What if he goes after Claire?"

A split second later, Erin jumped up. The fire mimicked her, crackling with angry sparks.

I stared. What was with Erin and fire?

I grabbed her arm before she stomped outside to give Harlon a piece of her mind.

"Wait. Come on, Erin." I pulled her back toward the fire. "Harlon could just as well have aimed this storm at the ranch and gone after all of you at the same time. So, maybe this was just a warning."

Erin huffed. "Just?"

I squeezed her hand. "Bad word choice. Sorry."

It took ages to coax her back to the fire. I made her sit, then settled down behind her in a loose hug.

"First, we need to warm up. Then, when the storm settles, we'll head back to town." Erin gave me a doubtful look, but I insisted. "Harlon can't keep this up forever. So, we need a plan for what comes next."

"Oh, I'll tell you what's next. My sisters and I march into that overpriced mansion of his and kick his ass," Erin growled.

I chuckled. "Much as I like the idea..."

She sighed. "Okay, maybe I'll make that item two. But I swear, that man is going to get a piece of my mind."

I grinned, picturing her sisters beside her, Pippa with a pitchfork, Abby with a bat. I would be next in line, ready to roast that warlock until there was nothing left but ash.

With a deep breath, I rested my chin on Erin's shoulder. It wasn't that simple, and I knew it.

"Can he do that?" Erin's voice shook with cold *and* anger. "I mean, can he just conjure up a storm?"

"You tell me," I murmured, careful to keep my tone even.

She tensed. "If you mean my father, no. He doesn't go around slamming cities with storms—" She cut herself off, making a face. "Okay, okay, there was that dust storm that hit Phoenix a couple of years back. But that was an accident." She bristled. "And this is about Harlon, not my father."

I thought it over, then shook my head. "Even the most powerful warlock can't conjure lightning or a storm out of nowhere. He can only amplify and redirect forces that are already in motion."

"Well, he did a pretty good job amplifying," she muttered bitterly.

I didn't answer. I just held her while the storm raged outside. The fire crackled angrily for a while, then slowly settled down. Erin's breath mirrored it — or was it the other way around?

I moved my hands gently over her back, comforting her as well as myself. I kissed her shoulder next, because that was comforting too.

And, oops. Maybe I comforted myself a little too well, because those kisses kept on coming, and I was just along for the ride. They inched closer and closer to her neck, then her lips...

Erin turned in my arms, meeting my lips, and our makeshift fire crackled in a whole different way. Before long, we were swept away by an entirely different kind of storm. One just as unstoppable — and possibly as dangerous — but nothing would hold us back now.

Chapter Twenty-Four

ERIN

I'd been aware of magic my entire life, but somehow, it took Nash — a shapeshifter, not a sorcerer — to make me *feel* it. Experience it. Live it. Swirling, thunderous, all-consuming magic that seeped into my soul and swept me away.

Every kiss we shared zinged with energy. Every touch sent fairy sparkles cascading through my mind. Every desperate breath fueled an inner fire.

Magic has its pluses, I remembered my dad saying, but it held dangers too. The trick was not to let it — or yourself — get carried away.

In which case, I was already failing.

"Nash..." I mumbled, slipping one leg around his side to come face-to-face.

In no time, I was straddling him, trusting him to keep balanced on the rock we used as a seat. Behind me, the fire crackled, urging me on.

"Seeing as this is wet..." He peeled back my jacket, then unbuttoned my shirt.

I cursed every inch of stubborn, drenched fabric. It clung to my skin, slowing down what felt like a life-and-death mission. I need this man, and I needed him now, dammit!

When he finally tossed my shirt aside, the fire sizzled and hissed. Nash bent to trail kisses down my chest, and when he reached a nipple—

Whoosh! A branch snapped, and the entire teepee of logs collapsed a few inches.

Gripping Nash's shoulders, I tilted my head back, greedy for more. But even that wasn't enough, and soon, I was dancing in his lap.

"Dammit." Nash broke contact with a frustrated growl and practically jumped to his feet, hauling me with him.

My wet jeans and panties were even harder to strip, and we cursed the whole time. We didn't bother with Nash's except for working down that poor, overstrained zipper. Then I practically shoved him back to the rock.

"Now, where were we..." I murmured, straddling him.

My voice cracked as I sank down, taking him deep. He slid his hands from my rear to my hips and then my knees, yanking me closer. I cried out at that perfect, piercing heat.

"I got you," he rasped, holding me firmly. "I got you."

Not thinking, just trusting, I leaned back and cried out again.

He groaned my name and plunged deeper still. And deeper...

Outside, lightning cracked, and the wind howled. But the storm outside was pushed to the periphery of my senses by the storm within.

Ha. Take that, Harlon. I pictured my inner lightning crossing and overpowering his in a burst of sparks. I imagined my own hurricane-force winds driving away his pitiful little puffs. All his forces retreated, at least in my imagination. I'd never felt more powerful or more possessed.

I rode Nash harder, faster, panting his name. It wasn't pretty or poetic, but dang, was it good. Our motions grew jerkier, and my vision faded until the flames of our fire blurred with the color of the cave walls.

"Yes..." I strained, close to releasing.

Nash's legs, chest, arms — every point of contact was stone-hard and fire-iron hot. Gritting his teeth, he leaned back, adjusting our angle yet again. When he jerked and released inside me, my breath caught, then escaped in a long, satisfied moan.

We stayed like that for a long time, suspended in a sensual haze. Then Nash pulled me closer, and I slumped over him in a tight hug.

I didn't dare speak, because I had no idea what to say. I just held him, inhaling his scent and basking in warmth. A short time ago, we'd been on the cusp of death. Now, we were at heaven's door, and I was in no rush to leave.

Chapter Twenty-Five

ERIN

Our — er, activities — made a mess of us, but we cleaned up as best we could, then snuggled, waiting for the storm to break. Over the next hour, I wondered if it ever would. But after a drawn-out wrestling match, the sun finally broke through the clouds, and light lasered down in long, brilliant rays. The rocky red landscape had never been so spectacular — not that we had time to admire it. As soon as it seemed safe to venture outside, we made our way back to the balloon and radioed in.

"Desert Skies One! So happy to hear you!" Chico cried, picking up a split second after we called. The man was truly a gem.

He'd dropped off Madden and the guests at the office, then headed back out into the storm to search for us, tuning in to the radio the whole time. Once we made contact, he maneuvered the van over punishing terrain to reach us. I was all for hauling the balloon out of the hollow there and then, but Chico and Nash insisted it could wait, and we drove straight back to town.

The storm had caused chaos there too, but that didn't stop a detail of police from appearing at the office in response to emergency calls about an out-of-control balloon. The press was hot on their heels, and we had to run a gauntlet of cameras and microphones on our way into the office.

I steeled myself for the worst, like *What the hell were you thinking going aloft on a day like today?* or *How do you feel about kissing your license goodbye?*

But their tenor was entirely different, and I blinked in surprise.

"Miss Sattler, Miss Sattler! How do you feel about saving so many lives?"

"Were you afraid to die, Miss Sattler, or are you as brave as they say?"

I stared. Huh?

Apparently, Madden had tried to make himself out as a hero, but Chico, John, and the guests had set the record straight. Instead of basking in attention, he was slumped in a chair in the back room, surrounded by officers taking copious notes.

The police split Nash and me up for separate questioning. But since Chico, John, and the guests had already reported their accounts, the police were patient — even friendly — with me, and the ranking officer finished with a smile.

"Flying isn't my thing, but if I ever go up, I'll make sure you're the pilot," he said.

So, whew. Maybe I didn't have to worry about losing my license after all.

Thank goodness the guests weren't the social media type. By the time they'd thought of whipping out their phones to film the action, the balloon had been far away. Good news, because I really didn't want to go viral as the pilot who'd headed recklessly out in a storm — or who was oblivious to the crew member dangling on a rope beneath.

The police even treated me to coffee and doughnuts once they'd finished questioning me.

"Sweet of them, huh?" John grinned.

Too hungry to groan at the pun, I stuffed my mouth with goodies.

Finally, we were free to go — but that put us at the mercy of the press gathered outside.

"Miss Sattler! Miss Sattler!" they all called out, competing for my attention.

I peered upward, ignoring them. The sun was shining, and the sky was blue, as if nothing had happened.

Then the hair on the back of my neck rose, and I scrutinized the crowd. Dozens of people had gathered by then — not just the press, but rubberneckers drawn by the commotion. An older lady with her shopping... A sweaty guy from the nearby fitness studio... A couple of sunburned tourists...

I froze. Harlon stood at the back of the crowd, casual as could be.

God, the nerve. I stuck my hands on my hips and glared.

Nash must have followed my eyes, because he tensed too.

"Meteorologists say that storm was completely unexpected," one of the reporters said. "Did it catch you unprepared?"

I kept my gaze pinned firmly on Harlon. "Any good pilot knows to expect the unexpected."

The warlock's lips quirked.

"In those two hours without contact, many assumed you were dead," another reporter observed.

I snorted in Harlon's direction. "Well, I guess I'm not that easy to kill."

Angelina was beside him, and her scowl deepened.

"From what we hear, you could have jumped out of the balloon to safety. Why didn't you?"

I mulled that one over. "My dad taught me not to give up and to fight to protect the things I value."

The warlock grinned openly and raised his hands in silent applause.

I kept my gaze steady. *Not amused, asshole.*

Angelina leaned in to kissing distance of Harlon's ear and whispered something.

Someone jostled through the crowd, blocking my view of them. A moment later, they were gone.

Good riddance, I decided, though I knew it was only temporary.

∞∞∞∞

It took a while, but Nash and I finally escaped the crowd and drove home. It was time for a powwow, for sure. I'd already texted my sisters, and Nash's contact at the agency had just returned his call.

"Hey, man. What have you found out?" Nash asked.

I listened in, privy only to Nash's side of the conversation. His expression filled in the ominous pauses, telling me the news wasn't good.

"She did what?" he yelped.

I touched his arm. Was *she* Angelina? And, yikes. What did she do?

Nash stared at the road, still listening to his friend. Then he sighed. "How can it get worse?"

I winced. We'd faced a year's worth of *worse* in half a day. What now?

Nash's brow creased more and more deeply. I'd never seen him so stunned.

Then he gave himself a little shake and said, "Yeah, I'm still on the line."

I pulled over slowly and not just because we were about to lose the cell phone signal.

Nash ran a hand through his hair, and it struck me how abruptly he'd returned to the hollow, weary look he'd worn when he'd first arrived in town. Over the past days, he'd slowly...well, *perked up* didn't exactly fit, but it was close. As if he'd come to Sedona a little lost but gradually homed in on whatever he'd been looking for.

His eyes met mine, and wow. I got a repeat of that glorious *sun bursting through the clouds* moment, all within the universe of his eyes. The dark, broody *something* lifted, and tiny points of light danced. They danced all the way over to me, lifting my soul.

Destiny, a voice in the back of my mind whispered.

I'd heard the stories, of course. That destiny wasn't just a concept, but a force. One with the power to bring people together — or tear them apart. And once destiny decided on one of those two actions, it was pointless to resist.

Old wives' tales? Maybe not, because my whole body warmed. My mind churned slowly, stupidly.

Nash... Me... Destiny?

Destiny, the glow in his eyes confirmed.

The phone crackled with a faraway voice, making Nash blink. Me too, as we both emerged from that momentary spell. Then he cleared his throat and spoke into the phone. "I'm putting you on speaker. Repeat what you just said."

"Um, Nash..." his friend said hesitantly, loud and clear now.

"You can trust her," Nash assured him.

My heart doubled in size, but his friend didn't sound convinced.

"Okay, but call me Frank for now," his friend insisted.

Ha. A code name. I couldn't blame him, though.

Nash rolled his eyes. "Okay, *Frank*. Go ahead and repeat what you just said."

Still, "Frank" hesitated.

"It's okay," Nash assured him. "She and I are in this together."

My heart thumped. Yes. Yes, we were. In every possible sense, good and bad.

Frank snorted. "Ha. What happened to *dragon shifters work alone?*"

I stared at Nash. Dragon shifter?

He squirmed in his seat.

Heat rose to my cheeks. Just when I thought I could trust him...

"You said wolf," I hissed.

Nash stuck up his hands. "You *assumed* wolf."

I nearly denied it, but when I played that conversation back in my mind, I found he was right.

"It never occurred to you to correct me?" I hissed.

Nash winced.

"If you two are too busy to talk..." Frank cut in.

Nash frowned and resorted to his favorite trick — changing the subject.

"Sorry. Repeat what you told me about Angelina."

I gave him the evil eye. Did I really have to hear about his ex, the vampire?

He really, *really* had to learn some tact.

"Go ahead," Nash insisted when his friend hesitated. "We don't have much time."

No, we didn't, because I was about to kick his sorry ass to the curb and drive away.

Frank hemmed, hawed, and finally spoke. "Angelina is no longer with the agency, but she's been in touch with the top brass. To warn them — about you, Nash. According to her, you've lost it. You're a danger to society and to the agency. She says you've been stalking innocent people and provoking supernaturals, including that class-four warlock up there."

My jaw hung open. What?

Nash might be the world's most tactless, annoying wolf — er, dragon — shifter, but Harlon was the one who'd done the provoking.

Nash huffed. "Innocent people, like Angelina?"

Frank made an equally frustrated sound. "You and I know she's poison, but when it's her word against yours..." After an ominously long pause, he went on. "She's made you sound so unhinged, they're putting together a team to come after you."

I stared. That spooky, mysterious agency was sending a team to Sedona — to nab Nash?

"That's ridiculous!" I barked.

The line went silent. Oops. Frank might be willing to risk his job to help Nash, but sharing insider information with me obviously pushed his limits.

Nash sighed, then waved at the phone. "Frank, meet Erin."

"Erin, huh?" Again, that hesitation. Why? A moment later, he went on. "Uh...nice to meet you?"

I laughed, though there wasn't much humor in it. "Nice to meet you — if you're one of the good guys."

Frank took a deep breath. "I like to think so, but I have to wonder sometimes."

I liked the sound of him. Wondering was a good sign.

Nash, on the other hand, had a hell of a lot of explaining to do.

A few seconds ticked by in silence. Then Frank cursed at some sound on his end of the line. "I have to go. I'll do what I can, but that might not be much. Once a train this heavy gets moving..."

Nash blew out his cheeks, then filled in the rest. "...it's impossible to stop. I get it. Thanks."

"Watch your back, man," Frank warned.

Nash nodded slowly. "Yeah. You too."

Chapter Twenty-Six

NASH

The moment I hung up the phone, Erin screeched.

"Dragon shifter? You're a goddamn dragon shifter?"

I ran a hand through my hair. Just when I thought things couldn't get worse...

"Yes. Sorry. I just..." I gave up and pointed at the road. "Can we just go?"

Erin glared at me. "You're changing the subject."

Trying to, yes. Though I preferred to put it in different terms. "I'm focusing on what's relevant."

"Being a dragon shifter isn't relevant? We slept together, dammit!"

A good thing "Frank" — aka Ingo — was no longer on the line.

I motioned at the road. "Just drive. We can talk about it on the way."

She shot me a slitty-eyed look. "Or not. What if I decide to leave you here?"

Would it help to point out that I could fly away? Probably not. I pursed my lips and waited as Erin pinned me with the evil eye. Yes, she had a right to be mad. And yes, I deserved it. But with a warlock and a vampire to deal with...

Erin huffed and tore down the road, sending gravel flying.

Funny how a car could talk for its owner sometimes.

"My mother is a dragon shifter," she muttered, as if that explained anything.

"And?" I asked as gently as I could.

Her dry laugh scared me. "She took off on me and my dad five weeks after I was born. Five weeks! Not that my dad isn't great — he is," she hurried to add. "But seriously, what kind of woman takes off on her own kid that way? She did it with my sisters too." She made a face. "Abby was the lucky — or unlucky — one. Apparently, Mom stuck around nearly two months for her. Not that that helped much in the end," she added mournfully.

"My mother is a dragon shifter, and she stuck around," I pointed out. "Hell, she still calls to check that I'm eating my vegetables."

Erin snorted. "Lucky you."

"I'm just saying your experience doesn't apply to all dragon shifters."

"I know that," she snipped. "I'm talking about liars. She lied to my dad about going for a walk but never came back." Erin glared. "She lied. *You* lied."

I stuck up my hands. "Those two things are on entirely different scales."

Erin huffed. "Maybe for you."

We rattled over a scalloped section of dirt road so violently, I had to brace myself — one hand to the dashboard, one to the roof.

"What other secrets have you been keeping?" Erin demanded when we hit smoother ground.

"No secrets. Just bad judgment. I'm sorry."

She huffed, then smacked the steering wheel. "And what the hell is a class-four warlock?"

Now, she was the one changing the subject. And man, oh man. What a detail-oriented mind. A mind I loved, like the rest of her.

So, you finally admit it, my dragon chuckled. *You love her.*

No, I wasn't ready to admit it — not out loud anyway — but I was getting there.

"The agency classifies witches and warlocks into five levels," I explained. "Class-one is the most powerful."

Her head whipped around. "There are warlocks more powerful than Harlon?"

"Maybe a handful, but I've never encountered one. Harlon is at least a two."

"So why would they call him a four?"

"To make him seem harmless, especially against a marauding dragon."

She huffed. "You haven't been marauding."

At least she gave me credit for that.

I sighed, trying to figure out how I'd ended up in this mess. I'd come to Sedona to clear my mind, not to pick a fight — especially not with Erin.

And, man. What irony. Just when I felt like I'd come back to life, I was facing death by Harlon, Angelina, or the agency hit squad.

I gulped. What happened to me didn't matter. All that counted was getting Erin out of this mess.

We drove along in silence, each lost in our own thoughts. Then we rattled over a cattle grid, and I looked up. We were nearly at the ranch.

"I guess you're not throwing me out?" I ventured.

"Not yet," Erin grunted, making the final turn.

∞∞∞∞

A short time later, Erin huddled with her sisters on the porch of the main house. Claire was in sight but out of earshot, brushing one of the horses, who swished its tail. Erin hadn't invited me in, but she hadn't banished me either, so I stayed in the no-man's-land of the stairs.

"So, now what?" Pippa asked once Erin had filled them both in.

"I knew he was trouble," Abby grunted, looking at me. Me!

Erin shook her head. "This isn't Nash's fault."

She said it begrudgingly, like I still had to prove myself to her. And, damn. Maybe I did.

"He didn't bring Harlon out here," Erin finished. "Harlon came all on his own."

I looked at my feet. True, but what about Angelina? Was it mere coincidence to encounter her out here?

207

Not chance. It's destiny, my dragon grumbled, and not in a good way.

I couldn't make any sense of it. Why would destiny make so many separate lives cross here? Who was doomed to fail, and who would prevail?

Abby threw a fierce *Momma Bear* look in little Claire's direction. "Fucking Harlon. I haven't even met him, and I already hate him."

Abby seemed to hate all men, so that wasn't saying much. But in this case, I agreed.

"You think they can actually find us here?" Pippa asked.

Erin shrugged and looked at me.

I rubbed my chin. The ranch entrance was blurred by a spell. A very old, very powerful spell that probably went back generations. I'd kept my senses piqued on the way in, but I'd still missed the visual cues. On the other hand, I had sensed a telltale tremble in the air once I knew it was there.

"Harlon might not spot the entrance on his first try, but I doubt it will trick him for long."

"How did he find out about the vortex?" Pippa asked.

Erin shrugged. "Madden pointed the ranch out to him from the air, but I had the feeling Harlon already knew about the vortex."

"How?" Abby demanded.

An excellent question. Too bad our investigation hadn't turned up anything about that.

"I have no idea," Erin said. "But right now, we need to come up with a plan. What are Harlon and Angelina likely to do next, and how do we defend ourselves against that?"

But the three sisters were stumped, and honestly, so was I.

Finally, Pippa sighed. "Maybe it's time to call in your dad."

Erin's expression made it clear she hated the idea. "Maybe it's time to call in *your* dads."

Abby's expression darkened, but she didn't say a word.

Pippa opened her mouth, then closed it, hesitating.

"What?" the other two demanded.

"What about Mom?" Pippa finally tried.

"No!" Erin and Abby shouted at the same time.

Pippa stuck up her hands. "You're right. Forget it. We probably couldn't track her down anyway."

All three fell silent, and my heart tore a little more. I'd never considered my family particularly close, but hell. I'd never appreciated my folks as much as I did just then.

"Maybe we shouldn't call in anyone," Erin decided. "Bringing in a dragon or a couple of warlocks could just escalate things."

True, but I was more in the *Get all the help you can* camp. I wasn't capable of holding off Harlon and Angelina on my own, and I doubted the sisters could either — no matter how determined they were.

Another silent spell ensued, broken by Claire's laugh as she shared a joke with Roscoe and the horse.

For a moment, we all smiled. Then, one by one, we each went serious again.

"What about that agency who's sent a unit here — the BDSM?" Abby asked.

ADMSA, my dragon grumbled inside.

"Well, maybe that's good," Pippa said. "I mean, having an entire supernatural SWAT team show up could help us with Harlon, and we can explain it wasn't Nash's fault."

If only it were that easy.

"They won't make it here before tomorrow morning," Erin said. "Harlon could make his next move before then."

"Why would he?" Abby asked.

Erin scowled. "If you were a warlock, how eager would you be to come across an agency tasked with keeping tabs on you?"

"Another reason not to call in my dad — or yours," Pippa decided.

Erin snorted. "They're not shady. Harlon is."

With that, she looked out over the ranch, and everyone grew quiet. It was late afternoon, edging toward evening and another fiery sunset. Shadows crept ominously over the arid landscape, and the air grew crisper.

"I have another idea, but I'm not sure I like it," Pippa finally said. "The vortex. Could we use its power to protect ourselves?"

Erin wrapped her arms around her middle and looked toward the cliff. "The only thing that terrifies me more than the idea of Harlon using it is trying to use it myself. And didn't Aunt Emma warn us never to go close?"

Pippa and Abby glanced at each other, then at the floor.

Yeah, those two had definitely gotten close at some point.

"Maybe it was one of those warnings adults give that only apply to kids." Pippa made air quotes. "Like, *don't smoke* or *don't have sex.*"

Erin broke into laughter, and even Abby cracked into a sly look — only to frown an instant later.

"Sex was pretty easy to figure out on my own," Erin said. "I'm not sure the vortex works that way."

They looked at each other blankly, then at me, but I had nothing either.

"Let me guess," Erin sighed. "Agency training didn't cover that."

No, it didn't. For all it had taught me about warlocks, it hadn't prepared me for seductive vampires, like Angelina, or for falling for the genuine appeal of Erin. Which just went to show that some things, you had to learn the hard way.

With Erin, I'd do it all over, my dragon whispered. *Again and again, a thousand times.*

As bad as the situation was, a smile played over my lips.

A horse nickered, and a bird flew by, slicing through the red-hued landscape.

"What about your own power?" I asked quietly.

Pippa laughed. "What power?"

I motioned at her, then Erin. "Your mother is a dragon, and your fathers are warlocks, right?" When they both nodded, I turned to Abby. "Is your father a warlock too?"

"He's a self-absorbed nutcase. That's what he is."

I stuck up my hands, coming to my point quickly. "Well, I'm guessing he has magic too. Look."

The sisters traded exasperated looks as I grabbed a box of matches and lit one. When I held it near Erin, the flame bent toward her, but she just laughed.

"That's the wind."

"Not the wind," I insisted. Could they not see what I meant?

Spotting a lantern, I lit it and held it high. Again, the flame bent toward Erin.

I tapped the glass of the lantern. "It's not the wind. It's you."

I got another one of those *You are unbearably stupid* looks. "The lantern is probably crooked or something."

But even when I rotated it, the flame tilted toward Erin.

"And if I do this..." I swung the lantern slowly between Erin and Pippa. At some point in the middle, the flame swayed a little, undecided, then jerked over to whichever sister was closer.

Finally, I took a deep breath and held it toward Abby. "Tell me about your father."

"None of your goddamn business!" she barked.

Whoosh! The tiny flame in the lantern exploded into angry crackles. They bounced off the glass hood, then escaped out the top, rushing toward me. I jumped back, holding it at arm's length.

"See?"

Abby crossed her arms. "You did that on purpose."

"Yes." I gestured around with the lantern. "Do you get it now? You have power. All of you. It's just that no one taught you how to use it."

Erin shook her head. "Just because fire reacts to us doesn't mean we can control it — or that we have any other kind of power. Even if we did, this is not the time to experiment with it."

I took a deep breath, praying circumstances — or Harlon — wouldn't force them to.

"It's not just fire. You can read the wind too," I pointed out.

Erin crossed her arms. "Like any good pilot or sailor."

I shook my head. She was on a whole different level.

"More like a wind whisperer," I murmured. "A person who can control the wind."

Erin snorted. "Ha. At best, I could make a few suggestions and pray the wind feels like listening."

I shook my head. Dammit, why hadn't her father taught her anything about magic?

My dragon snorted. *She's convinced she doesn't have any magic. And once Erin is convinced of something...*

I didn't know whether to laugh or sigh.

An errant streak of wind swept over the desert, making us all turn. Erin wrapped her arms around her middle, and Pippa sniffed the air. I did too, suddenly on alert.

A moment later, we all relaxed. No sign of Harlon, just the wind ruffling patches of sage and grass. That didn't stop Abby from stalking out to join Claire, however.

"Come on, honey. Time for Misty to go back to the barn."

We watched them go, half eyeing the sky. I observed the sisters at the same time. Did they even realize they were testing the wind the way I did? Probably not, but I was sure that was their dragon shifter blood coming through.

If these sisters harnessed their power instead of denying it... my dragon mused.

Watch out, Harlon, I agreed. Still, that was a big if.

"What if we bluff and tell Harlon we'll sell?" Pippa asked. "That would buy us time."

Erin thought it over, then shook her head. "That wouldn't stop the agency from coming tomorrow."

"So?" Then Pippa shot me an apologetic look. "Oh. You'd still get in trouble." She thought it over, then brightened. "But not if you leave before they get here."

I gulped. How could I leave Erin at a time like this? How could I leave any of them?

To my surprise, Erin spoke before I did. In fact, she practically barked.

"Nash stays." The pink in her cheeks intensified, and she cleared her throat. "I mean, in case we need his help. I mean, if he's willing to stay. I mean..."

She doesn't want us to go, my dragon cheered quietly.

Because her family is in danger, I pointed out.

And other reasons, my dragon hummed.

Our eyes locked, and the glow in her eyes confirmed those *other reasons.* My chest swelled, and for the next few heartbeats, all I felt was peace and hope.

A pretty good definition for love, I supposed, risking a tiny grin.

Erin's lips curled too. So, whew. It wasn't just me.

But it wasn't just the two of us either. Pippa was right there, studying us with a sly look.

I tore my gaze from Erin's and murmured in my grittiest *secret agent* tone, "I'm happy to stay and help."

"Good. Great. Thank you," Erin said, still flustered.

Pippa grinned openly. "All right, then. We still need a plan, though. Ideas, anyone?"

Chapter Twenty-Seven

NASH

I spent the night perched on a cliff top in dragon form, watching over the ranch. My leathery hide was the equivalent of a bomber jacket, but I was still cold. I shifted from foot to foot — er, claw to claw — half wishing I were a furry bear shifter instead of a dragon. Every fifteen minutes or so, I took to the sky and kept an eye on things from there. Movement kept me... Well, not exactly warm, but warmer and, above all, alert.

Part of me yearned to be back in the warmth of Erin's loft — and her arms. Just getting back to a point where she wasn't furious would be a good start.

My long triangular ears pointed forward, and my nose tested the air. A dozen constellations kept lookout with me as I swooped in slow circles, studying every inch of the ground. The desert was an undulating carpet that went on and on, torn here and there by mesas big enough to host a strip mall — though no one had tried that...yet. The blinding lights of Sedona were more than enough development, as far as I was concerned.

I leaned into a turn, concentrating on the ranch...the winding creek lined with huge cottonwoods...the long, dusty road...

Every once in a while, a light would flick on then off in the main house, reminding me why I was there.

Erin, my dragon hummed.

My heart swelled — so much, I had to steady myself with a deep breath.

Erin was what made this so different from the dozens of other stakeouts I'd endured in my time with the agency and the Marines before that. Erin — and her sisters and her niece — made this so much more than any other job.

Destiny, my dragon whispered.

Yes. Yes, it was — a series of events woven together by a mysterious, mischievous force. Loosely at first, then tighter and tighter until those threads formed a noose that dangled ominously in front of me.

Wisps of smoke escaped my nostrils, and my throat burned with fire. Fire I would gladly aim at an enemy, if one would only appear.

But there was no sign of Harlon's quiet, creeping magic or the odorless void that marked Angelina's place in the world. Just a peaceful world and a slumbering ranch — for now.

After three long, sweeping rounds, I glided back to the cliff, stuck out my claws, and thumped to a landing. Then I folded my wings tightly and tapped my tail with every passing second. Ironically, we had the next morning off work, but neither of us would be sleeping in.

An hour passed, then another, and another, until the stars dimmed in the first sign of dawn. The mountains to the east were a dark wall, but behind them, the sky slowly turned gold. Then, at a movement below, I froze.

A moment later, I relaxed. It was Erin walking silently toward her cabin from the main house, where she and her sisters had hunkered down for the night. Halfway along the scrubby path, she stopped and turned, scanning the cliffs.

My heart thumped. Was she looking for danger or looking for me?

Good morning, my mate, my dragon murmured wistfully.

My pulse quickened when she found me and went still. The cool breeze that had been chilling my back went warm, and I swear, every bird in central Arizona broke into song.

But then her expression clouded, and my mood plummeted.

My mother lied. You lied, she'd said.

Turning away briskly, Erin continued and disappeared inside her home.

My wings drooped, and I resigned myself to a lonely fate. Which shouldn't be hard, given all the resigning I'd done in the past couple of months.

A bitter taste filled my mouth, because the old me wouldn't have given up so easily.

And just like that, something snapped in me. I took to the air as an inner voice roared.

Enough giving up. Enough giving in. Enough being a shadow of who you used to be.

I flew at breakneck speed, trying to shake away that dull cloud that always hung over me. Then, laying my ears flat against my head, I dove. Using the footpath as my runway, I landed with a couple of noisy thumps, ready to roar. At Angelina. At fate. At everything keeping Erin from me.

The screen door opened with a creak, and I froze. Hesitantly at first, then a little more boldly, Erin paced across the porch and onto the top step, eyes locked on me.

Puffs of condensed breath rose from my nostrils, and I gulped.

You lied to me, I imagined her yelling. *You let me believe you're a wolf shifter, and now you're huffing and puffing outside my cabin. How dare you?*

I held my breath, preparing for her verbal assault.

She opened her mouth, then closed it again, and finally let out a weary sigh.

"Good morning."

I bent my neck slowly, giving her a little bow in reply. A better alternative to booming *Good morning* in my dragon voice.

She cocked her head. "Have you been up all night?"

I hunched my wings in a dragon shrug. Yes, I had been.

What about you? I wanted to ask. *Have you been up all night too?*

She must have caught the gist, because she yawned. "I'm not sure anyone got much sleep last night, except Roscoe and Claire."

For another long, quiet minute, we stood there, staring at each other. Then she moved. Or — oops. I was the one who'd moved, unconsciously stretching my neck toward her.

Her eyes went wide, but she held her ground.

A puff of hot air escaped my nostrils, and I winced, afraid of spooking her.

I'm sorry, I willed her to understand. *I'm sorry I didn't tell you sooner. I'm sorry about a lot of things.*

I cursed myself, because why should she forgive me? Not just for the dragon thing, but for so much more. For being closed off. For my past. Worst of all, for getting involved with Angelina.

My wings drooped.

But instead of rejecting me, Erin raised her hand slowly, palm up, and held it out the way she would greet a dog.

Not the best image for my ego, but I wasn't about to nit-pick. I stretched a little more, then cursed. I'd misjudged, stopping a few inches too far from the porch. Short of dislo-cating a vertebra, there was no way I would reach her hand. I inched a tiny bit closer, cursing silently. Dragons were made for gliding gracefully through the air, not waddling along the ground. *Not* the look I was going for.

But Erin inched forward too, and a moment later, my snout touched her hand.

"Oh," she exclaimed at my warm breath. Slowly, she cupped my chin with both hands, muttering. "Dragon, huh?"

I gulped. Um, yes. Yes, I was. And I was really, really sorry.

Not that I managed to get a single word out.

Erin rubbed her thumbs along my tough, bronze-colored hide, then murmured. "Wow."

I held my breath. Did that mean she didn't hate me?

My beast side sighed dreamily. Dragons didn't get a lot of cuddling. Normally, we didn't want to either. But now... My eyes dropped to half-mast, and my heart slowed a couple of ticks. When Erin stroked the hard plates of my cheeks, then scratched my brow, I nearly hummed.

Or maybe I did hum. It was hard to tell with that angels' chorus singing joyously in my mind.

My thoughts turned to fantasies. Erin hugging my dragon neck. Or better yet, dragon Erin winding her neck around mine. Even better, sliding her wings over mine in an intimate dragon move...

"Wow," she mumbled again.

So, whew. I wasn't the only one in Happyland right now.

As delighted as I was, I was sad too. Her mother was a dragon. Had she never seen one of us up close?

My wings twitched with the impulse to gently embrace her.

But a pair of bats flitted overhead, and Erin ducked. I bared my teeth, tempted to roast them. But that *definitely* wouldn't be a good look, so I swallowed my fire, singeing my throat. Ouch.

The commotion made Erin pull back, and just like that, our quiet moment was gone.

"I...um..." Erin started awkwardly, then motioned with one jerky hand. "I'll put the coffee on."

She disappeared inside, leaving me alone.

My dragon mourned at another lost opportunity. But at least Erin wasn't furious any more.

I closed my eyes, extended my neck, and wiggled the tips of my wings. My arched claws went cold as they transformed into bare feet on chilly ground, and my ears curved into their rounder human form. With a deep breath, I opened my eyes to the narrower, brighter vision of a human.

I paused, working out the kinks in my shoulders. Then I pulled on the clothes I'd left on the porch earlier and stepped indoors.

"Thank you," I murmured, taking a steaming mug from Erin. "And sorry. For everything."

Erin wrapped both hands around her mug and sipped. Then she licked her lips and whispered, "No, thank *you*. You could have taken off last night, but you stayed. Even with the agency coming, you stayed."

Of course I had. There was no way I would ever leave my mate. No matter what price I had to pay.

I didn't dare say as much, though I wondered if I should. Would I regret omitting that detail too?

When I took a sip of coffee, my inner dragon sighed. How nice it would be to start every day this way. Me, Erin, and a cup of coffee. Or, hell. Just her and me. A quiet life in a quiet place. Like this, with horses neighing and cows quietly mooing in the distance.

Then Erin spoke, reminding me how far that was from my reality.

"No sign of Harlon. Not yet anyway." She peered out a window. "So, now what?"

I'd spent the night considering every logical scenario of Harlon's next move — or ours. But maybe *logical* was a mistake, I realized when the phone rang.

And rang and rang.

We stared at it, then at each other.

"Not your sister?" I tensed.

Erin looked at the display, then frowned. "You're kidding."

When I leaned in, she turned the phone, showing me the caller ID.

For the next two rings, neither of us moved. Then Erin stabbed at the speaker button and held the phone between us.

"Harlon. What a surprise," she said dryly.

An amused chuckle floated across the line. "My dear Miss Sattler. I hope I'm not calling too early."

She refused to let that rattle her. "I'm a balloon pilot. Dawn means sleeping in for me."

He gave another condescending *Aren't you amusing* chuckle. "Glad to hear it. I was hoping to meet you for breakfast."

Erin cackled outright. "Pity I have other plans."

Somewhere in the distance, a horse whinnied, and the small herd of cattle lowed.

He's coming, my dragon rumbled. *They can sense it.*

Erin frowned and stepped quietly to the porch, looking around. I followed her, listening in.

"Going ballooning?" Harlon had the nerve to ask next.

Erin gritted her teeth. "No, I am going to hang up. Good-bye."

He cut in quickly. "We really must talk."

"Must we? I think not."

My eyes caught on the laundry hanging on a line outside the main house. A moment ago, it had been hanging limp. Now, it was gently flapping in the breeze.

My dragon rumbled, uneasy. How close was Harlon?

In the paddock, the horses grew more restless, tossing manes and stomping hooves. The air crackled with the pent-up energy of an encroaching storm.

My ears twitched, alerting me to the background sound on Harlon's end of the call. A car rattling down a bumpy road?

I turned, looking up at the point where the ranch driveway crested a rise.

"All I ask is a moment of your time," Harlon said as the engine in the background grew louder.

Two streams of light appeared on the rise, and a moment later, the sun glinted off metal.

Harlon, I nearly grunted, recognizing the bracket-shaped headlights of his SUV.

But the phone was on speaker, and I refused to give him the satisfaction of hearing me curse.

The cattle rumbled, making for the canyon at the far end of their enclosure.

"Are you asking or demanding?" Erin snipped, watching the road as intently as I.

The vehicle stopped, along with the engine noise on Harlon's end of the line.

"Asking, of course. I wouldn't dare intrude."

Erin snorted. "No? I suppose you missed the *No trespassing* signs, then?"

She motioned urgently to the main house, mimicking a second phone. I yanked mine out and held it out while she dialed her sister's number. Then I went inside and waited breathlessly for Pippa to pick up.

"Pippa, this is—" I started.

She cut me off. "I see the car. Is that him?"

"Yes."

"What about whatshername — that vampire?"

"Angelina is with him," I confirmed. I couldn't see, smell, or hear her, but I could sense Angelina as clearly as she sensed me.

Pippa cursed. "Okay. I'll get Abby."

Rejoining Erin on the porch, I stared up the hill — and the dark clouds gathering behind it. In the distance, a bolt of lightning forked across the sky.

"I told you, this ranch isn't for sale," Erin barked into the line.

Harlon sighed. "It's rather difficult to have a civilized conversation on the phone, don't you think?"

"I've made my position perfectly clear."

Harlon made a tut-tutting sound. "You have, but it's important to make an informed decision, you know."

Erin opened her mouth to retort, then froze as a huge, winged shape appeared over the ridgeline.

I lunged forward, ready to shift and fight. But Erin grabbed my arm, shaking her head.

My inner dragon roared as the intruder circled the ranch, then landed on a rocky outcrop to the northeast. It was another dragon — a big brown one that whipped its tail and extended huge wings.

Show-off, I grunted while my dragon raged inside.

Erin flinched as a second dragon appeared and perched on a cliff not far from the first. Clearly, Harlon had brought some hired muscle with him.

The instinct to challenge those rivals made me step forward, but Erin's touch said more than *wait.* She pulled me close, telegraphing, *Don't go. Please.*

Her gaze was just as determined as ever, but her hand trembled over mine. I took a deep breath and nodded. Whatever came next, we would face it together.

Erin puffed out a shaky breath, looked at her car, and then back to me. I hesitated, then dipped my head in a nod.

A moment later, she clicked off the phone and stalked to her car.

Chapter Twenty-Eight

ERIN

My hands shook on the steering wheel as I sped up the rise, my gut roiling in a mix of fear and rage. I'd really, *really* had enough of Harlon's bullying.

Vroom! I roared right up to the front grill of Harlon's fancy Range Rover. Angelina was in the passenger seat, and, oh, the sweet satisfaction of watching her go pale, yell, and brace her arms against the dashboard for impact.

Okay, okay, she was always pale. But I swear, she went even more white.

Harlon remained perfectly calm, which only angered me more. He thought I wouldn't dare?

I rammed into his bumper. My Chevy was already beat-up, and he had to know I meant business.

I left the vehicle there, bumper to bumper, and slid out coolly.

"Oops," I said without so much as a sideways glance.

Nash joined me, looking wide-eyed, like Harlon. Good to know I'd impressed them both.

Angelina slid out of the Range Rover, gesticulating. "Are you crazy?"

I shook my head. "No. Just fed up with your games."

"They're not games, I assure you," Harlon growled, as menacing as the clouds swirling behind him.

"No? Then cut the mighty warlock act," I demanded. "It doesn't scare me."

"It should," he rumbled, drawing a snarl from Nash.

A shadow raced overhead, making me look up. A third dragon raced in, followed by a fourth. They soared over the ranch, sending the horses into a panic.

My gut dropped, because my sisters and niece were down at the ranch too. That was one reason I'd driven up to face Harlon — to buy Abby time to hustle Claire to safety while Pippa hurried into position, according to the rough plan we'd settled on the evening before.

The dragons circled in opposite directions, crossed paths, then landed, each settling down beside one of the original two. I expected them to roar and spit fire, but they did something much scarier.

Nothing. Absolutely nothing. They just sat there as quietly as Alfred Hitchcock's birds.

I scanned the horizon, wondering how many others waited in reserve.

"Interesting spell you have here." Harlon waved around. "Child's play to crack, but interesting, nonetheless."

Had he broken the privacy spell entirely or simply found his way around it? Either way, I was fuming.

"You have some nerve—"

"No, I have a final offer," Harlon cut in. Switching tactics, he flashed a winning smile. "I like you, Miss Sattler. I really do..."

He did, I realized, feeling sick.

"...and I would prefer to do this in a way with the best possible outcome for you."

"You mean, I keep the ranch, you disappear, and never come back? Perfect."

He shook his head. "Unfortunately, this land has something I need."

"Well, too bad for you."

"Ah, but this property isn't just yours," Harlon pointed out. "Your sisters' names are on the deed too."

"They agree with me."

"They shouldn't," he grunted.

"Because...?"

"Because I would hate to see someone hurt."

I snorted. "Then don't hurt anyone."

Harlon tilted his head. "I wouldn't dream of it. But if an unfortunate accident were to occur, or even a natural disaster..."

My heart dropped as I thought of the cliffs above the ranch. If Harlon brought them down in a giant rockslide, would the rubble reach the main house?

Still, I kept a brave face. Or so I hoped.

"And no one will question the likelihood of another 'natural' disaster on the heels of yesterday's storm?" I challenged.

Harlon shrugged. "Climate change. Maybe people will finally take action to undo the mess they've made of this earth."

"Says the man who travels by private jet and creates his own flash floods," I muttered.

Angelina huffed. "Enough talking. Let's get this started."

"Before the agency arrives and catches you up to no good?" I shot back.

Angelina flashed a wicked smile. Truly wicked, with her canines extending into sharp fangs.

"The agency is not an issue. Well, not for me." She shot Nash a knowing look.

"What about Harlon?" I turned to the warlock. "So far, you've managed to stay off the agency's radar. How eager are you to appear in their records now?"

And, bingo. A tiny scowl played at the corners of his mouth. Then, with a glance at Angelina, he declared, "The agency will not be an issue."

Hmm. Was he counting on Angelina to sort things out for him? Bad idea.

Then he went on, making my blood run cold. "Not an issue, just like this friend of yours." With a glare at Nash, he motioned to Angelina.

She flashed a crocodile smile and turned her attention to Nash. In one instant, her too-red lips went from scowling to puckering into a coy, sensual heart. Canting her hips to emphasize her curves, she slipped into full-on seductress mode.

"You don't need to be involved in this, Nash," she said in a singsong tone. "In fact, you need to leave, because the agency is coming for you."

Ha. Did she think she could enthrall Nash? He was a dragon shifter, not an unwitting human.

But, shit. His gaze grew vacant, his body still.

"You never really had an interest in Sedona," Angelina went on, practically caressing him with her words.

Something flashed behind her. A bolt of lightning, half hidden in the dark clouds. Clearly, Harlon didn't like Angelina looking at another man like *that*.

Neither did I, at least when it came to *my* man. But I was sickened too. Did I mean nothing to Nash? Was he so easily swayed?

"Why don't you head back to California?" Angelina suggested, touching his shoulder. "Life is so much better there."

Nash turned west, as if in a dream.

"That's right," Angelina purred. "Back to California. Remember that little place we stayed in by the ocean? You could go there. I could meet you there."

Her voice dropped like she meant it, and ugh. Maybe she did.

I pictured Nash's arms around me after we'd made love. Then I pictured them around Angelina, and bile rose in my throat. How could he have fallen for her — then *or* now?

"That's right," she coaxed him into another step.

The nearest dragons swung their heads forward, and their eyes glistened.

No, no, no! I wanted to scream. Those dragons wouldn't even have to fight Nash. They could simply kill him while he was in that state. That would leave me alone, and I would be forced to negotiate. And if I didn't...

Storm clouds swirled, hinting at the destruction Harlon would wreak.

Down at the ranch, the dogs barked wildly. The barn was a quarter of a mile away, but I could hear the horses pace and fret. We only kept the oldest few in there, and now, one whinnied, while another kicked at the stall door.

Harlon's eyes shone, telling me, *There's so much you stand to lose. Do not test my patience any longer, you weak little thing.*

All the self-doubts I'd ever harbored crawled out of their hiding places in my mind. I had powerful parents, but no powers of my own. I couldn't shift into a different body or conjure a single spell. I could try as hard as I wanted to get ahead, but I would never succeed...

I cut off those thoughts and rolled my hands into fists.

I wasn't weak. I wasn't insignificant. And I would not be cowed into letting Harlon get the better of me.

He sighed. "My patience has its limits, Miss Sattler."

The wind swirled, rattling the shutters of the main house.

Meanwhile, Angelina remained focused on Nash. "Just walk away. No reason for you to get involved here."

I hated her for toying with Nash, and I'd hated him for having fallen for her. But maybe Nash hadn't fallen for Angelina so much as fallen for her trickery. She'd used her vampire charms to lure him in, and her bite had made him a marionette.

Rage swirled through my veins. How dare Angelina? How dare Harlon? I bared my teeth, wishing I could spit fire.

I couldn't, but ouch. My throat burned in a way it never had before.

"Last chance," Harlon warned.

"Or you'll what?"

His nostrils flared. "You don't want to know, Miss Sattler. You really don't want to know."

I itched to slap him, but I didn't. Why, dammit? Why? Men like Harlon could be assholes, but women had to be polite?

My hands shook with fury. I'd waged the same inner battle countless times in my life, but I'd never, ever broken those unspoken rules.

Until now. I wound up, formed a tight fist, and let a punch fly.

And, *crack!* My knuckles screamed in pain, but there was nothing more satisfying than the sight of Harlon's head snapping back.

Slowly, he blinked, rubbing his jaw. When he looked at me, evil glittered in his eyes. "Oh, you'll regret that."

Angelina went on crooning to Nash. "You can forget everything that ever happened here. You can be free of all this."

The dragons around us opened their wings, ready to swoop down on their prey.

"I want to be free." Nash stepped away dreamily. When he turned to look at Angelina, I was sure I'd lost him forever.

But his eyes snapped into focus, and his voice was loud and clear.

"I want to be free of *you*."

He didn't finish with *bitch*, but he did shift and spit a massive plume of fire.

I was no expert, but wow. I'd never seen a shifter change forms that fast.

The flame was huge, its heat scorching. I leaped aside. Angelina screamed and threw up her hands. The fire crackled and whirled, wrapping her in a fiery tornado. Meanwhile, Harlon jumped to safety, showing where his priorities lay.

It all happened so fast, I froze. Then Nash — huge, angry, dragon Nash — cut off his flame and looked at me.

As a dragon, he couldn't yell *Run!* But the scary expression he flashed, full of teeth and sparks, made that perfectly clear.

I took off running.

Nash's roar shook the earth. Then he leaped into the sky, beating his wings so hard, the rush of air made me duck.

Harlon hissed at Angelina. "Control him!"

"I'm trying! But it's not working!"

I peeked through my whipping hair, taking stock. Nash had four dragons to deal with. That left me to take on Angelina and Harlon.

Yikes.

Luckily, they were distracted — for now. Angelina crouched, gasping, while Harlon bent over her, checking for injuries once Nash's fire died out. I dove into my pickup and revved the engine to life.

Harlon and Angelina looked up, eyes wide.

You wouldn't dare, Angelina's expression said.

I backed up ten feet, then roared forward, heading straight for them.

Oh, I would dare, all right.

Harlon thrust out his hands, conjuring a spell. But either his magic didn't apply to engines or he was too slow, because a moment later, he dove out of the way. Angelina jumped clear too, so I spun the wheel and rammed the side of the Range Rover instead.

The impact nearly made me face-plant into the steering wheel, but heck. The adrenaline rush was worth it.

Hooting like a banshee, I took another shot at Angelina, then sped through a U-turn and raced toward the ranch. Harlon was raising his hands in another spell, and something told me to get as far as I could.

Furious, boiling clouds packed the rearview mirror and spilled over the edges, reflecting on the inside of the windshield. I wasn't even halfway down the hill when rain — no, hail — began to spatter, then pound the pickup's roof. Hurricane-force winds roared, jostling the vehicle as much as the bumpy road. Tumbleweeds raced past, faster than my poor old Chevy, and—

Crack! The rear window exploded, piercing my ears with sound, if not glass. I screamed and ducked, making the car spin out.

A second bolt of lightning struck the ground, even closer than the last. Clearly, Harlon was angry. Well, so was I. Even more so when the engine quit and refused to restart.

I looked around. I couldn't sit there helplessly while Harlon hurled an entire weather arsenal at the car — lightning, thunder, maybe a landslide. . .

I pushed the driver's side door open and told myself, *On three. One. . . Two. . .*

A bolt of lightning speared down, shoving me back.

After a deep breath, I threw myself out the passenger-side door. Lightning bolts followed me like machine-gun fire. I sprinted toward the cliffs, carving sharp turns all the way like a skier.

Boom! A lightning bolt fried the prickly pear cactus to my left. The next torched a juniper on my right. It sizzled despite the downpour that plastered my hair and clothes to my skin.

I ran on with a single goal in mind. The vortex.

What exactly I would do once I got there, I had no idea. But instinct screamed for me to get there, and fast.

So fast, I would have slammed into the cliff face if I hadn't thrown my hands up in time. My left hand slapped down an inch from the spiral symbol, and I yanked it away. Sensing another blast coming, I cringed and closed my eyes.

Lightning flashed inside my eyelids, and every hair on my body stood. I spun around, staring.

Harlon stood on the rise, gesturing madly, throwing everything he could at me. A line of hail accumulated inches from my feet, and a residual breeze bit through my soaked clothes. But whatever Harlon tried, he couldn't invade this safe haven.

Meanwhile, an aerial battle raged beyond the perimeter of that compact storm. Five dragons whirled and gushed fire, creating their own fiery tempest. One screamed, then plunged toward the ground in a blur of flames, wings, and a desperately whipping tail.

Then, *boom!* Bone and sinew crashed, making the ground shake.

My heart leaped to my throat. Was that Nash?

Then I exhaled. Nash was still up there, a flash of determined bronze battling his remaining three foes.

My foes, actually. I turned back to Harlon, ready to put an end to this. But how?

I cowered against the cliff face, watching Harlon gesture and fling. Dragon roars filtered through the noise of the storm, and I looked up. Another dragon had just arrived, circling those locked in combat.

Really bad had officially gone over to worse now. And where was Pippa? We'd agreed to meet at the vortex while Abby took Claire to safety, but she was nowhere in sight.

At least the horses had broken out and scattered. I prayed they hadn't injured themselves in the process.

Beside Harlon, Angelina pointed so furiously, I could picture her shrill commands.

Get her! Get him!

Harlon flashed a sour look, and his lips moved, grunting something along the lines of, *You said you would take care of the dragon.*

I threw a grateful look at Nash. I had no idea how he'd broken free of Angelina's hold, but he'd done it. And boy, was he mad.

And he wasn't the only one.

Slowly, I moved my right hand toward the spiral symbol and sent it a silent plea.

All right, vortex. Time to show your stuff. Please.

When I edged my hand closer, a burst of energy shoved it away. I shook my head and whispered, "I don't want to fight you. I don't want to use you. In fact, I'd rather not bother you at all. But I need you. We all do."

The vortex thrust my hand away, refusing to cooperate.

My voice grew tighter, more desperate. "If you don't help me, you'll be dealing with Harlon next."

Again, the vortex pushed my hand away, clearly wanting no part of this mess. And, heck. I could relate. But some problems didn't go away on their own. Sometimes, you had to dive headfirst into a battle and fight until you won — or lost.

And I sure as hell was not going to lose, not with everything I held dear on the line.

I braced myself and covered the spiral, fighting the force this time. Eventually, I was able to flatten my hand against the rock, though it took every scrap of energy I had.

Dammit, where was Pippa?

"I need your help. Please, just this once. Help my family," I begged.

Still, the vortex pushed back. It pushed images into my mind too — a blur of all the people who'd lived in this quiet, dusty corner of Arizona, from my great-aunt's time to her aunt's and her ancestors before that — all the way back to pioneer times and beyond. I saw the familiar outline of the ranch shrink, expand, and shrink again in a bewildering rush of time.

The vehicles parked outside changed from the Chevy I'd inherited to a rounder, 1940s model, then a wagon. My cabin faded away, as did the barn, while the main house changed from its familiar form, with one addition after another chopped off until it was reduced to a mere shack, then nothing at all.

For a moment, all I saw was swaying grass and silent rocks. Then people appeared — smaller in stature, but not in pride, and deeply bronzed by the sun. People who planted, sang, and carved symbols into stone. I saw harsh winters, brilliant springs, and towering lines of corn tangled with bean vines. Then those people faded away too, and I caught a brief glimpse of a different, migratory clan, before nature reigned, and reigned alone.

I moved my hand away from the spiral. Yeah, I got the message. I was only the most recent in a long chain of inhabitants. Not the first, nor the last. When my time was up, it was up, and that was that.

I smacked my hand back over the spiral and pointed the other into the storm. "Harlon isn't just coming for this land. He's coming for you. For your power."

The energy surged as if to say, *Let him try.*

"He will," I hissed. "He will try and try, and this land will never know peace again. He will bring in others to draw from your power too. Greedy souls who will mine you for any advantage they find."

Harlon gestured again, and the storm intensified.

"Please," I whispered. "Help me keep this place safe from him. Not just for me, but for you."

My fragile hopes plunged when the energy under my hand ebbed. Was the vortex shutting down altogether?

But then it came bursting back out in an entirely new way. Instead of pushing my hand aside, the energy flowed in and tingled all the way up my arm.

Do it, I imagined an earthy voice mutter. *Get rid of him, and fast, before I change my mind.*

I stared at my hand in one of those terrifying moments that followed getting what you wished for. Because, yikes.

The power flowing into me was *intense*. Invasive, almost, and I feared the side effects of calling it forth.

But, heck. I didn't have much choice.

Keeping my right hand over the spiral, I inched away from the cliff and reached my left foot and arm back into the storm.

Angelina shouted to Harlon in warning.

He lifted his arms and thrust forward. A lightning bolt formed out of nowhere, blazing directly at me.

I held my breath — and my ground — praying my gamble would work.

Chapter Twenty-Nine

ERIN

Lightning in the sky was fascinating. Lightning coming straight at you, on the other hand...

I cringed, sure I would die. One painful zap, and it would all be over.

And, bang! The lightning hit. It shoved my body backward, and every hair on my body stood. But its energy bounced away, sending the lightning bolt ricocheting back at Harlon.

His eyes went wide, and he jumped aside. Angelina, who'd been clinging to his shoulder, lurched too — directly into the path of the lightning.

She screamed, and for three horrifying seconds, her body glowed. The glow became a fire that consumed her skin and clothes. Her scream rose, then cut off abruptly. Her body crumpled.

I stared, as did Harlon, who cautiously toed the pile of ash and burned clothes. Was she really gone?

High in the sky, Nash roared. *Yes! She's gone for good.*

I flicked a hand dismissively. *Good riddance.*

And, whoa. A wisp of wind stirred Angelina's ashes into a tiny tornado, then scattered them.

I stared at my hand, then at the vortex. Was that my doing?

Harlon's face twisted as he followed the ashes. Not in grief, nor regret. Just the annoyance of a man who'd suffered an inconvenience to his carefully laid plans.

When he turned back to me, his eyes took on a fiendish glow, and his fingers curled, preparing his next blow.

Whoosh! Another bolt of lightning shot out. It bounced off my hand, but my teeth rattled with the force of it, and I was nearly flung back into the cliff.

Thunder exploded, mirroring the warlock's frustration. He wound up for another attack, then stopped, thinking.

My hand was still up, ready to ward off another attack. But the longer Harlon thought, the more I trembled. Now what?

Flashing a scary grin, he turned in the direction of the main house.

My jaw dropped. No. God, no. Please.

Harlon's lips curled, hissing something like, *Yes. Now, you will pay.*

He thrust forward, sending twin bolts of lightning through the sky. One speared the barn with an ear-splitting crack, while the other zapped into the old windmill beside the main house.

Once upon a time, my great-aunt had dazzled us kids by wrapping the entire rusty structure in Christmas lights. But that didn't begin to match the wattage the windmill lit up with now.

A terrified yelp sounded from inside the house. Roscoe?

My knees wobbled. I loved that dog, but I loved my sisters and niece even more. Where were they? I vacillated between cursing them for not meeting me at the vortex and hoping they were safe.

I was sure Harlon's next strike would set the house on fire, but he aimed it at the sky instead. The dragons scattered, and I screamed.

"Nash!"

My heart stopped when one of the dragons plummeted toward the ground — one with a dull brown hide, not Nash's bronze-tinted body. So, whew. Nash was safe. He roared at the last two dragons, setting off the next phase of battle.

Amid all the chaos, three stooped figures emerged from the back of the house. Two darted from bush to bush, then disappeared into the trees along the creek.

I could have cheered, because that was Abby with Claire.

The third — Pippa — cut sharply north, toward the mesa.

I nearly yelled out to her. *No, not that way! The vortex is over here!*

Thank goodness Harlon didn't spot them. But one of the dragons must have, because it dive-bombed Abby and Claire.

Nash roared and rocketed after it, tucking his ears and legs into a streamlined form. Once close enough, he sprayed fire. But his foe twisted away and fought back with his own stream of flames.

My heart jumped to my throat. Thanks to Nash, Abby and Claire had time to escape. But would his heroics come at the ultimate price?

One heart-stopping minute of aerial acrobatics later, the dragon broke away for a breather, and Nash did too.

Grumbling, Harlon hurled a bolt of lightning at the house. All I could do was watch helplessly as it hit the weather vane and exploded into sparks.

Not so helpless, an inner voice said, faint but fierce.

I wiggled my fingers, trying to focus. At the sound of a battle cry, I looked up, fearing an attack from the newest dragon on the scene.

But that battle cry wasn't the dragon. It was me, raging away. At Harlon. At the storm. At everything I had never been able to be or do. Raging enough to push my soul aside and reveal a bigger, bolder, braver me.

The next time Harlon released another bolt, I reached out — not just with a hand, but my mind.

Intercepting lightning should have been impossible, but it wasn't. At least, not in the picture in my mind. A split second later—

I gasped, rattled by thousands of watts of power. Not directly, but out at that extension of my body and mind, where I was hit by blinding white heat. And not just hit, but *consumed* by it.

As kids, Abby and I had played Jedi knight, while Pippa played Princess Leia with a seriously badass twist. We were pros at mimicking the sound of light sabers — exactly the sound that deafened me now as blazing white light flashed.

I stared through narrowed eyes. The lightning bolt was still flashing but suspended in place. Suspended, though not frozen — it went on crackling, kicking, and sparking like something in a mad scientist's lab.

It was working! I was holding the lightning back! Or rather, the vortex was. Now all I had to do was redirect it.

I gulped.

My hammering heart sent adrenaline through my veins. Adrenaline, and something else.

Nash's words echoed through my mind. *Do you get it now? You have power. All of you.*

Okay, maybe we did. But as Nash had pointed out, no one had taught us how to use it.

In my mind, I yelled at my father. *Why didn't you ever teach me?*

But he'd tried, I realized. I was the one who'd resisted his efforts, insisting I didn't have any power.

But I did. Lots of it.

And, heck. Maybe Pippa was right. Maybe magic came as naturally as sex when the situation called for it.

And boy, did the situation call for it.

My hair whipped in the wind, and a strand caught in my mouth. The lightning faltered, reflecting Harlon's surprise. Then he scowled and threw his arms forward again, doubling the power of the lightning.

I reeled at the impact, barely hanging on.

You wanted my help, I sensed the vortex grumbling. *Show me you're willing to do your part, or I'll quit.*

I was. Truly. But I was a novice when it came to magic. Didn't that earn me any mercy?

Apparently not. Not a bit.

Sweat beaded on my brow as I strained with each arm — one against the rock carving, the other in the air, aiming the vortex's power. The lightning went on crackling and zapping, scorching the patch of ground it hovered over. But inch by inch, it advanced, pushing toward the main house with menacing power.

Harlon was winning. I was losing. It was inevitable.

You should have accepted my offer, Harlon's triumphant look said.

Suddenly, the lightning bolt erupted into a shower of sparks, and he stumbled backward. I lurched as his resistance broke off, then jerked back as he recovered. The sound of dueling light sabers intensified. Now what?

Pippa's voice, choked with effort, sounded in my mind. *Well, don't just stand there. Help.*

I couldn't see her, but I could feel the boost in resistance. It was as if my sister had jumped in beside me, slapped a hand over the vortex, and pushed with me.

Except she wasn't beside me. I stared through the swirling storm. Where was Pippa?

Then I focused on repelling Harlon's lightning. The *how* didn't matter now, only that we succeeded in holding him back. . . somehow.

In my mind, I was leaning against a stone wall and pushing. Harder. . . harder. . .

It's working! Pippa panted into my mind. *Keep going!*

The lightning hissed and sputtered, angrier than ever. But it was scorching a new patch of ground now, a few inches closer to Harlon.

It was working! We were pushing Harlon back!

His face contorted in anger and exertion, and we stopped making headway.

If only Abby could chip in too. We three sisters had always made a formidable team. Surely, as a trio, we could overcome Harlon.

But Abby had to keep Claire safe, so that wasn't an option.

Dragon roars filtered down through the clouds, making me despair.

Dammit. . . Pippa cursed as Harlon clawed back some of our hard-earned headway.

Somewhere overhead, a dragon screamed, and another roared in triumph. Was Nash the winner or the loser?

My arms burned with effort. My whole body ached. But letting up now meant losing everything. Everything.

Well, not today, someone growled in my mind.

I nearly cheered. Abby?

Never count me out of a good fight, she barked. *Just tell me how the hell this works, and I'm all in.*

That was the hard part, because I had no idea.

You need to get to the vortex, Pippa told her, still straining against Harlon.

I am at the vortex, Abby insisted.

No, I'm at the vortex, Pippa retorted.

No, I am, I nearly said. *And you two are nowhere in sight.*

Then it hit me. My great-aunt had warned us all about the vortex, but she'd never brought us there at the same time. Was there more than one vortex — or more than one place to tap into its power?

Touch it, I barked. *One hand on the vortex. Point your other hand at the—*

The lightning bolt jolted before I finished my sentence. That Abby. Always a quick learner.

Holy smokes, she muttered.

Yes, that about summed it up.

A prickly pear burst into flames as our combined power pushed Harlon's lightning backward. The ground charred. A jackrabbit emerged and sprinted for new cover.

Keep going! Pippa urged as we kept up our combined efforts.

Okay, asshole, I sensed Abby hiss when the lightning wavered. *We're winning. You're losing. Now, get the hell off our property!*

Harlon backed up, looking incredulous. When he bumped into the front of his car, he cursed, and thunder boomed over the ranch. A moment later, he turned to flee.

I would have loved to chase him with his own lightning bolt, but the moment he dropped his arms, it fizzled, making me stumble forward.

I raced up the hill in hot pursuit. What I would do when I reached Harlon, I had no clue. Throttling him was high on my list, though.

I prefer kicking him in the balls and watching him whimper, Pippa muttered.

She, too, was panting and racing toward Harlon.

Unfortunately, the warlock had enough of a head start to hop into his car and take off. But when I crested the hill, I found him staring into the distance.

Several big, dark Suburbans were rushing up the dirt road, churning up huge dust clouds. Seconds later, the vehicles fanned out and screeched to a halt in front of Harlon.

"Whoa," Pippa muttered, nearly knocking into me from behind.

Doors flew open, and a dozen big men — some in secret service-style suits, others in combat gear — leaped out, brandishing weapons and IDs.

"This is the ADMSA!" one of them shouted. "Nobody move."

The storm clouds parted, and a dragon soared by, roaring.

"Nash!" I yelled, half in relief, half in warning.

A dozen weapons followed him, and I screamed. "Stop! Don't shoot!"

"Don't!" Pippa yelled, backing me up. "He's with us! Harlon is the problem!"

The agency men looked between us and their leader.

My hopes rose... until Harlon started talking in that hypnotic purr of his.

"Gentlemen, thank goodness you're here. I can explain everything."

Chapter Thirty

ERIN

The minute Harlon started talking, my heart dropped. Any minute now, he would convince the agency men to kill Nash, arrest me, and turn the ranch deed over to him.

"That dragon is a menace to society." Harlon pointed to Nash, who circled overhead, steaming — literally, with angry puffs emerging from his nostrils.

"An out-of-control, cold-blooded murderer." Harlon went on, indicating the pile of ashes. "He killed Angelina Saint James." He nodded sadly at the men's shocked expressions. "Just as she was trying to talk sense into him."

"She was hit by the lightning bolt you threw!" I protested.

Technically, I was the one who'd bounced it back in his direction, but I left that part out.

Harlon tsked. "Sadly, he's managed to infiltrate the minds of these poor, defenseless women. They're under his spell."

Pippa stomped forward, raising a fist. "I'll show you poor and defenseless, asshole—"

I held her back as a dozen rifles swung our way. How was this happening?

Pippa seethed, kicking Angelina's ashes. "This is our property! He's trespassing. You're all trespassing!"

The head agent flashed an ID. "Captain Edwards of the ADMSA. We're just here to help, ma'am."

I snorted. They were here to pin the blame on Nash, and I knew it.

"Then get this trespasser off our property." Pippa stabbed a finger at Harlon.

He tsked. "They signed a bill of sale last week. I have it back at my office. This is my property now, but they refuse to vacate it."

"We refuse to *what?*" Pippa and I screeched.

Harlon was lying through his teeth, but he was doing it so calmly and confidently, I was afraid the agents would buy it.

But, whew. Captain Edwards stuck up a hand, cutting Harlon off. "We'll take your statement in due time. Now, put your hands on your head and face the vehicle."

"Of course. Anything to cooperate with the law," Harlon hummed, sweet as honey, though he made no move to obey. "And anything to help bring in that renegade dragon. You'll need to get him under control right away."

My hopes sank. He was doing it again, dammit — playing tricks with people's minds.

But Edwards barked, having none of that. "Save the mind-bending for humans, and put your hands on the vehicle. Now."

I nearly cheered. What a relief to know the agents were immune to Harlon's magic.

Then again, I wasn't off the hook yet.

Edwards was a fit, square-jawed, sixtysomething man with a neat, salt-and-pepper beard. The kind of man who probably turned women's heads everywhere he went — and not just the over-fifty crowd. A little like Harlon, in fact — except Edwards was on the right side of the law.

Or so I hoped.

"You and you," he barked at Pippa and me. "Stay right where you are. And that dragon — I want him down here, pronto."

I looked at Nash, who was still circling. Why hadn't he fled when he'd had the chance?

Intense bronze eyes stared down at me, vowing never to leave as long as I needed him.

My heart fluttered, and I flashed him a broad smile.

"There's another dragon over there, sir." One of the agents pointed.

Edwards nodded curtly. "That one too." He jutted his chin and boomed at them both. "You and you. You have one minute to land. There and there." He pointed to two spots on the ground.

The guy had a hell of a voice — and a hell of a presence. Plus, neither the warlock nor dragon aspect seemed to faze him. But I supposed that was a requirement when you worked for an agency specializing in supernatural activity. Was he also a dragon shifter? A wolf? A warlock?

At his signal, four agents stepped behind a vehicle. A minute later, they were towering above it in dragon form. Without a word — or a growl — they stalked to one side and formed an intimidating line behind the other agents.

Pippa's jaw dropped. "Wow. Dragons."

I gulped. Yes, four of them. Just what we needed to top off this mess.

"How do you expect Nash to land with you crowding him?" I protested.

Edwards didn't blink. "He knows the procedure."

So, he knew it was Nash. Did they know each other personally? And, yikes. Was that a good or a bad thing?

Nash circled slowly, then glided in to land beside me instead of the indicated spot. He stood there, teeth bared, wings extended, tail lashing.

"Boy, am I glad he's on our side," Pippa murmured.

Me too. He'd single-handedly — er, single-clawedly? — fought off four dragons to save my ranch and my family. He could have run off to save his own hide, but he didn't. He'd stayed to fight — for us.

For me.

I faced him, trying to catch his gaze. Not easy, what with him glaring at Edwards and Harlon in a way that said, *If you make one move to harm this woman, you will die.*

How had I ever doubted him?

I edged closer, trying to keep him calm. "It's okay."

My pulse rose with every step I took. Approaching a calm, friendly dragon, as I had a few nights ago, was one thing. Stepping into the personal space of a raging, smoke-puffing dragon was another.

I bit my lip and kept going, gently tapping the leathery plates of his chest. Wow. They were so hard. Could Nash even feel that?

Apparently, because he craned his neck to look down. Straight down, since I was that close.

My heart revved as I looked up — and up. That was a hell of a lot of dragon up there. Enough to make my knees shake. Thank goodness I knew that was Nash in there.

"It will be okay. Somehow," I added a little lamely.

His frown said, *How?* but he did lower his wings slightly.

I patted his chest again.

Edwards pointed at the second, mystery dragon perched on a cliff — the one who'd been watching impassively all along.

"You there! I need you to land here. Now."

The agency dragons rumbled, reinforcing the order.

The dragon blinked at them, utterly unimpressed. A long minute later, it shook out its wings in a bored motion and stepped elegantly into a smooth glide.

My jaw dropped. Until then, I hadn't gotten a good look at it. Now that I had...

Pippa did a double take, whispering, "You're kidding."

The dragon's hide shimmered like leprechaun gold, and when it stuck out its feet for landing, its talons had a shiny, manicured finish.

I took a deep breath, bracing myself. My hair whipped as the dragon landed, but that was the least of my worries.

"Mom," Pippa whispered, as shocked as I was.

The dragon glanced at us briefly, then turned to the agents. Everyone went silent as she looked them over one by one.

Click, click, click went her talons, tapping the rocky ground impatiently.

Then Captain Edwards spoke, and things got even weirder.

Up to then, he'd been the picture of a cool, calm FBI-type. Now, his voice fell to a hoarse whisper.

"Virginia?"

I stared. He knew my mother?

She barely acknowledged him, maintaining her regal attitude with a distinct air of expectation.

"Oh. Right. Just a moment." Edwards gestured to another agent, who hurried to the back of the SUV and returned with two bundles. He tossed the first roughly at Nash's feet. The second, he laid reverently before my mother, practically bowing as he backed away.

"Hm-hmm." Edwards cleared his throat, and all his men looked away to let my mother shift in privacy.

Any normal woman — or shifter — would rush to pull on clothes in a situation like that.

Not my mother.

She shifted slowly, almost lazily — a process I'd never actually witnessed. Not even now, because Nash shifted at the same time, drawing all my attention. In dragon form, he was so different, yet instantly recognizable. Same fiery eyes, same strong shoulders. Same aura of vulnerability mixed with invincibility.

"Nash," I whispered, taking his hand.

He gripped mine tightly, and when he spoke, his voice was deep and scratchy. "You okay?"

I nodded. Yes. So far.

He nodded grimly, then nodded at Edwards. Clearly, someone he knew — like the dark-haired man over on the left Nash made brief eye contact with.

"Ingo," Pippa whispered at the dark-haired man in disbelief.

I stared. Huh?

Then it hit me. *That* Ingo? Pippa's ex?

Ingo went bug-eyed at her, then straightened. Neither he nor Nash acknowledged each other, which made me wonder. Where did Ingo's allegiance lie — with his friend or the agency? And how did he feel about seeing my sister?

Lots of questions. No time for answers.

When I glanced back at my mother, she was human, naked, and in no rush whatsoever. In fact, she held up the plain gray jumpsuit and contemplated it with disdain. Finally, she sighed and pulled it on, leaving the front zip low enough to reveal her cleavage despite the winter chill. Next, she cinched the belt tightly, showing off her curves.

Then she cleared her throat, signaling *You may turn* to the others as if they were her lowly subjects.

"Hello, girls," she murmured, barely giving us a second glance. "Nice to see you." Then she frowned. "Good God, Erin. Fix your hair, will you?"

My jaw fell open. By the time I opened my mouth to respond, she'd turned her attention, such as it was, to Captain Edwards.

"Virginia," he breathed again.

Pippa and I exchanged pained glances. Oh, they definitely knew each other. And as for how *intimately...* I really, really didn't want to know.

I sighed and did my best to untangle my storm-blasted hair.

Mom only acknowledged Edwards after checking her nails. "Good to see you again..." She paused, thinking. Finally, she added, "Tim."

His face clouded. "Tom."

My mother didn't actually say, *Whatever*, but her gesture did. Then she looked at Nash, who wore a matching jumpsuit. On him, it looked like a badass *Top-Gun*-type uniform, while my mother looked ready for a fashion show. And she hadn't even had time to accessorize.

She threw Nash an appraising look. The kind of look she'd probably once thrown at Tom — er, Captain Edwards — shortly before taking him to bed, only to disappear without a word the next morning.

Normally, I would have sighed. But since it was Nash she was checking out, I ground my teeth.

Nash leveled a look at her, then slid an arm across my shoulders and nodded at Edwards. "Captain."

The guy nodded gruffly. "Nash."

My mother shuffled, displeased at not being the center of attention.

"What are you doing here?" Pippa asked.

Our mother replied in a long-suffering, *Is this what I get for sacrificing everything for you?* tone she had no right to use.

"Your father called me." Then she frowned, turning to me. "Or was it your father? Maybe Abby's?" She shrugged. "It was late. I could barely think straight." Then she yawned. "God. It's still late. Or early. I need a coffee." She looked around, and though she didn't actually stick out a hand for someone to press a steaming Arabica blend into, the expectation was clear.

Sure enough, two agents practically stumbled over each other to reach the back of the SUV. The winner returned a moment later with a thermos and a paper cup.

And here I'd been thinking the BDSM would pack their trunks with weapons, radios, and magic-tinged restraints. But so far, they'd only produced jumpsuits and coffee. Did they carry doughnuts too?

Either way, Mom clearly hadn't lost her mojo.

She considered the paper cup for a long time, waiting, perhaps, for the guy to whip out porcelain. When none appeared, she reluctantly accepted it. She sipped the coffee, shot the agent an offended look... and sipped again.

Yes, mixed messages were my mother's specialty.

"Why would Dad — or Erin's dad — call you?" Pippa asked. "And, wait. He has your number?"

My mother shrugged as if to say, *It's not my fault my ex-lovers keep hounding me.* "He had the feeling something was wrong. He called Greg first — oh, there. It was Erin's father who called, not Pippa's — but neither were close enough to get here quickly. So they called me."

A deep sigh made it clear what an inconvenience that had been.

"I'm not sure why you bothered," I couldn't help snipping. "You didn't even help. Why?"

She took another sip of coffee. "You three seemed to have things under control. And your dragon friend did too." She shot Nash an appreciative look.

Not appreciative of his help. Appreciative of his looks.

I tightened my hand around his.

"We could have died, Mom," Pippa protested.

"Now, now. Don't be so dramatic." Still, she narrowed her eyes on Harlon. "On the other hand, this warlock *was* throwing lightning bolts at my daughters, and one has to wonder why."

Her tone dropped, and her eyes went icy.

Strangely enough, that warmed my heart. Maybe Mom did love us. Maybe she did care, in her aloof, distant way.

Edwards turned to Harlon, looking dangerous as hell.

Harlon stuck up his hands. "I had to defend myself. They attacked me."

Pippa and I huffed, while Nash stepped forward, growling.

My mother snorted. "They attacked you, did they?" She motioned to his car with her coffee cup. "Did they lure you out here too?"

The agents leaned in, waiting.

Harlon opened his mouth to speak, then closed it again. It was shortly past dawn on a Sunday. Even a warlock couldn't explain that away.

"And that storm that came out of nowhere," my mother continued. "Did they launch that at you too?"

I crossed my arms. "That's at least a class-two warlock, isn't it, Nash?"

He nodded. "At least."

Edwards frowned at Harlon, then at another agent holding a clipboard. Did the paperwork there categorize Harlon as a harmless class-four?

"Right. Hands on the vehicle, sir," he ordered.

Harlon huffed. "Do you know who I am?"

"No, but I can't wait to find out all about you." Edwards moved closer, flanked by two big men. "And I mean all. Finances. Business licenses. Unauthorized use of magic..."

I flinched, spotting Harlon's fingers twitch.

"Go ahead," Edwards said coolly. "We'd love more evidence of what you're capable of."

Harlon's jaw went hard, and he shot me a dark look. The glare he shot at Nash was even more murderous. "What about him?"

Tim — er, Tom — followed his gaze to Nash. "Oh, he'll be talking to us as well. As will the others." He looked at Pippa and me, though nowhere near as menacingly. "But I advise you to worry about your own business."

At a signal from Edwards, two agents escorted Harlon into one of the vehicles. They piled in after him and drove off, followed by two other SUVs — and two of the four dragons, high in the air, where more patches of blue appeared. The other two dragons shifted to human form and drove away in Harlon's Range Rover.

That left two vehicles, six agents, and Captain Edwards, all staring us down.

Well, three agents stared us down. Edwards had a hard time dragging his eyes away from my mother. I could practically count the sparkly hearts in his eyes.

Finally, he cleared his throat and barked orders at his men. Two pulled out some kind of forensic kit and got to work on Angelina's ashes, while the other four set off to measure the scorch marks on the earth.

I shot a covert glance at the petroglyphs, then jerked my eyes back to the ground. How the hell were we going to explain the vortex?

Maybe we can gloss over those details, Pippa's voice sounded in my mind.

I gave her a teensy-tiny nod.

"Now, I'll need statements from everyone..." Captain Edwards started.

"Yes, yes," my mother said impatiently. "But surely you don't have to do that out here. Or in that drafty office of yours."

Pippa and I exchanged looks. Mom had been to his office?

Pippa glanced back at my mom, then sighed. *I want to ask, but I don't want to ask.*

Mom showed Edwards her empty coffee cup — the most pressing misdemeanor on her list — and gestured toward the main house. "Can't we do this in a more civilized way? I'm sure it won't take long to clear everything up."

Edwards studied her, torn between protocol and my mother's charms.

Ha. The man might be immune to the magic of a class-two warlock, but not to my mom.

Pippa chimed in next. "Good idea. We could put on coffee — real coffee. And didn't Claire make muffins?" Then she faked surprise. "Oh! Mom, if you come over now, you could see your granddaughter. I know how much you've missed her."

Nash raised his eyebrows. I didn't say a word.

"What a shame it would be if you had to hurry away now. A crying shame," Pippa emphasized, going for the hard sell.

"Oh yes," my mother agreed with no emotion whatsoever. "I've missed her so much."

Ha. She missed coffee more, but we'd learned to take what we got.

"I suppose we could start inside," Edwards murmured.

And off we went, down the hill to the main house.

"So, the vortex..." Pippa whispered.

I shushed her with a sharp look at Edwards, then corrected her. "Vortexes." It sounded wrong, though, so I mulled it over. *Vortices*?

"Aunt Emma only ever showed me the one by the head of the canyon," Pippa whispered.

"She only showed me the one by the cliff," I added.

Pippa rubbed her chin. "And Abby was somewhere over by the mesa."

We chewed on that for a moment.

"One vortex with three outlets, or three separate vortexes?" Pippa wondered out loud.

I didn't know, and I wasn't sure I wanted to. Anyway, let my sister chew over that topic. I threaded my arm around Nash's and trailed behind her.

"So, are you still in trouble?" I whispered.

He weighed that up before whispering back. "Not sure. But I think I might let your mother handle things for a while."

I stifled a laugh. "Not sure if that's a good idea."

He chuckled, then stopped and took both my hands. "I'm not sure about a lot of things, except one."

My heart stuttered, and my breath caught.

He ran his thumbs over the tops of my hands. "I know I've never felt more alive than I have around you. I know I was meant to come here. And I know I never want to leave."

I bit my lip to keep it from trembling. When I finally spoke, all I could come up with was a jittery joke.

"Technically, that's three things."

He flashed a smile. "Call me greedy."

A thousand emotions choked me. Not one helped me come up with an intelligent response, though. The best I could do was, "Well, Sedona is a nice place..."

Nash shook his head. "It's not the place. It's because you're here."

I cleared my throat, trying to remain composed. In the end, I flung my arms around him, holding him tight. So tight, my chest squeezed, and it was hard to breathe. But easing up a little didn't change that, so I went back to a desperate squeeze in case another warlock, vampire, or shifter came along to take him from me.

"I'd like you to stay too," I whispered. "No — I'd love it."

He grinned. I couldn't see it, but I could feel it. Just as clearly as I felt so many other things. Joy. Hope. Energy. Desire.

And above all, impatience. I wanted to fast-forward in time to a point past coffee and muffins, past the interrogations and everything else we couldn't avoid. I wanted to pop back out at the point when all that was done and Nash and I could be alone. To talk. To love. To figure things out.

Nash kissed my neck, then my cheek, and finally my lips, promising we'd get to that. Soon.

Chapter Thirty-One

NASH

It had been a hell of a night, and it was shaping up to be a hell of a morning. We'd beaten back the threat of Harlon and Angelina, but now we had Captain Edwards and Erin's mother to deal with. Worse, I was fading fast.

"Are you all right?" Erin asked, helping me up the porch steps.

I tried answering, but all that came out was a mumble, and my vision blurred.

"Nash!" She grabbed my arm, barely keeping me from face-planting on the top step.

"*Post-eleftheros* withdrawal," Edwards grumbled, though he sounded miles away.

"Post-*what?*" Erin shrieked.

I moved my lips, trying to tell her what the agency had taught me.

In the rare case of a vampire's victim surviving the latter's demise, the body seeks to establish a new state of homeostasis by ridding itself of lingering chemical residue.

Like withdrawal for a drug addict, in other words, but it all came out slurred.

This life-threatening condition often disrupts brain chemistry and results in death...

God, I hoped not. Not now that things were finally looking up.

Or down, I thought as I toppled onto the porch sofa.

"Nash!" Erin cried.

255

Edwards didn't sound worried, though. "Just give him a couple hours. He'll be fine."

Erin wasn't buying it, and neither was I. But by then, the world was fading...fading...gone.

∞∞∞∞

How long I was out for, I had no clue. For a while, I was out cold. At some point, I was vaguely aware of mumbling feverishly and being heaped with blankets. Then came a nightmarish phase in which I relived my deepest, darkest memories — most of which related to Angelina. Those clung doggedly to my mind, but eventually, they faded, scrubbed away by brilliant sunshine. Only then did I doze for a while.

When I woke, the sun was high, the sky clear and bright.

I blinked. Wow. *Really* bright. *Sunglasses* bright, though the lumpy objects stacked on my chest cast a little shade. I felt around and lifted a...bunny into view.

Yes, a bunny. A fluffy pink stuffed-animal bunny.

Hopper, my dragon said dryly.

Next, I found a teddy bear — Fred, if memory served right — and a rainbow-colored unicorn whose name I couldn't remember.

Setting them aside, I rolled and slowly sat up. My foot found a free spot, but not by much, because a whole stable of model horses were lined up there, keeping watch over me.

I looked them over, identifying a few. Seabiscuit... Man o' War... Black Beauty...

Leaning over, I rubbed my eyes. Damn, was it bright. Not interrogation-bright, just a nice, cheery, *I can see clearly now, the rain has gone* kind of bright.

And, wow. My whole body felt... Well, maybe not *bright,* but light.

I stood, took a couple of wobbly steps away from the porch, then tipped my head back. Wow. The sky was an intense blue, the rocks redder than ever. Every breath that slipped down my throat was a crisp, clean delight. My shoulder sported a burn, and my left leg was sore, but those wounds were healing fast.

All in all, I felt good. Really good, in a way I hadn't in a long, long time.

"Oh. You're better," a cheery, little-girl voice said.

I turned to find Claire with another armful of stuffed animals.

"I am. Hopper helped." I waved a little — and oops. The bunny was still in my hand, exuding pink joy, like Claire. "So did Seabiscuit," I added, because setting up all those horses had to have taken a lot of time. "Thank you."

Claire's smile brought out her dimples. Then she turned to Abby, who'd just emerged from the house. "See, Mommy? It worked."

"It did. Thank you," I said, bracing myself for Abby's scowl.

She didn't, though. She just tousled Claire's hair, nodded, and whispered, "No. Thank *you*."

She made eye contact for all of two seconds before glancing at the rise behind me. Then she whirled and disappeared back into the house, muttering something about lunch.

I turned to check the road. The SUVs were gone, but a faint trail of dust still hung in the air.

Inside the house, Abby hollered, "Hey, Erin. He's up."

The door banged open, and Erin flew out.

Her eyes went right to the couch, and her brow furrowed. Then she spotted me and lit up.

And I mean, lit up, with every line of worry replaced by joy and relief.

My heart doubled in size. How often was a guy treated to a look like that?

Erin leaped to the ground, skipping the stairs, and raced toward me. Then she slowed, suddenly self-conscious.

"Oh. Good to see you," she whispered.

I laughed. "Ditto."

"My animals healed him," Claire reported.

I waved Hopper. "Sure did."

Erin's smile was a thing of beauty. Really beautiful, like the rest of her. I found myself staring, because, like the sky, the air, and the rocks, Erin was different from before. Well, the same, but more intense, somehow. More *there*.

That's when it occurred to me that Erin might not have changed. Maybe it was me. More intense. More here. More alive.

Free, my dragon whispered happily. *We're finally free.*

I was. The curtain Angelina had dropped over my soul was gone — and gone for good.

I turned my back to the hilltop where the vampire had met her demise. All that was behind us now. Ahead lay… What, exactly?

My heart pounded as Erin approached.

"You're really okay?" Erin asked.

I nodded. "Just a little sore."

Her chest rose as she looked me over, and she nodded briskly. "Good."

"Good," I whispered back.

For a moment, we stood perfectly still. Then something in me snapped, and I threw my arms around her.

Because, hell. We'd survived a balloon crash, a warlock, a vampire, and an aerial attack. We'd endured a lightning storm and destiny's meddling. Why play it cool at a time like this?

Erin melted into my arms and hid her face against my shoulder. Her favorite spot, it seemed.

Mine too.

I held her tightly, with my arms overlapping and my cheek nestled by her hair. I still had Hopper in one hand, but that was okay. He fit too, though his floppy ear tickled my skin.

At some point, Erin pulled back just enough for her gaze to meet mine. Her eyes danced, and primal drums hammered in my soul.

"Uh-oh," Claire stage-whispered to her animals. "I think they're going to kiss."

Erin's cheeks bunched, and her skin went pink. "Sorry, kiddo. I just have to."

"Like this?" Claire smooched her teddy bear loudly.

I laughed and held Erin even closer. Close enough for our toes to touch and her chest to press against mine. I closed my eyes, listening to her heartbeat.

"That's hugging," Claire pointed out.

Erin's laugh made her wiggle in my arms. Bliss. Then she nosed her way along my jaw, looked into my eyes, and finally delivered that kiss.

Double bliss.

"Now, *that's* a kiss," Pippa chuckled, joining Claire on the porch.

Yes, it was. Not our first, but the first with my senses switched back on. Well, nearly all. My balance was out of whack, and I nearly keeled over. Or maybe my balance was fine, but the kiss was that good.

So good, my dragon side hummed.

Unfortunately, the motion broke our kiss. It did give me another chance to gaze into those amazing eyes of hers, though — one green, one blue.

"Is everyone all right?" I asked.

Erin nodded. "Yes, thank goodness. The horses have wandered back too. And the really good news is, my mom talked Captain Edwards into keeping his questioning brief — for today, at least. We have to meet him at the county sheriff's office tomorrow morning at nine."

Wow. Edwards was a stickler for protocol, and I'd never, ever known him to grant exceptions.

"Your mother is amazing."

Erin sighed. "That's one way to put it."

"Are you sure she's not a witch?"

Erin shook her head. "No magic spells, thank goodness. Just good old-fashioned feminine charm. Or dragon charm, I suppose."

I looked around, looking for Erin's mother.

"Grandma had to leave," Claire said sadly. "Too bad."

"Yeah, too bad," Erin echoed, though it didn't sound too sincere. Then she took my hand. "That does give us time to talk, though."

Claire looked at us, puzzled. "What do you have to talk about?"

Erin's eyes met mine, and she bit her lip.

Thump, thump, thump, went my heart.

"Um… about tomorrow," Erin said when Claire fidgeted. "Do you think there will be repercussions from the agency?"

I shook my head. "If Edwards was planning to lock me up, he would have already brought me in. Waiting until tomorrow sounds more like routine questioning for his report."

She let out a long breath. "Thank goodness."

"Hey, Claire." Pippa motioned toward the kitchen. "You want to help me make brownies?"

I could have kissed her — Pippa, I mean. Well, not really — but I was grateful. Claire scampered inside, leaving Erin and me alone.

I raised an eyebrow. "You don't want to make brownies?"

Erin broke into a smile, then went all serious. "Not just now. We really need to talk." Then she gulped. "About tomorrow, I mean."

"Maybe about longer than tomorrow," I ventured, squeezing her hand.

Her eyes shone and she nodded, making my heart leap. So, whew. I wasn't the only one thinking long-term.

"That too," Erin whispered, leading me toward her house.

Chapter Thirty-Two

NASH

As impatient as I was to talk — and do more than talk — I paused on the way over to Erin's cabin.

"It's so beautiful here," I murmured, taking it all in. The ranch. The rocks. The peace...

Erin laughed. "You only figured that out now?"

"No. Well, yes. I mean, everything looks clearer now. Like a dirty window wiped clean."

The same applied to my hearing, my nose... Every single sense had been cleansed.

Erin tugged my hand, and we continued down the path. Other than our shoes crunching over the ground, the world was at peace.

Then we got to the *talking* part, though we danced around the big topics for a while. We discussed meeting Edwards the next day, then work. Apparently, Henry had called off all flights for a few days. Desert Skies had to repair the damaged balloon and regroup after all the media attention, so Erin and I had more free time than usual.

And boy, did I intend to use it well.

"And after that?" I ventured.

Erin stopped on the first step of her porch and looked at me, her eyes brimming with hope.

"I guess it depends. On how long you plan to stick around, I mean."

Forever, my dragon said immediately. *Tell her, forever.*

I shrugged, trying to play it cool. "I'm in no rush to leave. Especially with some new job prospects opening up." When she tilted her head, I went on. "Henry's going to need a new ground crew chief now that you'll be piloting more."

I could see her excitement, though she kept it in check.

"Not too boring a job for you?" she asked, moving up another step. "I mean, after being an agent and all..."

I shook my head. "Nah. Low-key is fine with me. Although I will need to add a side gig. Maybe work on a ranch somewhere... You got any ideas where I might start?"

Her eyes sparkled. "Oh, I definitely have ideas."

So did I, but just in case...

"Such as...?" I prompted, waiting breathlessly. A little like Roscoe did around the dinner table, wagging his tail hopefully.

"Well, we could use a hand around here." Her throat bobbed. "We can't afford to pay, but we could offer room and board."

I pointed to the barn. "There's space in the loft, right?"

She gestured toward her cabin. "I was thinking of another loft."

I inched a little closer, and my voice went all scratchy. "You got enough space there for two? For more than one night, I mean?"

She shrugged, but her eyes danced. "I'm sure you'd fit perfectly."

And, *whoosh!* The innuendo sent heat rushing through my veins.

I stepped closer. Right into her arms, in fact. Or maybe she stepped into mine.

"Oops." I stopped when we crushed Hopper. "We still have the bunny."

Erin plucked him out of my hands and set him on a porch chair. "He can keep watch out here."

With that, she slid her arms around my neck.

"Good idea," I mumbled, leaning into a kiss.

Erin slid her hands into my rear pockets and pressed me closer, making my dragon groan.

So good...

"Hang on." She broke off long enough to open the cabin door and pull me inside.

Seconds later, we were at the foot of the steep stairs, leaving the floor littered with clothes. Mostly Erin's, but she did peel my jumpsuit down to my waist. The dangling sleeves would probably be a liability on the loft stairs, but hell. We'd braved greater dangers together.

Erin shed her jacket, vest, and boots, then worked down the buttons on the oversized flannel shirt she wore as a sweater. I tried making myself helpful by coming up from the bottom but got sidetracked by her breasts. An arrangement that suited both of us, though it slowed progress on those buttons.

"Oh, screw it," she muttered, yanking the flannel over her head.

The shirt underneath went with it, and the motion funneled her hair, then let it cascade around her shoulders.

I dipped, eager to taste what I'd touched. The angle wasn't quite right, but Erin fixed that by rising to the first step.

Perfect, my dragon rumbled.

With one quick move, Erin popped her bra and tossed it aside. It fluttered past my head, though my eyes were on a different prize.

"Oh!" she exclaimed when I closed my lips around a tight bead.

She tipped her head back and rocked against me, then tapped my shoulders. "Up. Up." One-syllable orders my dazed mind could easily follow.

"Watch the—" she started.

I thumped my head on a roof beam. Ouch. It did, however, provide a cheap excuse to flop back on the bed.

"Poor baby," Erin murmured, crawling over my body to kiss me.

So, really, things could have been worse.

"You okay?" she asked a moment later.

I nodded, looking up at her. And oh, what a sight, with her straddling me in nothing but a pair of panties.

"I might have to lie down for a little longer. Just in case."

She went back to kissing me, murmuring "Poor baby" a few more times.

By then, it wasn't my head that ached. More like my groin. All the more as Erin slid down my body, trailing kisses over my chest. By the time she got to the waist of the jumpsuit, I was bulging inside.

"Poor baby," she purred in a totally different tone.

I raised my hips, letting her shove the jumpsuit away. She got it as far as my knees and left it there.

"So, you're trapping me? Is that how this works?" I teased.

"In the best possible way. Now, hush," she ordered, leaning down.

I closed my eyes just before her lips made contact, praying it wasn't all a dream. Then she slid down, sucking me in.

For the past weeks, thoughts and worries had crowded my mind. Now, that space went blissfully blank except for the sensation of her lips and tongue.

Best dream ever. Especially since it was real.

"Hang on," Erin panted a moment later, nudging me toward the center of the bed. "More headroom here." Then she laughed. "Get it? *Head*room?"

I groaned at the pun, then hissed as she went back to where she'd left off.

Her lips were firm, but her hands were gentle. Her panties rubbed on my thigh as she fell into a rhythm that drove me wild. I twisted my hands in the sheets, ordering myself not to explode — yet. Peeking only got my dragon further riled up, so I shut my eyes, imprinting that brief glimpse on to my memory.

Each time Erin came up for air, she panted harder. Each time she dove back down, I groaned in ecstasy. But shared pleasure was double the pleasure, so. . .

I tapped her shoulders, and she popped her head up.

"Had enough?" Her hair was a mess, and her eyes were bright.

"I will never have enough of you. But right now. . ."

Breaking into a huge smile, she crawled back up my body and sat up, straddling my hips. "Right now, you were thinking something like this, right?"

"Not exactly," I admitted, jerking my hips. "But it's a good start."

She huffed. "I'll show you a good start, buster..."

She pressed down over me, dragging her hips in slow, sensual circles. Her panties were soaked, and the soft cloth provided just enough friction to turn me on more. Not that I needed much more stimulus in that department.

She teased me a while longer, then broke away to strip those panties off.

"Dammit," she grumbled as they rolled, getting stuck. "Are you even helping here?"

"Sorry," I said, kicking the jumpsuit off. "I just need one second..."

She made exasperated sounds until we were both naked. "Now, where were we?"

She climbed back into position, teasing me with the barest contact where I need her most. Then she locked eyes with me and sank down, carrying us both into bliss.

For a while, I lay still, relishing the moment. Then I grasped her hips and echoed her movements with short, upward thrusts of my own.

"Nash..." she whispered, telling me how good she felt.

I rubbed a thumb over her skin, telling myself I could hold on through three more hits of that drug. But Erin only made it through two before rolling to one side.

"More. I need more..."

It was half plea, half order, and I was happy to comply.

We rolled without losing contact and picked up where we'd left off — which was very, very close to exploding. Being on top gave me the leverage I needed to take us to the next level. Erin clamped her inner muscles, milking me for all she was worth.

"Watch...your...head..." she murmured between short, hard breaths.

If I hadn't been that close to exploding, I might have laughed. I followed her back to the center of the bed, then I hammered down again.

Mate, my dragon cried as we rocked wildly.

I'd stopped denying it a while ago, but never had the notion been as crystal-clear as it was to me now.

Every other thought and sensation, however, blurred together. The rocking motion... the hot, hard glide... the sounds Erin made... the heady scent of desire...

I thrust deeper than ever, then howled and released.

"Yes..." Erin cried out, shuddering as she came.

For the next few seconds, the only sound was our heaving breaths. I sank down slowly, panting over her shoulder for a long time.

"Oh!" Erin cried out with an aftershock.

If I'd had it in me to punctuate it with a few more thrusts, I would have. A damn shame, really, until I thought of something else.

Something better, my dragon growled eagerly.

My chest heated, and my throat burned. I found Erin's mouth and smothered her in another searing kiss. Then, after a deep breath, I sealed my lips around hers and let my dragon rip.

Erin's eyes went wide, and her body jerked. For an instant, her nails dug into my shoulders in panic. Her eyes blazed, telling me she was on fire.

My fire, I willed her to understand.

Her expression went from shock to bliss. Her legs, wrapped around my waist, clamped me even closer, and she shuddered, surrendering to wave after wave of fiery pleasure.

For a few precious moments, we soared in ecstasy. Then we slowly keeled over and went limp. At some point, we cleaned up with a corner of the sheet and lay face-to-face. The curve of Erin's hips made the perfect notch for my arm to loop over, and I held her close.

"Wow," Erin finally managed, her chest still rising and falling in time with mine. "What was that?"

Apparently, she'd never had a mother-daughter talk about intimate dragon stuff. Why was I not surprised?

"Dragon kiss," I explained, smoothing her hair over her shoulder, then twirling a strand around a finger. A tiny pleasure, but still incredibly satisfying. Just like the tickle of her breath on my chest.

She smacked her lips a few times. "Dragon kiss or dragon fire?"

"Same thing." I cupped her cheek, suddenly worried. "No good?"

A sly smile spread over her face. "Very good. Can I get another?"

I laughed, then kissed her, sending a smaller lick of fire across this time.

Erin's fingernails dug in, and she wiggled, pressing her hips against mine. When we came up for air, she gulped and stared at me. "And another?"

I laughed. "I've created a monster."

She flopped to her back, laughing. "Maybe. But wow. Dragon kiss, huh?"

I nodded as my dragon danced in delight and relief.

She likes it! She likes it!

"Lots more where that came from," I promised, holding her close.

"I hope so," she whispered, then became more serious. "I don't know much about shifters, but I hear a lot about mating bites..."

My breath caught, and I nodded eagerly.

"Obviously, my parents aren't the world's best example." She frowned a little. "And I never thought I'd want to know. But now, with you..." She bit her lip, gazing deep into my eyes. "I guess I'd like to...uh, consider our options."

My grin was so wide, it hurt. Oh, we had options, all right. A lifetime of them.

"Mating is forever, you know," I warned.

"The opposite of my parents? Perfect." She kissed me.

And, oops. The kiss, like so many others, quickly slipped out of control. But, hey. We could work out the details later.

Now was the time to indulge ourselves in an equally important task — getting to know each other in the very best way.

"Just watch your head," Erin murmured as I rolled, taking the top.

I chuckled into the soft skin of her neck but didn't reply. Not with words anyway.

Chapter Thirty-Three

ERIN

Two weeks later...

"Mmm." I stirred, half asleep, trying to find a comfortable new position on the mattress.

Nash nuzzled my shoulder and tightened his arms around me.

I smiled. Some people talked in their sleep. Some walked in their sleep. My man cuddled.

A wonderful, wonderful complement to his more, um... *active* bedroom talents. The latter left me blissfully tired and oh-so satisfied, while the former proved how deep his love went.

Not that I needed the reassurance. Not after what we'd gotten up to a week earlier, when a few innocent kisses led to a raging inferno in which we'd gone at it on all fours, followed by—

I blushed just thinking about it.

We'd both sworn to take our time settling into a new normal after the whirlwind of the past weeks. Nash had been especially sensitive about not pressuring me into taking the next logical step — a mating bite. Which was a relief, or so I'd thought, because I hadn't been all that excited about the *biting* part, what with a nasty she-vampire all too fresh in my memory.

But that night, in the throes of passion, something deep inside me fought its way to the surface, igniting a craving like nothing I'd ever experienced. I'd ended up begging — full-on, teary-eyed, scratchy-voice, shameless *begging* — for a bite.

And, holy smokes. I'd never experienced a more explosive, dizzying high than in those next, unforgettable moments.

Except, ha. I'd gotten to experience it all over again the next night, and a few hours ago, because mating bites weren't a one-time deal. You got to repeat them as often as you wanted.

And boy, did Nash and I want. We wanted and wanted and wanted.

But I digress.

The glow must have shown the next day, because Pippa hustled me a safe distance from Claire and demanded to hear all the sizzling details. But I honestly didn't have the words.

"Try," Pippa growled.

That Pippa. Bossy as hell sometimes.

So I tried, but even *the best, most explosive sex of my life coinciding with a tiny flash of pain that sent fire searing through my veins and plunged me into ecstasy* didn't do it justice.

I doubted that would satisfy Pippa, who'd never shied away from smutty girl talk. But my expression must have conveyed the rest, rendering even her — mostly — speechless.

"Wow," she said, stunned.

Yes, that summed it up nicely.

And yes, I knew I was one lucky woman. I had a good job, a great man, and a wonderful life in a beautiful, peaceful place.

And yet, that night in my loft, I stared up into the roof beams, inexplicably restless.

Nash was sleeping as soundly as ever, his steady breaths conveying calm and satisfaction. Outside, not a dog barked, not a horse whinnied. The world was at peace.

Everything and everyone but me.

I checked the clock. Nearly midnight. Then I stared into the darkness, trying not to think. An eternity later, I glanced at the clock. Why was time moving so slowly?

Maybe it was me.

Ever since tapping into the power of the vortex — something I vowed to never, ever do again (unless another warlock or vampire came along to threaten us. But damn, I sure hoped not) — things were different. Before, I could track the wind if I made a conscious, concentrated effort — a little like using my limited high school Spanish. Now, I was suddenly fluent, comprehending as effortlessly as in my native language.

Yeah, comprehension. Fluency — those fit my new relationship to the wind perfectly.

But the wind was slumbering at that moment, as I ought to be.

I lay there, listening to my heart thump. Not a quiet nighttime thump either. More like an anticipatory, *the race is about to start kind* of thumping.

I frowned into the darkness. There was no race, only a four a.m. alarm looming. It was time to rest, not to lie around fretting.

I rolled and cuddled closer to Nash, trying to absorb his peaceful vibes. But when I closed my eyes, my mind filled with apocalyptic images of rushing landscapes and bursts of fire.

I snapped my eyes open and rolled to my back. Maybe if I counted sheep...

Okay, counting sheep never worked. But I had to try something.

And damn, was it hot. Even naked and with sheets long since lost over the side of the mattress, I broke into a sweat. I could see it glisten on my chest in the moonlight. Which would be normal for summer — or menopause, I supposed — but we were still in the dead of a high-altitude Arizona winter. And as for menopause, I shouldn't have to deal with that for another twenty years. Or so I hoped.

Twisting, I dug my shoulders into the mattress against a sudden itch. And, ow. Not just an itch, but sharp, stabbing pinches. I frowned. Abby had once suffered a severe case of shingles — the virus, not the roofing — and it had been utter misery. Was I coming down with it?

I lay there a while longer, wondering what was wrong with me. Then I took a deep breath and forced myself to push it all out of my mind.

Inhale. Exhale. Everything was okay.

There. *Mind over matter,* like my dad liked to say.

Or maybe not, because a moment later—

An intense, urgent *something* hit me. I threw my pillow aside, jumped out of bed, and hurried downstairs.

"Erin?" Nash called sleepily.

Bang! I pushed the front door open so hard, it slammed against the wall.

"Erin!" Nash called in alarm.

I wanted to stop and tell him everything was okay. But it wasn't, and I couldn't.

I raced out into the desert, barefoot, naked, and panting. I didn't feel the cold or the gravel underfoot, just the urge to get out under open skies and into a fresh breeze.

Open skies... Fresh breeze... Going faster and faster, something in me cheered.

I sprinted, following sheer instinct. But weird instinct, because if you wanted to run fast, you kept your arms pumping, not out at your sides like an albatross.

Not an albatross, a deep, throaty voice scoffed in my mind. It reminded me of my mother.

I cringed. She wasn't back already, was she?

"Erin!" Nash yelled from the doorway.

I wanted to run back into his arms, but something steered me onward. Faster and faster, with cold night air whooshing over my skin.

Yes, that deep voice murmured. *Faster...*

I was nearly at Picnic Rock, as my sisters and I had dubbed it — a big, flat slab of rock that slanted gradually to about four feet above ground. We really did picnic out there sometimes, and as kids, we'd held jumping contests that started with a run-up along the rock and ended with a leap off the high end. Pippa usually won.

My lips curled into a deranged smile. Something told me I was about to break her record.

"Erin!" I heard Nash's footsteps behind me. But they were interrupted by curses and hops, whereas my feet didn't register rocks, roots, or thorns.

I did register the wind, though. The moment I'd burst outside, it had perked up the way the horses did when we opened the barn door. Within seconds, it whipped into excited little gusts. Now, it settled in behind me and pushed, practically cheering, *You can do it!*

Do what? the last working section of my mind wondered.

The rest of me was on autopilot. I ran so fast, tears blurred my vision. I leaped so far, my breath caught. So high, the stars sparkled.

And I never landed.

The ground rushed by five feet beneath me. Ten feet... twenty...

"Woo-hoo!" Somewhere in the distance, Nash cheered. "You're flying!"

I blinked, catching sight of a wingtip to my left. And, wow. A matching one on my right.

I stared. Not a good idea. Just like staring to one side while riding a bike — your body tended to follow the shift in balance.

Right on cue, I tipped into a tight turn, bellowing in panic.

Really bellowing, as loud as an irritated heifer. Maybe even louder.

"Your tail!" Nash shouted. "Use your tail!"

Now, that's not very polite, a ladylike corner of my soul grumbled.

But, oh. Something whipped behind me, and I steadied out.

Whew. Or, crap. I had a tail now?

I wasn't sure how I felt about that.

The sentiment came out with a little yelp and, *whoosh!* A thin line of fire illuminated the space in front of my nostrils.

Nash ducked out of the way. "Careful!"

I sealed my hot, ashy lips, terrified but also recklessly thrilled.

Because, wow. Those weren't apocalyptic visions I'd had. They were glimpses from a dragon's point of view.

My point of view now.

I rose to fifty feet, then a hundred, then higher still. Cool air whisked over my cheeks and followed the lines of my body to stream smoothly over my chest and wings. I leaned this way and that, testing out the controls, so to speak.

Feeling bold, I sucked in a lungful of air, let it heat in my throat for a split second, then blew it out.

Whoosh! Flames burst out of my mouth. It was exhilarating, like pulling the burner cord in a balloon, but fifty times better.

When the airflow to my right changed, I glanced over to find a huge bronze dragon zooming up beside me.

That was amazing! Nash's deep dragon voice boomed in my mind. *It took me ages to learn to take off, and even then, I didn't fly much farther than the Wright Brothers. You're already soaring!*

I was, without even thinking.

The wind tickled my belly, demanding its share of the credit.

I hastily amended the thought to *Thank goodness for this amazing wind, without which this wouldn't be possible.*

Still, I had to quietly marvel. I really was flying, and not too shabbily.

It was all so new, yet strangely familiar.

The more I flew, the more I suspected that my dragon side had been with me all along — that gritty voice in the back of my mind that had always doled out advice, encouragement, and warnings.

This way, Nash called, turning toward Bear Mountain. *Just watch the eddies. . .* He glanced back to check on me, then went wide-eyed.

Wow. You're a natural. And it doesn't hurt to be a wind whisperer, does it?

I pursed my lips — big, hard dragon lips, as I discovered; maybe not so good for kissing — and replayed that last section of flight time. I'd felt the eddy, but I'd adjusted in time to avoid bobbling. So, yay me. Points for technical merit.

I flew on, thinking that over. But instead of clear thoughts, all I got were emotions — a whole tempest of them, all sweeping at me from out of nowhere.

As urgently as I'd taken to the sky, I dove toward the cliff tops to land.

Watch the— And the— Nash bit off his own instructions as I aced the landing. *Really* aced it, like an old pro, which was why my mind was spinning.

I slumped and bent my frighteningly long neck until my head touched my chest. I nestled my nose there and closed my eyes, panting. Sniffling. Wait... Crying?

Well, a dragon version of crying, though I didn't actually shed tears. My breath heaved, and I made pathetic little wheezing noises.

What's wrong? Nash landed and looped a huge wing over my shoulders — a move with serious potential to terrify, though I found it strangely comforting.

So why was I crying?

I blubbered incoherently. Because of everything, I supposed. Everything I was, and everything I'd spent years believing I would never be.

Why are you crying? Nash asked, sounding genuinely torn.

Well, lots of reasons, though they were hard to pin down.

One was joy — the sheer joy of flying. Something I'd grasped at my whole life, only to achieve now. Because, wow. I could transform into a dragon!

Another part was sorrow. All those years I'd wished for a tiny crumb of my father's magic or my mother's abilities... only to realize they had been there all along, deep inside me. I just hadn't been connecting the puzzle pieces properly. Now, they all clicked into place, and I felt whole — really whole, and really *me* — for the first time ever. Not the me I *wished* I could be. The me I was destined to be.

Which brought me back to joy again. The bittersweet kind you only tasted after a long period of struggling.

So, I supposed that was why I was crying. For all that, and for Nash, who'd made it possible.

For so long, I'd harbored a lot of dreams, but finding a man like Nash was a little like dreaming about world peace. A nice idea, but unlikely ever to be achieved.

And yet, here we were. Amazing.

So, hey. Next stop, world peace?

One thing at a time, I reminded myself. *One thing at a time.*

I pulled myself together and whispered into his mind. *You know how you said you only came alive once you were free of Angelina?*

He nodded tersely.

I feel like that now, I explained. *Alive. Free.*

Nash nuzzled my head with his chin. A huge, chunky, battering ram of a chin, but it felt like heaven to me.

I sniffled a little longer, leaning into him. When my breaths steadied out again, I looked up.

Sorry.

Nothing to be sorry about, he assured me.

I nuzzled him. And oh, was that good, especially when I rubbed my thick brow against his chin. I made a mental note.

Maybe not sorry, I agreed. *Just grateful for so much. Grateful for you.*

His smile came with a puff of warm air. *I'm grateful for you.*

We stayed there, enjoying a dragon cuddle — not at all as counterintuitive as it sounds — for a few minutes. Then I took a deep breath and straightened.

I'm ready now.

Nash cocked his head. *Ready for...?*

Flying, silly, I said, as unabashed as I could manage, seeing as I was the one who'd rushed into an emergency landing to bawl my heart out for a while.

Nash's eyes sparkled, and he stuck out a wing, indicating the miles of wild, open landscape we could fly over. Heck, we could do better than just fly. We could soar. Glide. Spiral upward and swoop downward... All over a stunning landscape bathed in moonlight and blessed by a friendly breeze.

After you, my mate, Nash rumbled happily. *After you.*

Epilogue

ERIN

Four weeks later...

"Good news or bad news first?" Henry asked, pressing a cup of coffee into my hand at dawn.

I took a quick sip and shut my eyes. Whatever the bad news was, I refused to let it faze me. I'd survived a scheming warlock, a jealous vampire, and two killer storms. Both Desert Skies balloons were repaired and back in operation, and I was cleared to pilot anytime — the job of my dreams in one of the most beautiful corners of the country.

Far more importantly, I had Nash. Partner, friend, colleague, lover.

Mate, my dragon side murmured happily.

So, as long as Henry's bad news didn't involve marauding demons or my mother popping in for another surprise visit — God, please no — I could cope.

"Good news first," I murmured, sipping my coffee.

Henry motioned at the huddle of eager guests waiting for lift-off.

"All the spots in the balloon are sold out today, tomorrow, and the day after. Wednesday would be fully booked too, but we're saving a spot for our aviatrix-in-training." He smacked me on the shoulder. "Brilliant idea, by the way. The press coverage has been great advertising — and even without that, it still would be worthwhile."

I tapped my coffee cup against his in a toast, genuinely proud.

277

"Glad to hear it."

I'd spent most of the past year desperately trying to scrape together flight hours — a hurdle many prospective female pilots faced. But it was only one recent morning that I'd had a brainwave for a way to address the problem on a bigger scale. Henry had been skeptical at first, but our two-week trial period had proven such a success, he'd committed to it for an entire year — and made national news in the process.

Once a week, Desert Skies saved a spot for a local girl or woman to fly with us. Some were disadvantaged kids recommended by counselors I'd contacted in the local high school. Others were adults, young to "old," who'd nearly given up on childhood dreams because ballooning was too expensive or too difficult to get into.

The first four months of our aviatrix-in-training program were already booked solid, and spots in the following months were filling quickly. It was such a success that balloon companies across the country were following our example.

I was tickled pink, as was Henry. Would some of those women go on to become balloon pilots? I hoped so, but that didn't really matter. The point was, they had the opportunity.

"So, what's the bad news?" I asked.

Henry sighed. "John won't be coming in this week, so we're one man short on the ground crew."

John was competent and easy to get along with, so that was a pity, but not an insurmountable problem. With Nash leading the ground crew, together with the ever-reliable Chico, we could get by.

Plus, being a man short didn't affect my chance to fly. Madden had left the company abruptly, citing "issues." Nothing to do with his botched handling of the bachelor party storm, he'd insisted.

Yeah, right.

Since then, I'd been Desert Skies's permanent number two pilot, after Henry. So, not much ground crew duty for me, unless I chose it.

The irony was, I didn't mind any more. As a dragon shifter, I could fly any time I wanted. In fact, most nights, I did.

Just last night, Nash and I had soared over Bear Mountain, meandered with the bends of Oak Creek, and glided silently over downtown Sedona. We'd headed home tired yet satisfied and fallen asleep after making slow, sweet love.

I took a deep breath to remind myself I wasn't dreaming. Life really was that good.

But, oops. Back to the ground crew problem.

I glanced over at Ingo, who stood a little apart from the other guests. Maybe he could help?

A moment later, I dropped the idea. That wouldn't really be fair. Besides, he was here on official business — though incognito, so to speak.

That was another silver lining to our whole ordeal. Captain Edwards of the ADMSA had let Nash off lightly in the debrief after the altercation with Harlon. In fact, Edwards had offered Nash a new position the agency was establishing in Sedona.

Thanks, but I like my new jobs, Nash had said. *Ballooning and ranching.*

That, and teaching his own private recruit — me — everything about dragoning. Shifting, flying, breathing fire... You know, all the usual things.

In return, I taught him everything I knew about ranching and ballooning. A win-win for everyone.

To Nash's delight and surprise, Ingo had taken the agency position.

To *my* surprise, Ingo was the *Frank* I'd "met" on the phone — Nash's insider at the agency.

To Pippa's surprise, Ingo was *the* Ingo, her ex-boyfriend. I couldn't decide whether she was delighted or dismayed to have him in town indefinitely. A little of both, I suspected.

Nash and I had spent a lot of time with the wolf shifter since then, and I'd learned a lot about the supernatural world, as well as the secret government agency.

In fact, I was still reeling from Ingo's biggest bombshell.

Word is, the agency tried to recruit your mother, way back when, Ingo had said.

My jaw had dropped, though it made sense, in a way. Secret agents had to be tough, unattached types — and unfortunately for my sisters and me, that fit my mother to a T.

Apparently, she turned down that offer, but she might not have turned Edwards down entirely. . . Ingo had added with a sly grin.

That explained how they knew each other. But, yikes. Captain Edwards and my mother?

I'd stopped asking questions after that, because, well. . . too much information. I barely had the headspace to keep track of three of my mother's ex-lovers — my father, Pippa's, and Abby's, the "only" three she'd had children with.

In any case, this flight was a business expense for Ingo. Part of his brief was developing a risk-assessment report for Sedona, which included getting an overview of things — literally.

Nixing the idea of enlisting his help as ground crew, I thought about Pippa next. Could she help?

Yes, my younger sister was there too, smiling and joking with the other guests, though studiously ignoring Ingo. It was a week past her birthday, and friends all over town had pitched in to gift her a voucher for a balloon flight.

I was delighted. For the first time ever, I could fly with one of my sisters.

Not about to ruin that, I folded my arms and stared down Henry. "The good news better be that you found a replacement."

"I did!" Henry grinned and motioned someone out of the shadows. "Amanda, come on over."

His eyes danced as he watched my reaction.

"We might be one man short, but we're one woman up. Erin, meet Amanda."

I shook hands enthusiastically. Amanda was a pretty Hispanic woman a good ten years older than me, and though a little shy on her first day on the job, the brunette was definitely not a pushover.

"Nice to meet you," I said, and boy, did I mean it.

"Nice to meet you too."

I introduced her to Nash and Chico, who took a shine to her immediately.

"I'll show you the ropes," he promised, puffing out his chest a little.

Nash winked and spoke into my mind.

Who knows. Maybe we won't be the only happy couple to have met on Henry's crew.

I laughed, thinking back to those days.

When our eyes locked, my heart swelled. Nash's step was so light, his eyes so bright. The same old Nash in all the best ways, but an entirely new version too. He was happier. More easygoing. *Alive,* as he liked to put it.

Alive, my inner dragon murmured just as happily.

So, yeah. I suppose the same applied to me.

"Coming, boss?" Chico called.

Nash popped a kiss on my lips and turned to go. Then he turned back and snuck in a second kiss, which nearly turned into a third. . . a fourth. . .

Someone bumped me, and I forced myself to focus on flying instead of getting it on with my dragon shifter lover.

Nash's eyes held a hint of a glow as he stepped away, murmuring, "Sorry, Captain. Gotta get that balloon ready."

"Oh! Oh!" One of the guests hurried over to me. "Can I get a selfie with you, Captain?"

That was part of my new reality — the minor celebrity that came with being "that lady pilot who saved all those guys," as I'd heard over and over.

I almost felt sorry for Madden. Almost.

"How about we do that after the flight, when you know whether you really want to thank me?" I suggested.

Everyone chuckled, leaving Henry and me to work out a flight plan. Then, after the safety briefing and preflight check, I got everyone aboard and pulled the burner cord.

Whoosh went the flames, thrilling my inner dragon.

The fire reflected in Pippa's eyes, thrilling her too. After all, she was also half dragon shifter. Did our mother's side of the family call to her the way it had always called to me?

Again, I felt lucky. Thanks to Nash, I was now a full-fledged dragon shifter. But Pippa was as earthbound as I'd once been.

Well, not for the next hour, she isn't, my dragon side consoled me.

The light breeze swirled enthusiastically around me, promising a smooth journey.

Another burst of hot air lifted the balloon gently into the air, and we were off. As we gained altitude and drifted west, I glanced down, keeping one eye on the van following our journey.

"Two-ninety degrees at four point two," Henry reported from Desert Skies One.

I sensed a change coming, but I echoed him anyway.

"Two-ninety degrees at four point two."

It was silly, but I still got a thrill knowing Nash was listening over the radio.

Not for long. His voice sounded in my mind. *Wind shift coming up.*

I grinned. We'd turned that into a little game — who could spot a change in conditions first. I usually won, but sometimes, like now, I let Nash think he had. Or did that go both ways?

"Wow, this is amazing," Pippa gushed. "Now I know why you rave about flying."

She winked at the private joke, then added into my mind, *Flying as a dragon, I mean. Along with raving about Nash. And all the — er, activities — you two have gotten up to.*

My cheeks heated. I'd tried not to gush about my man too much, and I certainly hadn't indulged in any dirty girl talk. But, heck. I guess soul-deep satisfaction showed. Was that my fault?

Your fault, I play-accused Nash.

What is? he asked.

Um. . .I'll explain later, I mumbled.

"Oh! There's the ranch!" Pippa pointed.

The view had become familiar now that I'd seen it so many times from a dragon's-eye perspective. Still, it never got old.

The scorch marks still showed, but we'd fixed the rest of the damage — all relatively minor, thank goodness. But, yikes. The shutters would still be askew and the barn door jammed if we hadn't had an extra hand — Nash — to tackle the repairs with us.

Like I said, I'm happy for a little mindless work, Nash joked into my mind, reading my thoughts from a distance.

I stifled a laugh. That was the plus side to the damage — an opportunity for Nash to prove himself to my sisters. Even Abby had warmed to him a little.

Okay, I have to hand it to him, she'd admitted. *He's pulled his weight around here, and then some.*

Very true, though I found myself sighing. Maybe someday Abby would finally find a good man. She deserved one.

My mind wandered to Ingo. He seemed like a good guy. Too bad he wasn't Abby's type.

But Ingo and Pippa, on the other hand...

One problem, though — they'd broken up years ago for reasons Pippa had never gotten into. She claimed to be over him, but I saw the longing in her eyes when she looked at him.

"So, how are you enjoying Sedona?" I asked Ingo, speaking loud enough for Pippa to eavesdrop.

Would you cut that out? Nash admonished. *He's not interested in getting back together.*

No, Ingo *pretended* not to be interested. But I'd definitely caught him peeking.

He's not her type, Nash added, clearly out to protect his friend.

True — Ingo and Pippa were total opposites. Ingo was a wolf shifter *and* a super-serious agent. But he would be a great influence on my impulsive, fly-by-the-seat-of-her-pants sister. And she sure could help loosen him up a bit. Another win-win, in my humble opinion.

"Sedona really is beautiful." Ingo nodded in answer to my question.

Still, I caught him watching Pippa more than the landscape. And who could blame him? Pippa was the peppiest and prettiest of us three sisters. The wind toyed with the wisps of blond hair that stuck out under her baseball cap, and her ready smile was impossible to resist.

Of course, that didn't mean there was a happy reunion in the cards. But a girl could hope for a nice brother-in-law, right?

"Three-oh-five degrees at three point nine." Henry's voice came over the radio.

He'd taken his balloon higher than mine, but we were nearly on the same course.

"Three-ten at four point zero," I reported.

The wind toyed with my hair, hinting, *We could go even faster.*

God, no. But thank you, I nearly murmured.

I opened the right vent to slowly rotate the balloon, treating every guest to three-sixty views. Below us, a couple of javelinas darted across the scrubby ground, and the sun glinted off Oak Creek as it meandered through the arid landscape.

"Oh! I see Robber's Roost!" Pippa exclaimed.

As she regaled the guests with bootlegging legends, I chuckled into Nash's mind. A place we knew well.

He laughed back. *Thanks — or no thanks — to Harlon.*

A good thing the agency had hauled Harlon in and put him through the wringer. His businesses were being scrutinized, and though he'd been released — after submitting to a restraining spell cast by the agency's panel of class-one warlocks — he remained on their "red" watch list. Hopefully, his days causing trouble for folks like us were over.

The sun climbed higher, coloring the rocky landscape in ever brighter hues. I marveled as much as the guests did. So much beauty packed into one area. So many memories. So much to look forward to in the future.

Sometime later, Henry announced our landing spot — Angel Valley — where the vans were already waiting.

"That Nash is almost as good at predicting our landing spots as you are, Erin," Henry marveled.

I couldn't see Nash, but I sensed his smile. If only Henry knew the extent of our talents.

The thing was, even I didn't know the full scope of my abilities. The lightning storm had been a hell of a wake-up call, though — literally, with my new, intensified connection to the wind. My dad had promised to visit soon and teach me everything he could.

Time would tell how much of his ability I had inherited. For now, I was grateful to be a dragon shifter — plus a fully certified and insured balloon pilot.

We touched down gently, barely requiring any braking action from the ground crew. Nash appeared at a corner of the balloon, all business at first. But once we were firmly on the ground, his lips twitched with the smooch he sent into my mind.

While Henry invited the guests to the traditional postflight champagne and breakfast picnic, I helped Nash, Chico, and Amanda with the equipment. Once everything was loaded into the van and trailer, Nash and I walked a few steps away with the flutes of champagne Pippa had saved for us. Just a sip each, but that's all we needed for a heartfelt toast.

In the distance, we could hear Henry reciting the traditional balloonist's prayer for the guests. We held up our glasses in our own private toast.

"May the winds welcome you with softness..." Henry started.

I thought of all the times they had, and the few times they hadn't.

"May the sun bless you with its warm hands..."

I tipped my chin up, savoring the sensation. Warm, like Nash when he held me every night and every morning.

"May you fly so high and so well that God joins you in laughter..."

Nash's eyes sparkled, reminding me of my first flying lessons.

You certainly do, he promised me. *Fly high and fly well, I mean. Causing joy and laughter.*

"And sets you gently back into the loving arms of Mother Earth," Henry finished.

The author of that particular piece was unknown, but they sure had captured everything I loved about flying.

Nash and I clinked glasses, then sipped.

"Speaking of loving arms..." Nash tapped me gently.

My cheeks stretched into a huge smile as I wrapped my arms around him. We held each other for a long time, rocking contentedly.

"Now, where's the captain?" Pippa called loudly. "She promised me a selfie. . ."

Nash and I broke apart, laughing. Several guests race-walked toward us, cameras in hand.

"I'll leave this part to you, Captain," Nash murmured, stepping aside.

As always, my dragon side grumbled at having him "so far away." But soon, this part of our workday would be over. Afterward, we could head home for brunch and a nap before tackling ranch chores in the afternoon. All in all, a perfect daily rhythm.

"Ha. Got here first," a guest said, nabbing me ahead of the others. "Could I get a selfie, please?"

I had to pose for six in total, but my smile was genuine in each. All I had to do was keep my mind on Nash.

Finally, with everyone loaded back in the vans, I squeezed his hand.

"Time to head home, amigos," Chico announced, winking at Amanda.

"Home sounds good," Nash agreed.

His smile was a thing of beauty, and mine matched it. Because home was my — er, our — place.

"Home," I couldn't help echoing.

Nash kissed my hand while whispering into my mind. *You and me together, my mate.*

Sneak Peek: Fire Dancer

**What to do when the customer you can't afford to lose
is a thirsty vampire?**

Fire Dancer? I wish. Just because I'm part dragon shifter,
part pyromancer doesn't mean I can control or breathe fire.
Lately, though, I've started to show signs of magic — and
that's not the only unexpected development in my life. My
wolf shifter ex is back in town and more consumed by his job
than ever. Ingo is sweet, loyal, and in serious need of some
work/life balance. As an agent in supernatural law enforce-
ment, he sees enemies everywhere — including in my best customer. A customer I can't afford to lose, given my financial
problems.

But what if Ingo is right and that customer is a vampire?
I've never met the reclusive Victor Jananovich, but Stacy, his
assistant, is looking paler and paler, and she always wears three
things: a pegasus pendant, a scarf that hides her throat, and a
necklace with a blood vial. Is Ingo right about those warning
signs, or is he just paranoid?

As a glass artist, I'm used to delicate problems, but I might
be out of my league on this one. Still, I'm reluctant to confide
in Ingo. Wolf shifters have their own ways of solving problems,
and *finesse* is not one of them. But the stakes are high, with
everything at risk — my struggling ranch, my fragile heart,
and even innocent lives.

Books by Anna Lowe

Spellbound in Sedona

Wind Whisperer (Book 1)

Fire Dancer (Book 2)

Dream Weaver (Book 3)

Sherwood Forest Shifters

Tempting the Sheriff (Book 1)

Tempting the Outlaw (Book 2)

Tempting the Maiden (Book 3)

Aloha Shifters - Jewels of the Heart

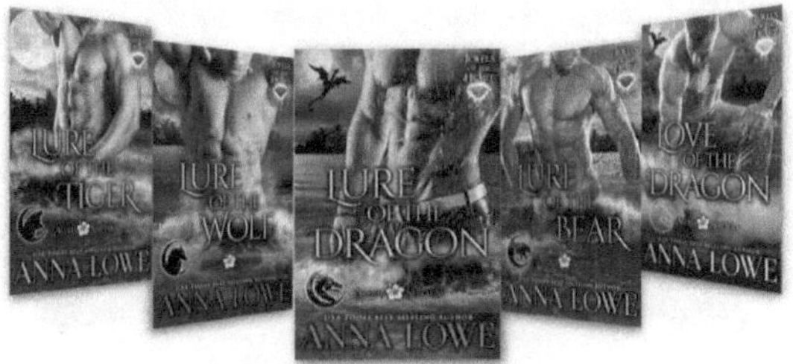

Lure of the Dragon (Book 1)

Lure of the Wolf (Book 2)

Lure of the Bear (Book 3)

Lure of the Tiger (Book 4)

Love of the Dragon (Book 5)

Lure of the Fox (Book 6)

Aloha Shifters - Pearls of Desire

Rebel Dragon (Book 1)

Rebel Bear (Book 2)

Rebel Lion (Book 3)

Rebel Wolf (Book 4)

Rebel Heart (A prequel to Book 5)

Rebel Alpha (Book 5)

Fire Maidens - Billionaires & Bodyguards

Fire Maidens: Paris (Book 1)

Fire Maidens: London (Book 2)

Fire Maidens: Rome (Book 3)

Fire Maidens: Portugal (Book 4)

Fire Maidens: Ireland (Book 5)

Fire Maidens: Scotland (Book 6)

Fire Maidens: Venice (Book 7)

Fire Maidens: Greece (Book 8)

Fire Maidens: Switzerland (Book 9)

The Wolves of Twin Moon Ranch

Desert Hunt (the Prequel)

Desert Moon (Book 1)

Desert Blood (Book 2)

Desert Fate (Book 3)

Desert Heart (Book 4)

Desert Rose (Book 5)

Desert Roots (Book 6)

Desert Destiny (Book 7)

Sasquatch Surprise (Book 8)

Desert Yule (a short story)

Desert Wolf: Complete Collection (Four short stories)

Blue Moon Saloon

Perfection (a short story prequel)

Damnation (Book 1)

Temptation (Book 2)

Redemption (Book 3)

Salvation (Book 4)

Deception (Book 5)

Celebration (a holiday treat)

Shifters in Vegas

Paranormal romance with a zany twist

Gambling on Trouble

Gambling on Her Dragon

Gambling on Her Bear

Gambling on Her Panther

Serendipity Adventure Romance

Off the Charts

Uncharted

Entangled

Windswept

Adrift

Travel Romance

Veiled Fantasies

Island Fantasies

www.annalowebooks.com

About the Author

USA Today and Amazon bestselling author Anna Lowe loves putting the "hero" back into heroine and letting location ignite a passionate romance. She likes a heroine who is independent, intelligent, and imperfect – a woman who is doing just fine on her own. But give the heroine a good man – not to mention a chance to overcome her own inhibitions – and she'll never turn down the chance for adventure, nor shy away from danger.

Anna loves dogs, sports, and travel – and letting those inspire her fiction. On any given weekend, you might find her hiking in the mountains or hunched over her laptop, working on her latest story. Either way, the day will end with a chunk of dark chocolate and a good read.

Visit AnnaLoweBooks.com